Heartsick for Country

Stories of Love, Spirit and Creation

edited by
Sally Morgan, Tjalaminu Mia
and Blaze Kwaymullina

 FREMANTLE PRESS

To all our ancestors
who have gone before us,
we honour you by still carrying
our country in our hearts

Contents

AMBELIN KWAYMULLINA

belongs to the Palkyu people from the Pilbara, in the North-West of Western Australia. She is an Indigenous lawyer currently employed at The University of Western Australia.

Introduction: A Land of Many Countries

When I walk in the footprints of my childhood, the years just fade away and I feel like I am there again as a young girl. I am flooded with wonderful memories of the sounds and smells of the bush, the joy and laughter of my sisters and me, and the connectedness and security from the voices and words shared with us kids from our Elders. Going bush was something we did all the time when I was young and it kept us grounded in culture and closely connected to our land.[1]

The stories in this anthology speak of the love between Aboriginal peoples and their countries. They are personal stories that share knowledge, insight and emotion. Each story speaks of a deep connection to country, of joy and pain, and of feeling heartsick because of the harm that is being inflicted on country even today through logging old-growth forests, converting millions of hectares of land to salt fields, destroying ancient rock art and significant Aboriginal sites, over-use of water by industry in semi-arid areas, and a record of species extinction that is the worst in the world. Each contributor's voice represents an ancient continuum, a way of being in the world that forged a mutually nourishing relationship between people and country that sustained succeeding generations for millennia. This anthology was driven by the need to speak of deeper things, and to share what is often only shared among Indigenous people. It has taken courage to tell these stories, and the telling has re-awakened many feelings — old grief, past joys, and questions about the future and what will happen when these writers, too, have passed on. In an era of global environmental challenges, we all need to listen to the voices that offer a way of seeing and relating to country that will allow the earth not only to survive, but also to thrive. These stories provide an insight for other people everywhere to gain a better understanding of the relationships to country that Indigenous people hold close to their hearts. These are the diverse voices of lived experience and they share one passionate desire — to protect country for all the generations to come.

This continent, named Australia by Captain Matthew Flinders early in the nineteenth century, is a land of many countries — and for every country, there is a people. We are the Nyungar, Palkyu, Martu, Gumilaroi, Worrimia, Bardi, Indjarbandi, Palawa, Tanganekald, and Meintangk, and we are many others. We were formed with the hills and the valleys, the water and the sky, the trees and the plants, the crows and the kangaroos, created by the ancestors who gave meaning and life to our world. And for each of us, our country is not just where we live, but who we are. The countries of our hearts are the red sands of the desert, the green gullies of the forests, the white shores of the coast and all the places in between. Our blood is carried by the rivers and the streams, our breath is on the wind, and our pulse is in the land. There was a time when the rhythm of our hearts was strong and steady and sure, but now we all struggle in our different ways to care for country, to hold up the connections between all life that *is* our life, in a world where those connections are so often unseen and unheard.

Aboriginal people in country

Long, long ago, when this land was without form, the ancestors journeyed across the world singing and dancing, laughing and crying, fighting and loving — and everywhere they went, life sprang into being. The ancestors created all life, and gave all life knowledge and law. Each country has its own people who hold the stories of these great events. Len Collard tells of the powerful Rainbow Serpent, the Waakal:

> … *the Waakal is the Creator, the keeper of the freshwater sources. He gave us life and our trilogy of belief in the boodjar — the land — as our mother and nurturer of the Nyungar* moort — *family and relations — and our* katitjin *Law — knowledge so that we could weave the intricate tapestry known as the 'web of life'.*[2]

All Aboriginal people are descended from the creation beings. Today, we can still follow the paths they travelled, see their tracks in the land, and feel and honour their presence in country. And, through the world that they made, the ancestors continue to teach us, showing us how all life is interconnected and interdependent. Dr Joan Winch tells of the Butterfly Dreaming:

> [There] *is a women's Dreaming site in the Perth area that is called the Butterfly Dreaming, and it is tied to the*

beautiful blue and black butterfly. The butterfly lays its eggs in ants' nests near a small shrub we call a bacon-and-egg plant. The ants carry the larvae up to get the nectar from the shrub. Then they carry the larvae back down again at night and the larvae exude this nectar, which the ants collect for food. This is a symbiotic relationship, where what is good for one is good for the other. That is how we have to think about the natural world, because in the long run, when everything is in balance, what is good for the earth will be good for us as human beings too.[3]

As Aboriginal people, we are a living, breathing, thinking physical manifestation of our land — a thread in the pattern of creation. Dr Bob Morgan writes that '… my culture and worldview is centred in Gumilaroi land and its people, it is who I am and will always be. I am my country.'[4] Country is not simply a geographical space. It is the whole of reality, a living story that forms and informs all existence. Country is alive, and more than alive — it is life itself:

Imagine a pattern. This pattern is stable, but not fixed. Think of it in as many dimensions as you like — but it has more than three. This pattern has many threads of many colours, and every thread is connected to, and has a relationship with, all of the others. The individual threads are every shape of life. Some — like human, kangaroo, paperbark — are known to western science as 'alive'; others, like rock, would be called 'non-living'. But rock is there, just the same. Human is there, too, though is it neither the most nor the least important thread — it is one among many; equal with the others. The pattern made by the whole is in each thread, and all the threads together make the whole.

Stand close to the pattern and you can focus on a single thread; stand a little further back and you can see how that thread connects to others; stand further back still and you can see it all — and it is only once you can see it all that you can recognise the pattern of the whole in every individual thread. The whole is more than its parts, and the whole is in all its parts. This is the pattern that the ancestors made. It is life, creation, spirit, and it exists in country.[5]

The world the ancestors made is one in which all life is joined in a web of relationships, a web that exists both within and outside us. And it is by maintaining and renewing the connections linking life together, that country — and so all of reality — is balanced and sustained. This is why, to Aboriginal people, our relationships with all shapes of life are of vital importance. As Dawn Bessarab comments:

Spirituality to Aboriginal people is connected to country and is about relationships; spiritual relationships with the trees, the land, the animals, the sky, the water. Country is not viewed as a bit of dirt with economic value but as a living entity ...[6]

Country is the source of all creation, all beauty, all wisdom. It sustains us, nourishes us, guides us. It gives us life, and teaches us how to live so that life — in all its shapes — will always go on. Country is our joy, our love, our hope.

Our country is our heart.

Other peoples in country

For thousands of years, Indigenous peoples cared for their countries, and were cared for in turn. Our Ancestors were not to know that, far across the seas, other people saw country in a very different way. One day the peoples of Europe would come seeking the place they called the Great South Land. It was the British who ultimately prevailed, with James Cook claiming our east coast in 1770, and the establishment of a penal colony in 1788. Those who arrived in our Ancestors' time did not understand that the bush they saw around them was not a wilderness, but a culturally managed landscape; that life in all its shapes watched them anxiously from the ground, the water, the sky; and that there was not a single grain of sand beneath their feet that was not part of a thinking, breathing, loving land. In their language, the British described and catalogued the land as an object, not as grandmother, grandfather, mother, father, sister, brother and family. And by being named as the land, country became hidden — for, as Greg Lehman writes 'words like "mountain", "tree" and "wind" are no invitation for them to show us their presence.'[7] Unlike Indigenous people, who had lived in cooperation with country for so many, many years, the British would cause the rapid extinction of numerous plant and animal species. This devastation was itself a product of a worldview in which land was, and could only ever be, an inert possession:

> [The British] *had left their Mother country far behind, and sought no new Mother here. They came to tame, conquer, subdue; not to be nurtured, taught, cared for. To them the continent was harsh, strange; empty of meaning except what*

they themselves brought to it; a place of which they were often afraid. These invaders — these strangers to country — could no longer feel their Mother's heart as it beat beneath the green lands of their home. They tried to understand the world by breaking it apart. Without their Mother to guide them, they could not see how the parts fit together to make the whole, or that the whole was more than the parts. Their science told them that human reason could make small and known a vast and mysterious universe; their religion said that of all the life there was, only they had been made in their Creator's image.[8]

Paradoxically, with every action taken to 'claim' this continent, the British only succeeded in creating greater and greater distance between themselves and the territory they wanted to make their own. For there can be no belonging in country without honouring and respecting the spirit of this living land.

Change in country

In the thousands of years before the British arrived, this continent had known transformations, not the least through extremes of climate change. But never before had there been a people here who could not hear the voices of the land, could not see that everything around them was alive, and could not feel the pain of country as pain to self. Greg Lehman writes:

... problems began when the British decided to stay. Killing began. Not just of cartela the seal, but us palawa mob too. That's the simple truth. Lots of killing. All of this

happened because of one thing: the sons of England did not know tunapri manta. *This is our knowing that comes from the Old Stories, handed down for a thousand generations. It give us our law and a way to know the world that works for everyone. But the sealers and soldiers would not learn!* [9]

The invasion of this land was an assault, not just on Aboriginal peoples, but on all life in country. Aboriginal peoples were killed, forced out of their lands, and confined in prisons, lock-hospitals, reserves, missions and other institutions. Country was attacked with the axe and the plough, scarred by roads, fences and mines, and subjected to a barrage of foreign species. And even when we were able to remain on our land, Aboriginal peoples were prevented from practicing the culture that sustained country. As Jill Milroy notes:

Land becomes real estate, an economic commodity, and a source of tradable wealth, duly assigned a particular value based on productivity or use. Land is packaged and parcelled: towns, parks, gardens, farms, stations, missions, reserves, mines, factories and prisons. There are desirable and undesirable places. Fences are erected, people are locked out and country is locked up. [10]

And Tjalaminu Mia comments:

We were forbidden to use language or undertake men and women's business which also included environmental sustainability practices; like seasonal burn-offs of particular tracts of land, maintenance of gnamma holes and ochre

13

deposits and the maintaining of food resources, like the fish traps along the Kalgan River near Albany.[11]

Traditional food sources dried up as native species were hunted, habitats were destroyed, and waterways were poisoned, by ignorance or design. Country struggled to provide for her people, and Aboriginal people were forced into working for those who were harming their land. Elder Beryl Dixon recalls:

It ... [was] impossible for us to look after the land the way our old people would have done in the times before the white people came. Our lives were hard. We had no opportunity and little access to a proper education or regular jobs with decent pay. The farmers employed us because they couldn't get anyone else to do the work cheaper. They also took advantage of our situation because they knew that we needed the work to survive. It was the only way we could put food on the table for our families. There were no hand-outs to talk of in those days, only the rations the Native Welfare Department gave to Nyungars, but this didn't amount to enough to survive on ... Looking back now at some of the jobs our people did, especially labouring to clear the land for farmers in the South-West, I think sadly of some of the consequences. The felling of all those trees has degraded the land and caused the water to become salty. Also, there are fewer places for the birds and animals to live. This could have all been avoided if, when white people first came to Nyungar country, they had listened to the wisdom of our Elders.[12]

Aboriginal people continue to be affected by the violence of dispossession. This is not distant history but a living experience that is held within people and country. The sorrow, pain and trauma are still felt deeply, both where the stories are known, and where there are gaps in memory and history that might never be filled. Bill Jonas reflects on the world of his childhood:

Now, when I think about the valley which nurtured me, I see this lovely part of the world in yet another light. In some ways it is a gloomy, even sad and tragic imagination that now takes hold of my thoughts. I find myself constantly wondering about what happened to the people who once lived here. Did the original inhabitants suffer the same fate as Aboriginal people in the surrounding valleys? Was that spearing at Hells Gates an isolated incident or, as now seems likely, was it part of a broader pattern of Aboriginal people being forced to defend their country and their lives? What awful secrets may lie hidden in that large lagoon? [13]

It was not only Aboriginal people who were, and still are, affected by colonial violence. The land remembers where blood was shed. Tjalaminu Mia speaks of visiting a place where a waterhole had been deliberately poisoned in colonial times, killing many Nyungar people: 'I felt depressed like I wanted to cry out in pain. It was like I was experiencing pain that did not personally belong to me but belonged to someone else.'[14]

The consequences of damaging the connections between people and country are profound, both for Aboriginal people and the land itself. Dr Bob Morgan comments:

When Indigenous people become disconnected from country, the teachings, steeped as they are in generations of traditions

*and wisdom, are open to abuse and indeed systematic
erosion. Disconnection from country is a pivotal factor in
understanding the level of dysfunction that sadly can be
found in the lives of far too many Indigenous people across
the nation.*[15]

And in her story, Dawn Bessarab writes of how waterfalls
in the Dampier peninsula dried up and no longer flowed.
Elders in Derby had told her uncle that:

*Dat country im lonely, people dey'll gone, no-one dere to look
after im anymore, so dat country lonely, im sad, dat why dat
water bin dry up, ee missing ees people.*[16]

Like all colonial nations, Australia must reconcile its
history. There has been violence here, and harm, sorrow and
pain. But there is also joy in this place, and wonder, and
creation. For despite all she has suffered, country yet lives. So
there is still an opportunity to heal the connections that have
been broken, a chance for us all to work together for country.

Healing in country

Despite the damage done to Aboriginal peoples and
countries, the spirituality of this land remains strong.
Connections have been damaged, but they are not yet
broken. Our ancestors are still with us, teaching us and
guiding us along the right path. And because the land holds
memory, then for as long as it remains, nothing is ever truly
lost. Songs, stories and knowledge that have passed from
human memory can still be brought back to us. Pat
Dudgeon tells how she dreamed of the death of her

grandfather, who had died many years before:

… in this dream, I was a man who was drowning in a violent storm out at sea. Amid the terror and desperation of the situation, I knew I wanted to live, I wanted to grow old with my family and my last thought was that I would die far away from my country, and they would not know that I had died, would not know where my body was, and would not mourn me properly.[17]

Other stories speak of the spirits of our old people still operating in our present lives. Dr Joan Winch writes:

The spirits have always guided me throughout my life, so I am following in their footsteps. My mum and dad told me that even when I was a little baby the spirits worked through me. It was me they used to warn them of impending danger.[18]

This land is still not the inert possession the British thought it was when they arrived over two hundred years ago. There are still powerful spirits here, in the deserts and the forests and the beaches, beneath the cities and the houses and the roads. As Noel Nannup tells:

People don't realise it, but there is some very strong country here around the City of Perth. Take a place like Kings Park, for example. It's an important place now, but it was important in the old times, too. The spirit in that land is so strong that it has saved itself from development. That happens sometimes, the land protects itself.[19]

The stories in this anthology speak of the relationship between Aboriginal people and the land, and they all share the theme of love. A love for country, of both its hard and soft faces, of our relations in the animal and plant worlds, of the fresh and salt water, and of the ancestors in the land and sky. They are also stories of the awe-inspiring way the land loves and cares for us all. But it is the deepest love that causes the deepest grief. To be heartsick is to be broken-hearted, or full of sorrow. To be heartsick for country is to speak of a feeling deeper still. It encompasses the emotions of loss, loneliness, sadness and grief. It is a profound wound of the heart, mind, body and spirit. Aboriginal people are heartsick over what is happening to the land; it is a stress we carry in our bodies. As Dr Joan Winch writes in her story:

My mother's family ... feel very concerned with the damage done to the land. In our way of thinking, if the land is in bad repair, then so are the people. If the rivers dry up and become polluted, then this can be equated with the body's lifeblood; and it means that life can't be sustained.[20]

And as Irene Watson says in hers:

Caring for country can invoke romantic images of Aboriginal people and the land and it can be all of those images but it can also be a lot of worry, sadness and hopelessness over our dealing with a dominant culture that doesn't care in the same way that many Aboriginal peoples care for the land.[21]

The destruction of the environment, of our relationships

with other life, is mirrored in the vast damage within us. We are all made less when we make country less. But perhaps there is now an opportunity, not just for Indigenous peoples, but also for all who dwell within country to work together to heal the wounds of the past. As Joe Boolgar Collard comments:

> *While it is our responsibility as Aboriginal people to maintain and protect our natural and cultural heritage, there is also a collective responsibility to take care of this country and to be strongly involved in environmental sustainability. This hasn't happened in the past, but it must happen in the future if we are to survive and look after this country.* [22]

If we are to solve the multitude of environmental problems that we face, then we must begin with our connection to country. We must repair and regrow the relationships between peoples and peoples, and people and country that have been damaged by dispossession. Despite the environmental devastation that has been wreaked upon Australia, this ancient continent continues to nourish and sustain all who live here. It gives us our water and food, and it protects us in ways we often do not imagine. We cannot survive here without a loving land that cares for us, and all Australians, Aboriginal and non-Aboriginal alike, are bound to its rise and fall. And if this ancient land is to survive, then all who now make their homes here must learn to see the land as a living, connected being, to realise we are all a part of something so much greater than ourselves. And if we can come together to return that care, that nourishment, that protection that the land gives us, then perhaps it is this love of country that will, in the end, redeem us all. For, as Sally Morgan writes:

> *If we, as human beings, continue to cut ourselves away from the web of life, then we embrace a story that, like* terra nullius, *can have only one ending — death. Far better then, to embrace a story which not only honours life, but returns it a thousandfold to all those who will come after us.*[23]

Gladys Idjirrimoonya Milroy

is a Palyku Elder, whose country is in the Pilbara region of Western Australia. Gladys is a poet and storyteller.

Jill Milroy

is a Palyku woman and Gladys' daughter. Jill is Dean of the School of Indigenous Studies at the University of Western Australia.

Different Ways of Knowing: Trees Are Our Families Too

Aboriginal people have different ways of knowing. One of the ways we know and make sense of the world around us is through stories given to us from the Dreaming. Stories tell us about the spirit of the world, and they come from trees, animal, rocks, rivers, the moon, stars, and country itself. Sometimes these stories come as dreams, or messages from our old people whose spirits are still with us, even though they have died. A dream can be a warning, given because you've gone the wrong way. Or there may be something you need to know to prepare for what is coming, or something you must do. It can be a way of reassuring and comforting us by letting us know we are going the right way. It's like a message stick, a way of communicating. In dreams we can be taken to other places, times, and the worlds between spaces. In dreams we must listen whether we like it or not; it is hard to walk away. We may do so when we awaken, but by then we will have been given the knowledge. Sometimes we do not know what we have been given or why, so it may take a long time to 'know'. Timing is uncertain; it goes its own way. Things can change. Knowing may come in the depths of sleep, between sleeping and waking, or when we are awake but restful and quiet. In these times it is easier for us to listen to those other ways of knowing that are available to us. This is when we can tap into the deep knowledge all around us, not just the surface. So knowledge comes in many different ways and these ways are common to Indigenous peoples around the world. As Leon Secatero, Spiritual Elder of Mother Earth and Headman of the Canoncito Band of Navajo explains:

> For a while when I talked about sacred things like this, I used words like 'revelation' and 'prophecy'. But those words do not represent real Indigenous thought. More appropriately, I would speak of 'a way of being', or a 'knowing' — the knowing that's in us.[24]

This kind of knowing is not unique to Indigenous people: knowing lies within us all. Unfortunately, it is a way of knowing that has been discarded by many of the world's cultures, and removed from their formal knowledge and learning systems. Western knowledge, as it is currently constituted, excludes or marginalises many ways of knowing, including its own ancient ways. Western knowledge is increasingly problematic because of its dominance over other people's world knowledge and learning systems, its innate belief in its superiority over *all* other forms of 'knowing', and its claims to universality when it is only a 'particular' way of knowing. The westernisation of knowledge has meant that many Indigenous ways of knowing have been labelled as myth and described as anecdotal and unreliable. This type of denigration has damaged people and their relationships with each other and with the natural world around them. As one of the senior Aboriginal women of Coober Pedy, who fought successfully to keep a nuclear waste dump from being built on their country, Eileen Unkari Crombie says:

The learning isn't written on paper, as whitefellas' knowledge is. We carry it instead in our heads and we're talking from our hearts, for the land. You fellas, whitefellas, put us in the back all the time, like we've got no language for the land. But we've got the story for the land.[25]

For Aboriginal people, the land is full of stories, and we are born from our Mother the land, into these stories. The old people tell us stories that nurture and sustain us through life into old age, so that we can tell children the stories they will need to sustain them. The great life-story cycle has been the way for millennia. It is the birthright of all Aboriginal children to be born into the *right* story. Indeed, it is the birthright and greatest gift we can give all children. The *right* story connects us intimately to our country, giving us our place and our identity. The *right* story embeds us deeply in nature, connected to the living spirit. As Bill Neidjie, the legendary Kakadu man, explains:

Tree
He watching you
You look at tree,
He listen to you.
He got no finger,
He can't speak.
But that leaf,
He pumping, growing

Growing in the night.
While you sleeping
You dream something.
Tree and grass same thing.
They grow with your body,
With your feeling.

If you feel sore,
Headache, sore body,
That mean somebody killing tree or grass.

You feel
because your body in that tree or earth.
Nobody can tell you,
You got to feel it yourself [26]

My grandmother Daisy could not read or write but gave all of us kids' stories. My mother Gladys and I continue to see the world in stories. When we began to talk about what story we should write for this book, what kept coming to us was a cry from the trees to help them tell their story. Not just because it is important for them, because it is important for us. To help us begin, my mother, Gladys, was given a dream about the first tree.

The first tree
In the dream I was a young girl again, about twelve years
old. I was walking around, searching for a tree to sit under,
but everything was desolate and empty. There were no trees,
just dried grass. All the trees were gone; it was as if they had
just walked away. So I sat down on the dry grass by the road,
and even though the sun was shining, it was very cold. Then

I saw a man wearing a business suit and carrying a suitcase fly down from the sky and land a few yards away from me. He opened his suitcase, took off his wings, folded them up and put them inside his case. Then he picked the case up and walked to the side of the road. A yellow bus came and he got on it. I called out to him, but he took no notice. I walked over to where he had been and picked up a little grey feather he must have dropped. The feather stuck to my hand and carried me up to a high mountain all made of crystal. When I landed there, the feather flew from my hand and stuck in my hair, I noticed that it had got bigger. I walked into the beautiful crystal mountain and saw a lot of people, like nurses, running around carrying babies wrapped in baby blankets. They were placing them all together in a large room and took no notice of me, they all seemed to be in too much of a hurry.

I wanted to look at one of the babies so I pulled the blanket back from its face and saw tiny little leaves growing out of the blanket. I realised they were baby trees, not people. When I lifted the blanket, all the baby trees started crying. A nurse hurried into the room to see what was happening. She saw me standing there with the grey feather sticking out of my hair and looked shocked. She grabbed my hand and called out to the others, who all crowded around talking loudly, only I couldn't understand their language.

They took me into an enormous room, so high you couldn't see the ceiling. A beautiful, old, wise-looking tree sat at the end of the room, it was ancient and had thousands of branches reaching in all directions and disappearing into the ceiling. I thought it was so beautiful and so old it must be the earth's first tree. A little branch reached out and plucked the feather from my hair. A strand of my hair clung to the *feather as the branch placed it in the tree. The feather started growing bigger and bigger turning red and gold. I saw the crystal mountain starting to disintegrate and realised it was made of ice. I felt cold now the feather had left me, so I stood in the glow that was melting the ice. As the feather grew larger it became a beautiful golden-red firebird. The branches of the ancient tree started glowing, they reached out and began picking up all the baby trees. The ancient branches covered the world, planting the baby trees all over the earth. The firebird flew around the world three times, then came back to its nest in the ancient tree. I looked out at the landscape and saw it was covered with wonderful trees of all colours. I wanted to find my own special tree, I turned back to thank the first tree and the firebird for bringing the trees back, but they were no longer there. I felt so happy the trees had returned, I laughed and danced among them looking for my special tree friend. The sun was warm again, black cockatoos flew from the earth, singing and calling to each other. They gently lifted me up and flew with me across a shining blue lake with a mirror-like surface. I glanced down at my reflection on the lake and saw that I was no longer a young girl; I was a lovely red-tailed black cockatoo flying with my family back home to country.*

It is through the eyes of our children that people will see the empty world we have created. We, who have folded away our spiritual lives and packed them into suitcases, expect our children to do the same. We wish them to find wisdom on wheels within the Western education system, not in an Aboriginal one with living trees. Trees are families too, and they give birth and nurture and care for their babies, just like humans. Children, trees and birds are all meant to grow up together. When we make our children pack away their spiritual lives in little brown suitcases, they learn only half of what they need to know. The full knowledge of the world gives children the feathers from their suitcases, the means to fly. In my mother's case, she became the red-tailed black cockatoo because this is her special bird (what is often referred to as her 'totem'). Of course, red-tailed black cockatoos need old forests to live in. They are big birds and need the large old trees to provide hollow logs big enough for them to nest in. Trees, birds and people are intimately connected; we are meant to be in the same story. It is people who break this connection, and create separate stories.

The story nomads

In Western scholarship, those writing about Aboriginal people have often called us 'nomads'. This really had a pejorative meaning, labelling us as wanderers, with no fixed home. 'Nomads' were the opposite of 'settled' people like the British and other Europeans who lived in agricultural and industrialised societies, and who had cities from which had come civilisations. The label, 'nomads' of course, has been very useful in undermining Aboriginal claims to land. Yet Aboriginal people never 'wandered' far from country and always struggled to stay close to it. We did not leave it but were taken from it and we still grieve for country we lost, as country grieves for us. We did not seek other peoples' country to make our own, we lived in our country and moved as country showed us. We followed song lines, Dreaming tracks and stories within our country, keeping country healthy through our presence and ceremony, which in turn kept us healthy. We cared for country, and country still cares for us.

The real *nomads,* of course, were the people who gave us that name: the British never stayed home, they have wandered the world. As a consequence, Aboriginal people have had to contend with what we could describe as *story nomads.* These *story nomads* wander about in other people's stories, mucking them up and changing the endings; disbelieving most, stealing some, selling others. They often come too late to understand what the story is about, starting in the middle of a story but claiming it is the beginning. They may leave before the end, so they don't have to face the consequences of broken stories. They are the perpetual travellers of the story world because they have 'disremembered' their own stories, consigning them to myth, mysticism, religion, allegory, metaphor or narrative: the 'not quite true' category. By dis(re)membering stories, they create limited knowledge systems. Telling other people's stories for them, *story nomads* believe the 'new' stories they create are true and more important than any others. Aboriginal people know these aren't proper true stories, but they are often trapped in them nonetheless. So are trees, and we can gain some insight into this strange situation through two Aboriginal storytellers, Dingo and Wombat.

Dingo and Wombat

It is important to understand who Dingo and Wombat are. To begin with, they inhabit a real world. Wombat guards the green world, the inner world. We can't see his secret life, as he sleeps deep in the earth. Dingo guards the outer world and talks to the moon while we sleep. Dingo is always finding things that are lost and Wombat is always trying to help him with them. Together, they give us lessons in how to restore everything to its proper place in order to ensure the future. They also help us understand what is important and what isn't. Their wisdom is useful to all people, particularly *story nomads*. If the current attorney-general, Philip Ruddock, had had access to Dingo and Wombat's wisdom in 2000, then he might not have been reported in the French newspaper, *Le Monde,* as attributing the then Aboriginal disadvantage to the nature of Aboriginal society itself, by virtue of the fact that 'Aborigines were hunter-gatherers not familiar with the wheel'.[27] Similarly, the prime minister, John Howard, might not have agreed that no apology or censure was needed, because Ruddock had been merely stating a 'historical fact'. But like a coin, there are two sides to a wheel, as Dingo and Wombat discovered.

The lost tree

Dingo walked restlessly outside Wombat's burrow; he was anxious for Wombat to wake up because he had found something very special. Dingo thought everything he found was very special, but he wasn't allowed to wake Wombat, not when Wombat was dreaming about how to change the world. Wombat could hear Dingo walking up and down outside, so he eventually gave in and asked Dingo what he wanted.

'I've found something very special and I need you to help me put it in my cave. It's a round tree', he said showing Wombat his latest find.

'Don't be silly', said Wombat, 'It doesn't look like a tree

to me'. But he helped Dingo try to put it in his cave anyway, only it wouldn't fit.

'Let's stand it up and try that way', suggested Wombat.

When they stood the round tree up, it started rolling down the hill. Wombat and Dingo chased after it, but it rolled faster and faster until it flew off a high cliff, fell into a deep ravine and disappeared out of sight. Dingo was very upset and in his heart he blamed Wombat for standing it up in the first place. He went back to his cave and drew a picture of his round tree on a rock, so if he ever found it again he would remember what it looked like.

That night, Dingo went to see his friend, the moon, and told him of his special find. 'It wasn't like anything I've found before', said Dingo.

'What did it look like?' asked Moon.

'I drew it on my rock over there', said Dingo.

Moon shone his light on the rock and saw Dingo's drawing.

'Oh that's no longer a tree,' explained Moon, 'though it was once. That's a wheel.'

Dingo got so excited his lost object had a name that he couldn't wait to tell Wombat and he raced off while Moon was still talking. When he found Wombat, he proudly told him he had found a 'wheel'.

'Now, we'll have to go and get it', said Dingo.

'No, Dingo', said Wombat, 'it has fallen back into Time, we can't go there, that's someone else's story.'

The wheel of time

The British valued the wheel, but they did not value its connection to the tree. The invention of the wheel is tied inexorably to the progress of Western civilisation, but at the heart of the wheel, was the death of the tree. And allied to the 'wheel', for Aboriginal peoples worldwide, was another dead tree, the sailing ship. The wheel and the sailing ship were instrumental in disconnecting people from country and the natural world. Similarly, the spiritually rich nature of Aboriginal cultures, where knowledge and relationships between people, country and all living things are highly prized, went unappreciated by the *story nomads*, because they could not see beyond the missing wheel to the living tree. What they valued was the resources and material wealth the land could provide, with no understanding of, or care for, the deeper story. Western progress required the plunder of the world.

Ordering the landscape, disordering country

The first thing the *story nomads* do when they arrive somewhere is to begin to order the 'landscape' to establish their 'view' of country, what they want to see in their field of vision, and what they want to exclude. What they really do is *dis*order country, removing it from its own story. They write the storybook they want to read. Land becomes *real estate*, an economic commodity, and a source of tradable wealth, duly assigned a particular value based on productivity or use. Land is packaged and parcelled: towns, parks, gardens, farms, stations, missions, reserves, mines, factories and prisons. There are desirable and undesirable places. Fences are erected, people are locked out and country is locked up.

Felling trees begins the destruction of memory and the usurpation of place. In 1829, the *story nomads* arrived in force in Western Australia and the founding of the new British colony was marked with the death of a tree. Mrs Dance, with axe in hand, made the first cut to fell a sheoak, to the accompaniment of rifle volleys, speeches and cheers. The ceremony is said to be accurately rendered in George Pitt Morrison's *The Foundation of Perth*, painted in the Centenary year, 1929, with copies distributed to Western Australian school children. Emblematic of the occasion, the imagery remains quintessentially Western Australian. Trees were an impediment to progress and development, so they had to be cleared. As the ancient giants were hacked to death, the birds, animals, insects were all cleared, along with Aboriginal people. The British imported into Australia their own plants, their own animals, their own birds, and their own people and made up their own story.

As Aboriginal song man Archie Roach laments in *The Native Born*:

> *So bow your head old Eucalypt and Wattle Tree*
> *Australia's bush is losing its identity*
> *While the cities and the parks that they have planned*
> *Look out of place because the spirit's in the land.*[28]

The old ones

In Australia, there is ongoing conflict over the continued logging of old-growth forests. Prior to colonisation, all Australia's forests were old-growth, but in a little over two hundred years, ninety per cent of old-growth forests has been cleared. Just like shooting birds and animals for 'sport', there were popular contests to see who could fell the largest tree. This usually meant the oldest tree, the tree with the most knowledge. Old-growth forests are always in danger in Australia. Thankfully, the trees have made deep friendships with many non-Aboriginal people who continue to fight for them. By supporting trees to keep their stories going, their friends live in the right stories too. This is a wonderful thing to do.

'Old-growth' and 're-growth' are very deceptive terms when applied to trees. They are meant to persuade us that it's a natural transition from one story to the other, to see not change but continuity, progress inherent in re-growth. Tourism mostly uses the more evocative term 'ancient forests', but this is a less desirable nomenclature in the forest logging debate. Ancient forests are made up of trees of many different ages, sizes and shapes, as well as fallen logs, and other plants that grow with them. This biodiversity supports a large variety of animals and birds. Trees themselves are in large extended families and communities with lots of support, love and care: grandparents, parents, aunties, uncles and children. In contrast, re-growth forests are biologically simple. They are made up of trees that are nearly all the same age, where it's a bit like growing up in institutions, with lots of children, some foster parents, no grandparents, no family to grow you up. It's hard to imagine a world where everyone's the same age. It's a restricted view of life systems to believe that young trees will simply be able to grow without the support and guardianship of older trees. We *can't* really know if trees will be able to reach such great ages and sizes again; we can know that the minimum waiting time will be hundreds of years. This seems a needless and heedless risk to take, to break the story now. The destruction of the earth's green mantle has enormous consequences for country and for what we pass on to future generations.

The tree of life

The tree is the symbol of life itself and trees actively support our life on earth, through all its cycles and in all its dimensions, physically, emotionally and spiritually. We all know what trees give us, but we act as if it isn't true. We know the right stories for trees, but tell the wrong ones. Everyone talks proudly of their family trees, but not everyone talks about the trees in their families. Trees are our relations. In the Dreaming, everything is related, as Yanuwa Elder Mussolini Harvey explains:

> *The Dreamings are our ancestors, no matter if they are fish, birds, men, women, animals, wind or rain. It was these Dreamings that made our Law. All things in our country have Law, they have ceremony and song, and they have people who are related to them.*[29]

Trees have always cared for humans and offered shelter in life and in its passing. For millennia, even for the *story nomads*, the tree was the child's wooden cradle, to hold the baby close to the mother, rocking as she worked. In death, the coffin was the loving rest, protection from bare earth. For Aboriginal women, trees are the midwives when children are birthed on the banks of dry riverbeds where the tall gums grow, and where each child has a birth tree. To protect mother and child, there is cleansing and healing smoke from gum leaves, with ashes rubbed into the child's head. To cradle the child, the *coolamon* is taken carefully

35

Birth tree, Palyku Country
Courtesy Gladys Milroy

from the tree and the mother carries the child nestled in its soft curves. At the end of our journey here, in our passing, we are held once more in the loving embrace of trees, held aloft, wrapped in paperbark, hollow logs, a resting place.

Trees are the very breath of life. An average tree produces enough oxygen in a year to keep a family of four breathing. As well as absorbing harmful carbon dioxide, trees provide shelter, shade, warmth and cooling. Trees and plants freely give us essential foods and medicines. It is now well recognised that Aboriginal people have a diverse and sophisticated pharmacopoeia in Australia. The eucalypt provides a powerful antiseptic, used worldwide for coughs, colds and sore throats; the disinfectant and antiseptic properties of melaleuca makes it particularly good for healing skin infections; acacia is used to make medicine for colds and flu and its bark for covering sores, wounds and burns. The smoke that results from laying leaves and twigs over a fire was used widely to keep people healthy as well as healing sickness. Aboriginal people have always known how trees look after our health and promote our wellbeing. They cure sickness and despair. Western studies now also show that patients heal more quickly when they have a view of trees; workers are more productive. Trees make us feel good; like the backbone of the universe, they lift us up and hold us there.

Trees protect water and soil quality, and replenish our water supplies. The world is facing a water crisis and several world leaders warn that this century, wars will be about water. Yet the rainforests that are needed to seed the rain clouds are fast disappearing. Australia is the oldest and driest continent on earth. Seventy five per cent of its vegetation is eucalypts, whose roots store water, a valuable reserve known to Aboriginal people. For Aboriginal people our most powerful spirit, the Rainbow Serpent is associated with water. While Australia continues to kill our trees, it fails to protect our most valuable resources: soil and water. Such thinking pervades all levels of Australian society. In suburbs along Perth's Swan River foreshore, trees are occasionally found poisoned or ring-barked, the suspected culprits nearby residents or developers keen to enlarge their river view and enhance the value of property. They cannot see the beauty of trees right in front of them. They don't realise that trees anchor the earth; they provide the eternal maternal bloodline that nourishes us all.

The smell of home

Aboriginal people can tell you that country recognises people by their smell, just as we recognise our country by its smell. Most of the world's eucalypt species are endemic to Australia; eucalypts, or gum trees, are the essence of the country. Gum trees are part of Australian folklore and national identity. Every Australian knows what gum trees look like and what they smell like. It is a unique and evocative scent. Soldiers returning by ship from the two world wars are said to have been able to smell eucalypts from many miles off shore, long before land was visible. Trees have always been the first to welcome us home. The cleansing, healing scent of eucalypts refreshed the weary traveller and restored the battered soul. What does our country smell like now? Can we still smell eucalypts far from shore? The genocide of the trees in Australia leaves a bloodied landscape, that's why the land is so salty and there's a metallic smell beneath the surface of Australia now. It makes people restless, anxious; it's hard to sleep. Trees have always been our spiritual reservoirs, but many trees are invisible now. In the invisible forest, the ghosts of gums wander aimlessly, for there is no resting place. The tree spirits still cling to country, protecting the spirit of the land, for the land is never empty. But the deep healing wells are hidden. When all the trees and all the forests are invisible, will our children cry in despair, 'Where are the gums gone, the smell of our nation is killing us'?

The bone tree

Wombat was dreaming peacefully when a blob of dirt hit his face, waking him up.

'What's going on?' he spluttered, getting another face full of sand. 'Oh, it's you, Dingo. What are you doing digging near my burrow?'

Wombat saw that Dingo had a big bone in his mouth. 'Don't bury that bone here,' said Wombat, 'Why have you got it, anyway? There's no meat on it.'

'It's lost,' said Dingo. 'I'm looking after it.' Dingo was always looking after lost things.

'Don't be silly,' said Wombat, 'Bones don't get lost, now go away!'

Dingo was so upset that Wombat was not interested in his lost bone that he wandered off and sat on his own. But that night, Wombat dreamed that Dingo's lost bone was knocking on his burrow, calling 'Help me, help me!'

The next morning, Wombat went looking for Dingo and found him fast asleep, hugging the large bone. 'Dingo, wake up!' Wombat said, 'Where did you find that bone?' Dingo jumped up, pleased that Wombat was finally interested in his lost bone and ran ahead to show him the tree where he found it. Wombat looked up, and saw that the tree was covered in bones, except for one branch, where there was an empty space.

'What sort of tree is this?' asked Wombat.

'I call it dog's heaven,' said Dingo.

'Don't be silly,' said Wombat, 'We have to put the bone back where it belongs.'

Then the tree started singing, 'Put the bone back, put the bone back!'

It was very high but they pushed a rock under the tree to stand on, and Dingo stretched up and just managed to put the bone back in its place. Suddenly, beautiful green leaves started to grow and when they covered the tree, golden blossoms appeared. A small willy-willy swept across the tree and carried the golden blooms high into the blue sky.

That night, when Dingo was sitting talking to his friend the moon, he was amazed to see the sky completely covered with shiny new stars. 'The sky is so beautiful tonight, Moon,' said Dingo.

'Yes,' replied Moon. 'You did a great thing today, Dingo, you saved the spirits of the children not yet born, they are the stars you see.'

Now Dingo always guards the bone tree.

The living tree

We are the guardians of children and of all life on earth. But what is happening to the Tree of Life in this country? We have stopped valuing the living tree, seeing *who* the tree is, body and spirit. In Australia now there are two knowledge trees. One springs from the *story nomads* and represents Western ways of knowing, while the other arises from Aboriginal ways of knowing that come from the living tree. Aboriginal people have been taken from our sacred tree, and some of our stories have been broken. Aboriginal people collectively have the oldest living knowledge system in the world. Our 'tree' is made up of many living trees. Aboriginal Australia has more than two hundred languages and some six hundred 'nations'. Aboriginal people are culturally and linguistically diverse, but share a holistic, animate, interconnected system of knowledge that knows the stories for country, the spirit in the land and the relationships between all living things. This is entrusted to us from the Dreaming, the boundless, eternal enduring spirit of time. Aboriginal communities no longer have the resources to protect, sustain and grow our knowledge. The *story nomads'* tree has grown very large. It is highly prized, well fed and well watered, but it takes all the resources from the trees that Aboriginal people have to nurture and care for, our family trees and the trees in our families. Resources and funding overwhelmingly and disproportionately privilege Western knowledge, which, however prominent, is only *one* of the knowledge systems that exist in Australia and should not dominate all available resources. There is a national failure to formally acknowledge and value Aboriginal knowledge systems and Aboriginal ways of knowing. There is a national failure to protect Aboriginal knowledge holders: people, places, rock art, trees, animals, and birds. This has disastrous consequences for Aboriginal children and ultimately all of Australia's children. If we put the Western and Aboriginal systems together, Australia would have one of the most complete and unique knowledge systems in the world and one that all Australians could share. In such a partnership though, Aboriginal knowledge has to be *privileged because it is the knowledge of the land itself.* If Aboriginal knowledge is not sustained in this country, if it no longer exists in Australia, it will no longer exist anywhere in *this world.* If Western knowledge no longer existed in Australia, it would be very difficult for us, but Western knowledge would still exist in the world, in other countries, and we could always pack our suitcases and visit it there.

The great difficulty is that some *story nomads* call their story the nation's story and think it is the only one. Its essence is encapsulated in a verse from a poem, *Old Botany Bay*, written by Dame Mary Gilmore, one of Australia's most popular poets, and whose portrait adorns our ten-dollar note. To demonstrate the currency of the sentiment (and well matched to Philip Ruddock's comments about the wheel in the same year), the poem was recited by Australian actor Jack Thompson at the 2000 Sydney Paralympics. In *Old Botany Bay*, the verse concerned is:

I split the rock;
I felled the tree:
The nation was –
Because of me! [30]

This is one of the many illusions that can keep us from

knowing our country. We should not mistake 'nation' for country. Nations come and go, but country is forever. The land speaks true; there are no lies in country. When we lie down in country against our mother, skin to skin, she enfolds us in her arms. Our spiritual heart connects us to country; there can be no lies. The Tree of Life that exists here is Aboriginal. Yet Aboriginal children continue to be born into a disconnected, inanimate world that mistakes the idea of what a nation is, for the truth of *country*, the surface for what lies beneath. This interferes with children's birthright and pushes them into someone else's story. Aboriginal children have a right to be born into the right stories, their own stories that connect them to country, and to Aboriginal ways of knowing that are respected and valued. All Australian children deserve to know the country that they share through the stories that Aboriginal people can tell them and through the different ways of knowing country. This is what gives children the feathers to fly with the birds and grow with the trees. To deny non-Aboriginal Australian children this knowledge is also to deny them a part of their birthright (the other parts, of course, are all the trees of life and knowledge that they are also tied to by their ancestors). If all Australian children are given their proper birthright to be born into the *right story*, then this country will have a future in which all Australians can share and all children proudly recite:

I saved the rock;
I saved the tree:
The country is —
Because of me!

DAWN BESSARAB

is of Bardi/Indjarbandi descent and is a saltwater woman from Broome. A social worker, she recently completed her doctoral thesis, which explores the experiences of Aboriginal women and men and how these experiences have contributed to the development of people's masculine and feminine identities.

Country is Lonely

As a child growing up in Broome, I had the privilege of parents who were great storytellers. My father was a Bardi man, whose country is on the Dampier Peninsula, at a place called Boolgin.[31] From him I grew up hearing many saltwater stories of his childhood and learnt from him that I was Bardi.

My mother met my father when he came to Woodstock station in the Pilbara as a stockman; she moved to Broome, where they were married. Mum was also a great storyteller and many were the times when she would trade stories for doing jobs, such as washing dishes and sweeping floors; such was the calibre of her stories that we would do anything to hear one. Mum's stories ranged from childhood antics to culture, and no matter what the topic, the results were the same: she held us captive to her magic. I learnt from Mum that her people had come from Millstream in the Pilbara and that I was also descended from the Indjarbandi people.

Today, as a Bardi/Indjarbandi woman, I can no longer ignore other aspects of my identity and even though they do not form the dominant characteristics that define who I am, I must acknowledge them because they are also a part of me. Those aspects are my non-Indigenous identity: French and

English. As a woman of colour, I identify strongly as an Aboriginal woman of Bardi/Indjarbandi descent whose socialisation as a child was heavily steeped in Aboriginal culture. Because he was a saltwater man, my father taught me to love the sea, and my mother, being a desert/river woman, taught me to love the bush. From both I learnt about country.

Yarning one day with my elderly uncle[32], sitting at the kitchen table with a mug of tea, he told me a story about country that he had heard from male Elders from the Mowanjum community, in Derby, Western Australia. My uncle also had grown up on the Dampier Peninsula and as a boy had accompanied his father on a lugger, regularly sailing up and down the Kimberley coastline doing postal runs and delivering supplies. As my uncle reminisced, he talked about how the coastline had many waterfalls cascading into the sea, something that had left a strong impression on him as a young child. When he returned many years later as an adult revisiting the same coastline, he had been astonished to discover that many of the waterfalls that he remembered had dried up and no longer existed.

Natural Temple, Cape Leveque
Courtesy Dawn Bessarab

Upon returning to Derby, my uncle met and talked with the Elders and in his discussion mentioned the disappearance of many of the waterfalls and his astonishment at how the country had changed. The Elders' response surprised my uncle:

'Dat country im lonely, is people dey all gone, no one dere to look after im anymore, so dat country im lonely, im sad, dat why dat water bin dry up, ee missing ees people.'

The significance of the Elders' response, and their explanation about why some of the waterfalls had dried up struck me, highlighting how different their understandings were and would be to Western understanding.

Western understanding would probably attribute the lack of waterfalls to things such as drought, summer, and changed watercourses: all scientific and all logically reasonable. Whereas the Elders' explanation, in its simplicity, was much more complex and profound. Their understanding and reasoning lay in a completely different paradigm, one that is grounded in Aboriginal philosophy and spirituality.

For many non-Indigenous people, the concept of spirituality is tied up with religion. For Indigenous people, spirituality was not connected to religion until the introduction of Christianity, in which many people think they are one and the same. While religion can encompass spirituality, it is not the same thing. For an Aboriginal person, to talk about spirituality is to talk about the connection of country and relationships, and the Dreaming, which provides a guide and spiritual roadmap for people to follow. This chapter will explore through narrative the deep relationship and connection that Aboriginal people have to their spirituality and the implications that this has.

Spirituality to Aboriginal people is connected to country and is about relationships: spiritual relationships with the trees, the land, the animals, the sky, and the water. Country is not viewed as a bit of dirt with economic value but as a living entity, which is often referred to and described in masculine and feminine terms. Leroy Little Bear[33], talking about the philosophy of the Plains Indians, in the United States, says most Aboriginal languages are 'verb rich' and do not allow for the categorising of dichotomies. According to Little Bear, there is no 'animate/inanimate dichotomy'. Everything is more or less animate. Consequently, Aboriginal languages allow for talking to trees and rocks, an allowance not accorded in English. If everything is animate, then everything has spirit and knowledge. If everything has spirit and knowledge, then all are like me. If all are like me, then all are my relations.[34]

Aboriginal women and men throughout Australia have similar philosophies. Land is not considered inanimate; it is seen to have feelings. Within the land there are messages and stories that have their foundation in the Dreaming, and through spirit beings these messages were left in the landscape to be relayed to us through stories that instil a strong belief in spirituality.

The Elders' explanation to my uncle describes the 'country' as having feelings and explains the dried-up waterfalls as a result of the disruption of relationships, in particular that between the country and its people. The spirit beings that inhabit the country feel the absence of the people who had been given the responsibility to look after the land, and, in loneliness, the land suffers.

My uncle's story is one of many that abound in the Aboriginal community. Children growing up in families are fed a steady diet of stories about the birds, trees, rocks and the sky, learning that these are all connected and represent different manifestations of Aboriginal spirituality.

Nyungar colleagues have told me how the entrance of a willy wagtail (*djidi djidi* [35]) into a house signifies the arrival of bad news. The strength of this belief unfolded at a workshop I was attending where several local Nyungars were present. During the workshop, a little willy wagtail flew in through the door and landed on the floor at the front of the room. The Nyungars reacted by getting up and chasing the bird out, loudly exclaiming that its presence could signify bad news. Similarly, in *My Place*, Sally Morgan talks about how the call of a bird heralds the message that her grand-mother has died.[36]

Through people's experiences, stories heard in childhood confirm 'the spiritual nature of the [Aboriginal] world [which] is incorporated into the socialization of Indigenous children' ... 'Indigenous spirituality encompasses the inter-substantiation of ancestral beings, humans and physiography'.[37] They are a physical fact because they are experienced as part of one's life, and through these experiences are confirmed as real and substantial.

A non-Indigenous anthropologist, whom I will call Karl (not his real name), gave me an example of this. When I first met Karl he was working in a remote community and though he had considerable experience working with Aboriginal people, he struck me as somewhat aloof and distant. We had had a discussion about Aboriginal spirituality, and Karl said that while he accepted that Aboriginal people had these beliefs, on a personal level, he did not really believe. At the time I could not articulate to myself what it was that I felt about him; now I would say he lacked connection with his spirit, but this was after he told me his story. This telling happened after our paths crossed again, several years later. After social pleasantries had been exchanged, I noticed there was something different about him; he seemed to have changed in some way. So I asked him what had happened to him since our last meeting. Karl found it surprising that I had noticed any change and proceeded to tell me about something that had happened to him for which he had no scientific explanation. This experience had completely changed his view of Aboriginal spirituality from a metaphysical concept to an experiential one. He told me he had been doing some work with Aboriginal people and some of the men from the community had taken him out to their ancestral lands, to visit a site. Karl described the excursion:

The day was bright and clear, not a cloud in the sky, when we drove our Land Rovers into the area. There were two Land Rovers and we were following a road through the long brown Kimberley grass as the wet season was over and the grass was beginning to dry. We parked under a tree and proceeded to walk down towards the billabong, which was at the base of the cliff and in the direction we were headed. We were halfway between the tree and the billabong when out of nowhere this dark cloud gathered overhead, it started to rumble and then lightning flashed; one struck down near to where we were parked. Before we knew it, the grass was on fire and it was heading towards us, threatening to cut us off from our vehicles. We started running as fast as we could back to the Land Rovers, we jumped inside and took off out of there. We got out just in time. The sky cleared up and once again was bright and sunny, with no cloud in sight. On the way back, the men in our vehicle were rapidly talking among themselves in language, and then one of them turned to me and said, 'We bin tryin' to figure out what we done wrong for the country to get wild with us, we shoulda introduced you early on when we bin pull up and not wait till we got to the site ... that country 'e bin wild with us for bringin' a stranger in and not telling 'im who you are and your business'.

Karl was pretty shaken by this experience and said that in all his years of working with Aboriginal people he had never experienced anything like it. He said there was no logical explanation for the appearance of the black cloud that had disappeared as quickly as it had appeared after they had left. He said he had not only been frightened, but also experienced a feeling of 'something else', something which had moved his spirit and confirmed for him that Aboriginal spiritual beliefs were real and not mythical. The difference I sensed in Karl was a shift in his spiritual belief system and a connectedness that somehow made him more real, more substantial.

I tell you this story because usually it is Aboriginal people who tell stories, and now here was a non-Aboriginal man telling me something with which he was still struggling to find meaning. Physically, his body had told him that he had experienced something beyond scientific explanation; mentally he was still struggling. Karl knew that in telling me his story he wouldn't receive a denial, or a challenge, or a scientific explanation of what had happened. From me he received acknowledgement of his experience and a confirmation of the Aboriginal men's explanation and belief as to why.

Growing up in my family and learning from my Elders, I was told that whenever I visited someone else's country I should always yell out and tell them who I was, where I came from and what my business was. By showing respect for the spirits of the country, I would not come to any harm. But if I failed to do so, then something could happen to me and the people accompanying me.

When I lived in Derby and my children were little, I regularly used to take them out to the river on picnics. One particular day, I took my children as well as a *gadiya* [38] friend and her children. We visited an area that is a women's site and a lovely place to picnic. While we were there, my sandals disappeared from the riverbank; I asked the kids if anyone had taken them, they all swore black and blue that they had not touched my sandals. As we were the only ones there, it was a mystery how they had disappeared. Later, as my friend and I were paddling in the shallow water and talking about the sandals, I was trying to figure out what had happened, when I suddenly remembered that I had not introduced myself or my friend to country. I said to her, 'I know why those sandals disappeared, the country is telling me something!' And to her surprise I started to call out and speak to country, saying who I was and that we were visiting for the day and meant no harm. After I had finished speaking, I had this strong feeling to put my hand down under the water and touch the riverbed in front of me, I did this and touched a broken bottle with very sharp and jagged edges sticking up in the sand. If I had taken one more step,

I would have seriously cut myself. I removed the broken bottle from the water and showed my friend, saying to her, 'See, the country has sent me a message, now it is saying it won't hurt me and is looking after me.' My friend looked at me as though I was slightly mad, but in my heart I knew that, in response, the country had spoken back to me, acknowledging my greeting.

How did I know this? Because my Bardi grandmother, whom I was told to call *Goli* [39] (grandmother), had taught me how to listen and communicate with country when she took my children and me out to her traditional country near Djarindjin, on the Dampier Peninsula. Her country was called *Miligoon* [40] and it was the first time that I had visited with her. When the Toyota stopped and we got out of the car, my children started to run down to the beach. We followed, laughing and talking, and then my daughter, Kalimba, suddenly stopped in her tracks (she was about three years old) and said loudly to me as she bent down to

Gift from the Heart of Country
Courtesy Dawn Bessarab

pick something up, 'Look, Mummy, a pretty heart.' When I looked to see what was in her hand, she had a beautiful smooth white stone in the shape of a heart. My *Goli* looked at the stone and said to my daughter, 'See, the country likes you; it has sent you a gift, a love heart'. I learnt from my *Goli*'s words that day that if you know how to listen and what to look for, the country speaks in many different ways.

Marika and Bunthami, women Elders from the Rirratjingu Clan of the Yolngu nation, say that 'Nature telling stories, and we're connected to these natural stories. We don't write it down and give to the kids; we teach through talking, telling and showing.'[41] Similarly, Nona, from the Torres Strait, says when she is talking about the sea, 'When we see the shark jump or the stingray jump, doesn't matter if the sea is calm, we know it's going to become rough because the shark and the stingray know this by the sea inside.'[42]

What my Elders have taught me is an integral part of the Dreaming. The Dreaming is a complex network of knowledge, faith and practices that derive from stories of creation and dominate all spiritual and physical aspects of Aboriginal life. The Dreaming sets out the structures of society, the rules for social behaviour and the ceremonies performed in order to maintain the life of the land.[43]

The Dreaming, or Dreamtime, as some people call it, is not the same for all Aboriginal people throughout Australia. What is the same is that, like the Bible, the Dreaming is rich with creation stories of how the world began and the spirit beings that came down to form and create the world.

During the Dreaming, ancestral spirits came to earth and created the landforms, the animals and plants. The stories tell how the ancestral spirits moved through the land, creating rivers, lakes and mountains. Today we know the places where the ancestral spirits have been and where they came to rest.[44]

In the West Kimberley, the Ngarinyin people talk about a great flood that came and the few people who were left to populate the earth. The Nyungar people, in the South-West talk about the *wakarl* [45] (spirit water snake) and how, as he travelled across the land, he formed the riverbeds and the mountain ranges. Wave Rock at Hayden forms part of the Nyungar Dreaming stories.

Aboriginal people across Australia have stories about how the landscape was created and how specific features in the landscape were formed during the Dreaming. I grew up hearing from my mother about the constellation known as the Seven Sisters, and at night, when the sky was clear and lit with a multitude of stars, she would point them out to me and my siblings, telling us how the sisters got to be in the sky. What made this creation story more real for me was that on extremely cold winter nights, when the dew lay heavy on the land and dripped off the roof like rain, my mother would say, 'Them old people in the Pilbara, they would tell us: "It's those Seven Sisters, they weeing on us tonight."'

On cold damp nights, when the dew is heavy, I can still hear my mother's voice and remember the Seven Sisters. I never questioned her belief or thought to challenge it as I got older. I accepted her story because it made sense to me and made the sisters real, being incorporated into my spiritual belief system. I, too, now say to my children on damp nights, 'Those sisters, they having a big wee tonight!'

For Aboriginal people, Dreaming stories offer another way of looking at the world. Christianity has used Aboriginal ways of looking at the world to spread the message of Christ. For example, Hart, talking about the Aboriginal Evangelical Fellowship, relays the story of fire.[46] Hart describes how the fire spirit came down to earth as a person, bringing fire for the people to warm themselves and to cook food. However, the fire spirit was too fiery and everything he touched burst into flames, and some of the animals and people died from the heat. The fire spirit overcame this problem by painting the symbol of the flame on his body and in this way was able to approach people and show them how to use fire. Christianity has used the symbol of fire, explaining the coming of the Holy Spirit on Pentecost Day as the tongues of fire. 'Like the fire spirit, *Kurta*, coming to bring fire to the earth, the gift of the Holy Spirit would bring a great change to their lives and social situations.'[47] Through Christianity, this traditional story of fire has been converted so the flames represent the Holy Spirit. Christianity, identifying a cultural match between the Aboriginal story and the story of the Gospel, has compared fire to the Holy Spirit and applied it to its teachings to convert Aboriginal people. [48]

Healy says that 'many religious discourses focus on the non-material world beyond our earthly existence' with belief in the after-life.[49] Where Christianity focuses on God as a higher being, Indigenous spirituality is 'embedded in the natural environment ... and may focus on one's relationship with the land and one's ancestors, or the "Dreaming".'[50]

According to Healy, a 'primary purpose of religious and spiritual oriented activities, is to promote spiritual wellbeing'[51]. This position concurs with Aboriginal people's beliefs about spirituality and the impact of colonisation on Aboriginal people as a group. Aboriginal people feel the loss of cultural autonomy and the disruption to their spiritual practices and belief systems as having had a major impact on the wellbeing of their communities, families and individuals. Loss of connection to land severed the spiritual relationships of entire communities and groups of people, resulting in loss of identity and spiritual wellbeing. Understanding how spirituality can affect an individual's and/or community's wellbeing has huge ramifications for service delivery and people attempting to work in a cross cultural setting.

In medical settings, for instance, an Aboriginal person could attribute his or her illness to a spiritual cause. Any attempt to heal the person by conventional medical means may fail because the spiritual element has not been acknowledged or addressed. Similarly, a psychological disorder could be interpreted as a symptom of mental illness, whereas the patient's community or family may believe the individual has been sung, has trespassed on taboo country, or has touched and taken an artefact, or a stone, away from the area.

The implications for anyone working with Aboriginal people are huge, and unless practitioners acknowledge and allow for spiritual or religious issues to emerge, their work, and its effects, can be seriously limited. Healy points out that 'understanding the religious and spiritual needs of service users is a key dimension of holistic care for service users, inseparable from attending to material and emotional needs.'[52] Much of the focus of helping Aboriginal people has tended to centre on the material, the financial and the physical, with little attention to how their spiritual and emotional needs should be met. For a race of people whose existence and identity were grounded in the Dreaming, the impact of the disruption to their spiritual life was catastrophic, resulting in I believe, a spiritual and emotional crisis that has affected the wellbeing of our communities and families. Until this spiritual crevasse is filled, Aboriginal people will continue to fill it by other means such as alcohol, drugs and violence. McLennan and Khavarpour, talking about their research into health and spirituality, point out that a 'common thread arising from the literature is the need to recognise spirituality as influential, if not the driving force, in the healing of Indigenous peoples.'[53]

Regardless of its dark history, Christianity has had both a positive and a negative impact on the lives of Aboriginal people. For some, Christianity has provided an alternative that has filled the gap, enabling them to move on and heal their lives. But for those who do not find solace in Christianity, other means need to be provided to bring back spiritual meaning and wellbeing into their lives.

McLennan and Khavarpour confirmed that, from their study in New South Wales, which looked at spirituality and wellbeing, spirituality was central in the lives of the people they looked at:

The strong connection between spirituality and wellbeing was expressed by feelings of protection, energy, confidence and pride. The spiritual connections within the community, such as those with ancestors and with the tribal area, help to maintain a sense of belonging, community cohesion and wellbeing.[54]

The diversity in the Aboriginal community today means that while spirituality may mean different things to different people, as a central value it plays a critical role in Indigenous wellbeing. Its importance cannot be ignored.

For Aboriginal people like me, who now live in urban locations and whose children are growing up in the mainstream community, maintaining a connection with country is difficult, because we are living in someone else's country and it is not as familiar as our own. Teaching our children about culture is also more difficult in the mainstream community, where the focus is on different aspirations and values. As a parent and grandparent, it is a struggle to hold and balance the traditional Aboriginal values that were handed down to me and to pass them on in an urban environment of bricks and mortar. Nevertheless, as I grow older (though I am not at this stage yet), I am beginning to understand what it means to be an Elder, the responsibilities that will come with that status, and the importance of passing on my knowledge and understanding to my children. Children take in information in different ways and at different times throughout their lives, so we cannot always be sure that what is being taught has been understood and remembered. Fortunately, as Aboriginal people become more comfortable with putting their thoughts onto paper through anthologies, handing on their stories is made easier. If we have done our work well and laid down strong foundations, in their own time and when the time is right, our children and our future generations will be able to read what we have written and their learning will occur.

In conclusion, the importance of spirituality and the impact of its presence or absence on the lives of Aboriginal people cannot be underestimated. What must be recognised is that Aboriginal people, whether they live in cities, rural communities or in remote country, have a different worldview and understanding of spirituality from Western people. If workers are to be effective in Aboriginal communities where social, emotional and health problems are rife, this must be considered, especially in communities where social cohesion and wellbeing have been severely disrupted.

LEN COLLARD

is a descendant of the Whadjuck and Ballardong Nyungar of the South-West of Western Australia. He is Chair of Australian Indigenous Studies at Murdoch University and a highly respected academic leader in the field of Nyungar culture.

Kura, Yeye, boorda
'from the past, today and the future'

Pindjarup Nyungar boordier *Mr Joe Walley said 'so these old stories, White people don't believe them; they think are not true. Well, how many stories going right back, can you say is true? I am a firm believer in the old Aboriginal ways. How many stories can you say is true? The Bible, because it is written down? When we speak, it is verbally a handed-down story. They say they are just words, you make it up. What is the difference between a man's written word and a person's word that is not written down? There is no difference. Well, one is written down and one is spoken. Yes, but it had to be spoken for it to be written down, ha ha ha. There is no difference at all.*[55]

Kaya noonankoort[56], my name is Len Collard and I am a Whadjuck/Balardong[57] Nyungar man and my Nyungar *katitjin*[58] has been passed on to me by many of our Nyungar Elders, family and extended family members. However, the *katitjin* I am going to share with you comes from a few of my *moort,* or in other words from my Nyungar relations who gave me the privilege of recording a few of their oral histories about country, family and knowledge. I did these when I headed up a Nyungar research team doing some work here in Perth a couple of years ago. I chose to talk about them here in this book because our oral histories are central to how we pass on our knowledge and they also highlight how the lives of Nyungar people are intrinsically linked through our connection to *boodjar*, *moort* and *katitjin*[59]. These are at the very heart of defining who we are, for our identity and our sense of belonging, they help us to make sense of who we are as Nyungar.[60]

To me, this type of research work is important because since early colonial times in Australia, *wedjela*[61] have largely controlled the documentation of the history of Nyungar. Up until recent times there have been few attempts to undertake a comprehensive understanding of how us Nyungar create and interpret our worldviews.

My research team started out by discussing how we could help other people understand who we are and how we understand our Nyungar world. We thought about how religion can actually help other people define their universe, and give them a sense of who they are and where they belong in the world. So, we began with a Nyungar cosmology and used it as one of our guiding principles to develop a theoretical and cultural framework for our research work. My team then engaged a set of propositions that enabled us to look at how Nyungar knowledge is constructed, passed on and supported in creating history narratives. The foundation of our theory is the trilogy of *boodjar*, *moort* and *katitjin*, which provided the structure for our cosmology, or, in other words, the Nyungar universe which began *kura kura*.[62] Our approach shows that the three are intrinsic; one cannot apply our Nyungar theory by using one of the major components without the others. On this basis, *boodjar* is the first major theoretical component, *Moort* is the second, and *katitjin* the third. If you want to learn more about this, go to the Murdoch University website and you can read all about it in our Nyungar website.[63]

Waakal, or Nyungar Rainbow Serpent

In our Nyungar cosmological theory, the *Waakal* is the Creator, the keeper of the freshwater sources. He gave us life and our trilogy of belief in the boodjar — the land — as our mother and nurturer of the *Nyungar moort* — family and relations — and our *katitjin* Law — knowledge so that we could weave the intricate tapestry known as the 'web of life'. Nyungar believe the Waakal is the giver of life because of its role in maintaining freshwater sources. My old pop passed away *kura*, he was a Whadjuck/Balardong Nyungar and he was the keeper of the stories; his name was Tom 'Yelakitj' Bennell:

> *There are two different sorts of carpet snake. If anybody ever see them, the old bush carpet, he got white marks on him. The old water carpet snake, he is purple and oh, he is pretty. He is purple. I saw them myself. I saw them, oh, up to fourteen or fifteen feet long, very pretty. But the old forest carpet snake, he is only just an ordinary old carpet snake. But the real water snake oh, he is pretty, that carpet snake. I don't think too many people have seen him. They wouldn't know he was a carpet snake, but he is a carpet snake all right, but the Nyungar call him Waakal.[64]*

The Rainbow Serpent is always connected and associated with tracts of water in specific country. An old *wedjela* writer from *kura* provided an insight into the power of the Rainbow Serpent's connection to man through ritual. Coming with showers and storms, which fall from above onto a thirsty land, the Rainbow Serpent is credited with a causative role in rain and depends on it.[65] Another *wedjela*, whom most us have read about, was old George Fletcher Moore, an early Swan River colonial who described the Nyungar Rainbow Serpent, or *Waugal*, as:

> ... *an imaginary aquatic monster, residing in deep dark waters, and endowed with supernatural powers, which enable it to overpower and consume the natives. Its supposed shape is that of a huge winged serpent.*[66]

Rainbow Serpents are said to be powerful entities and hold control over life and death. They live in deep rivers or water sources and there is protocol that must be followed when anyone visits the abode of a Rainbow Snake.[67] These yarns are clear examples of how Nyungar are bonded historically with land or country in a cosmological and spiritual way.

Nyungar *boodjar* lies in the south-western corner of Western Australia. It extends eastward of Esperance, or Wudjari Nyungar *boodjar*, moving in an arc to the north-west, close to the small Wheatbelt town of Nyoongah, in Njakinjaki Nyungar *boodjar*, and west-north-west towards Coorow, or Juat Nyungar *boodjar*, and south of Geraldton across to the west coast of Western Australia. These are the general boundaries of Nyungar *boodjar*, where all Nyungar *moort* have geographical and *moort* affiliation.[68] For Nyungar, your *moort* is your family or your relations. The

Waakal gave us the foundation of our Law, knowledge about kinship systems and how we relate to one another, for instance, whom we could marry and what our obligations are to one another. As Nyungar descendants, we suggest '*nitcha ngulla Whadjuck un Pindjarup and Balardong Nyungar boodjar*', which, in *wedjela* language, means, 'These are our relations and our ground.'

A piece of history my old Pop recounted went like this: 'The old Nyungar, the tribal Nyungar, they used to have their mob and travel in tribal mob. Your tribal mob would have been your *moort*, that is the Nyungar name for 'relations'. Nyungar, they used to call their [69], when she was carrying a baby, *doordajee doordajee*. Now that means she is going to have a baby. *Kooboorl, kooboorl, koombar kumbariny*. That means the belly is getting big.'[70]

In Nyungar culture, all *koorlangkar*[71] take their mothers' *gnarnk gnoorp*.[72] This is because 'Nyoongar culture is matrilineal and our cultural identification is recognised through our mothers' heritage, not our fathers' affiliations.'[73] If a Nyungar knows who the *koorlangkar ngarnk*[74] or the child's mother is, or if the mother does not have a partner, the Nyungar always knows who the *moort* of that *koorlangkar* is and therefore knows to whom he or she belongs. In *moort* theory, a Nyungar man might have had several *yok* and inherited many *koorlangkar*, and thus becomes the *maaman,* or father, but through the birthmother of the *koorlangkar* their heritage is always 'true'. Therefore, a *koorlangkar* knows who their *ngarnk* is even if the *maaman* of the *moort* is not their biological father.

As you can see, I have used a fair bit of Nyungar *wangkiny* or language because the commitment to our knowledge is central to our history and identity. Much of our Nyungar *wangkiny* and *katitjin* has been rejuvenated by and among Nyungar, but in my family our *wangkiny* and *katitjin* were part of our life and we still continue to use our language and knowledge in everyday conversations. Our *katitjin* and *wangkiny* are part of our identity, so we must keep them and use them and teach our kids, because this is our cultural heritage and it is a very powerful way of letting people know that we are Nyungar. An old *wedjela* [75] said this many years ago about our *wangkiny*:

> [Nyungar] *retain only those characteristics of man which it is impossible for him to lose, under any circumstances; namely, the power of language. The language of Derbal* [of the Perth waters] *seems to possess a great deal of originality. But there is something very peculiar in its construction; or, it is characterised by great irregularity in the declension of its nouns and conjugation of its verbs. In either case, to acquire it accurately, and commit it to writing correctly will be no easy task.*

I can certainly agree with Mr Lyon, because I have struggled for many years in trying to decide how to spell our language; but I believe I am pretty consistent with the spelling when I use Nyungar *wangkiny* in my writings. The most important issue here, though, is to try to make sure it is spelt how it sounds. I am not a linguist, so I leave it up to the experts to tell people about sounds, spelling and so on.

The *katitjin*, or Law knowledge, that the *Waakal* gave to the Nyungar included all things connected to our *boodjar*. The *Waakal* gave us our knowledge about the sacred sites such as Boyagin Rock, Mandikan, Karta Koomba, Pinjarra, Mundaring, Walwalyalup, Waakal Mia, and the Derbal

Len Collard
Courtesy of Len Collard

Yerrigan or estuary, and our relationship to them.[76] *Waakal* gave us our knowledge about Nyungar and our relationships, responsibilities and obligations to one another. The Rainbow Serpent gave us our *katitjin* and law about the animals, plants, bush medicines, trees, rivers, waterholes, hills, gullies, the stars, moon, sun, rocks and seasons, and their interconnectedness in the web of life of the six seasons in the Nyungar world[77].

The Nyungar Rainbow Serpent also gave us our *katitjin* about the spirits or *wirrin* in our *boodjar*, *wirrin* and *moort* in the cycle of life. Some Nyungar people were given *boolyada*, or magical powers, to heal or kill and to protect all things sacred created by the *Waakal*. The *Waakal* also gave us our *koorndarn*, or *kaarnya*, which are the fundamental and underlying principles that give all cultures their values and belief system or their 'commonsense, respect and shame'.[78]

I hope that the *katitjin* I have shared with you will help you understand a little bit more about Nyungar culture, but I am sure the oral histories you are going to read will also give you some insight into the Nyungar world. So, in keeping with our Nyungar speaking oral history tradition in the South-West, which is still shared by Nyungar and *yorkga* today, here are three oral histories about our *boodjar*, *moort* and *katitjin*.

Kaya.[79]

Oral history by Dr Richard Walley

As you know, in our culture, regardless of where you go, you are part of a family tapestry and that's your sort of visa, I suppose, on your passport to the different communities. I just came back from Jigalong and, for example, when I went onto the community they asked me two questions. Those two questions put me exactly where they found I fit within their tapestry. The first question was: 'You related to the Walley family in Meekatharra?' and I said yes.

They said, 'Do you know Madeline Walley?'

I said, 'She's my sister,' and they said, 'Ah.' So they knew where I fit then, because my sister married into some of the people from that area, relatives of that area, and a cousin of mine was up there living as well. So they knew exactly where I fit in.

I can go right back to, say, the Perth connection, or the connection from around this area goes right back to my great-great-grandmother, Fanny Balbuck, who was actually born on Heirisson Island. Her family used to go between Heirisson Island right up to Kings Park and then they would come south, right around to this area here, towards following the swamps more than anything else. It was really the swamp country. My mother was actually born in York; she's a Balardong mob, then the Indich/Winmar clan. My mother is a Winmar and my father was actually born in New Norcia. His mother was an Evans that came right through from Yalgoo or the Yamatji run, up that way. His father was from down the south, the Pinjarra area; that's where his father's and grandmother's country is, from there.

Len Collard: What's old boy's name?

His name was Steve Walley, my old grandfather, and we found that his father was what they called Whan (Juan), or John Walley, and he was actually one of the first ones who, in the early days, went to New Norcia. So his grandfather was one of the early ones they recorded, but before him, the other old fella just came straight out of the bush. They [New Norcia priests] just had him as Aboriginal from the south. The name Walley, itself, is a bit contentious. Some say that it's got the connection to the Walley name that came out of England and places like that. The other names, which I found through research, came from Wallibunger and Walleyup — where all the Walleys was short for these names. They used to name people where they came from, so that's the story that I am still researching at this particular moment. It is hard to find because so many things change and in the New Norcia archives, they put them into Spanish as well as English.

So Walley was the first part of a name and, as you know, in our country down there, there are lots of things starting out with the name Walley. This reinforces our connections to this part of the land, I suppose. I find that there are two things about a location or a place. One, that you're a part of it and it's like a family that you could recognise: the environment, the animals, the seasons and you could fit in quite well with it. The other one is that you are adopted to it, into it, like, that's when people are born in another region/country and they come and marry into a family or settle close by. They like the lifestyle or they like the people or you find they stay for long periods of time. When they find that they stay for great periods of time, they become adapted to the land and adopt it. To the older people, well, I was lucky enough to be around them as a young fella; the

Nannup family, the Ugle family, down that way, the Mippys and Kellys — I was very lucky to be a young boy, a young lad (I was about eleven or twelve years old), to be speaking to people like old Granny Doorong Abraham. His grand-daughter married a cousin of mine, Jim Corbett, and he used to live just down in the back of the Reserve, where Jim lived in Pinjarra.

People just did not marry within their own little circle. Sometimes they'd go out of that circle and marry someone from another region. Well, the Ugles were a good example. When the Ugles married into some of the families in Pinjarra, a lot of other Ugles would come from the Narrogin and Williams area. They would come to Pinjarra for a while to catch up with their families and whilst they were there, they'd sometimes get hitched up with local people local girlfriends and boyfriends. That turned into a relationship, and you'd find that this created relationships in areas that might not have had connections before.

So what happens then, you got children of those couples who've got affiliations in both countries, so they can go between both quite easily. Thus, when I start off with my story, I can travel quite easily through Yamatji country 'cause that's my grandmother's area. I can travel right through the Perth area quite easily, because that is my great-grandmother's area, and I can travel through the Moora area without any problems, which is quite prominent through the Indich connection. I can go through the Balardong country, through the York and Quairading area, which is my mother's country. So what it does is, it opens up the whole landscape for you but, you still have an affiliation back to one part of the country. So, even though I have a connection all the way through, my affiliation is still back in Pinjarra, and this is what I'm talking about. You can't explain it, even though I wasn't born there. It's my grandmother's country and great grandmother's and great-grandfather's country [on the Walley side]. You go back all through those areas and you'll find that it is something beyond. That there is a spiritual link that pulls you back. It's not necessarily just me; it's a lot of people who are looking for a place of belonging. Sometimes they find that place of belonging in very unusual places, or sometimes they find it exactly where they are looking for it.

Oral history by Janet Hayden (Aunty)

Len Collard: Janet, I want to talk about some of the family issues. You say you're from Wilman and Balardong. Now what about the Swan River area? Because it's my feeling that the Bennells are Swan River people, and they are out at York and a whole lot of other places. Can you tell us a little about what your understanding is of the relationship between the Nyungars at York, Brookton, the Swan River and places like Pinjarra?

Well, I will only tell you what my grandfather taught me. My grandfather was Norman (Dooram) Bennell. I grew up with this old man and before he died (he was ninety-two when he died), he lived with me, my husband and kids for the last twelve years of his life. All the stories that he told me are a little bit contrary to what a lot of people are saying today about the Swan River. He was born just out of York and, as a young man, he married a girl from York also. Her name was Kate Collard. The Collard and Bennell families are two of the oldest families who came to Brookton to live. The Bennell family was the first Nyungar family ever to live around the Brookton area and the Collard family moved there looking for work. Grandfather Collard was involved in brick making and he got a contract with a guy who made him a partner. Granny Kate Collard was one of the girls who grandfather liked, and a relationship started. The Bennells originally came from York, as far as I know or what I was taught. That came about because of a relationship between a white man and a tribal woman. The white man was John Monger and grandmother (I can't recall her name). They had one son, whose name was John Monger-Bennell, and this is where my grandfather Dooram came from. His mother was Kandianne and she was a Serpentine woman. She came from the Serpentine area and her father was named Cleetland and her mother was named Annie.

That relationship was in the Serpentine region, where they used to go to from York, Beverley, Dale right back through the Wandering area and back through to the Swan River or Avon River. I have never, ever known people to say that the Bennell people originated from the Swan River area. That could only have come from the Monger side of it. It could not have come from of the Bennell side, because, as far as I know, all the Bennell family, all the girls, were born around Brookton and the boys from around Beverley, Wandering. I could give you the names of every town that grandfather told me where the relationships were from or where these families came from. The Garletts and the Humes family originated from the first marriage, where Grandfather John Monger-Bennell married Minnie. They used to call her Fanny. She was the first sister and she died in childbirth. She had five children. After she died,

Grandfather John Monger-Bennell took all his children back to give them to Cleetland and Annie, but they were too old to look after them. So he [Cleetland] gave his sixteen-year-old daughter, [Granny] Kandianne, to [Grandfather] John Monger and that is where we all come from, fifteen kids in the Bennell line.

They did a lot of travelling along the Swan River, from York to the Swan and around Beverley. They were cattle droving and they came down here to Fremantle and to get cattle from the Fremantle docks and take them back around the York area and the wheat lands for the farmers. This was the only link that I know of. Grandfather Jack Bennell, Grandfather John Monger Bennell, his oldest son from his first marriage, came down and met a young girl in Fremantle. Her name was Sarah Isaacs. Most of our Bennell families in the early days were drovers. They were bringing sheep, cattle and horses from the city. This was their link to the Swan River and that is the only link that I know of. My grandfather Dooram was quite able to speak very, very well, right up until his death. If we were Swan people, I think he would have told me that his only link to the Swan River was that they were droving cattle in those areas.

Len Collard: So from what you can figure out from the oral history that you're aware of, it seems that Serpentine might have been the boundary of the family history that you are talking about. Keeping it in mind, how long do you think it would take to walk from Serpentine say up to the Swan River?

Probably about a week, for young men, maybe. It would take a couple of days but if it was a family say, dad and the kids or grandfather, dad, mum, grandmother and the kids, it might take about a week, because they would stop and rest then go on. Why I am saying this is because this is exactly what my mum used to do when we lived around the Wheatbelt area, when there was no horse and cart. We would tag along behind Dad and Mum. We would do about twenty miles in two days or so, sometimes it might take a week. If Mum weren't feeling too good, it'd take longer. It might take a family about a week. If it was young people, it might take a couple of days, it all depended on the area.

An old man, John Seabrook, and old Robinson, I think they asked Grandfather John Monger if his boys could work. Granny Felix was the first one they asked, and Granny Dooram, so these young men worked for him. He gave them horses and they had to drive cattle. First of all York to Brookton, and then the Collard family came to Brookton and Grandfather Collard started working with the young blokes. They set up a partnership to do [build] houses and these old fellas were working really hard, opening up the land. They cleared the land and old Granny Bert Bennell, Grandfather's old brother and Grandfather Jack, who had Granny Sarah Isaacs, they were the eldest and they worked really hard opening up a lot of the land around there. For the first twenty or thirty years, it was only the Bennells there. It was the Bennells working with the farmers, opening up the land.

The old farmers started to respect the old Nyungar people. I spoke to one old Nyungar when I ran for the local shire up there and I spoke to some of the old White blokes there, too, and they referred to my grandfather as the last king of the Nyungars in that area. They opened up all the land around here. It was opened up by the Bennells. When the Collards arrived here, Grandfather Collard's daughter, Kate, married my Grandfather Dooram. Grandfather Collard asked Grandfather Dooram if he could marry Granny Katie [next generation]. He would give him a horse and a cart and that was his dowry. Her dowry was a spring cart and a beautiful big horse. He gave it to Grandfather Dooram to marry Granny Kate and she had two sons, Pop George Collard and Pop Tom Bennell.

But when Grandfather Jack married Granny Sarah Isaacs, she came back to Brookton. She came back to York and lived there for a certain time, then they came back to Beverley, Brookton, Pingelly and Wandering. That was their run, and the only time they ever came back down this way was when Granny Jack and them used to come back either through the Hotham or down through the Serpentine run. I was reading a story about one bloke who did a story on the Serpentine run right back down to Dale. The Nyungars were still doing that run which was very much a part of, that was the link up to Grandfather John Monger. One of the questions you would like to ask is, how did he get down there in the first place and marry Granny Minnie first, and then after she died, go and marry Granny Kandianne? Did he go around the Guildford area or did he go right down to Serpentine? Because that is the run they always spoke about. The Serpentine run was a major run.

Len Collard: And York and Brookton. It seems that there is a relationship to the Swan River.

Yes, there is, there would have to be, I think. You look at Granny Sarah Isaacs, she was born in Fremantle on a hill there, that is her birthplace, I often heard her talk about it as a little girl and I used to listen to the stories she told about Fremantle and the fear they had of the white man. As a little girl, she feared the white man. Her grandmother used to say, you have nothing to be afraid of, but she feared white men, because they had these guns and horses. Her whole family died out there, they never went away, they died around the Fremantle area. Her grandmother reared her up. If you look at the link Brookton had with a lot of the regions, and you look at where the Garletts went, they went around Merredin and that was the Bennells, Granny Yoorleen.

Len Collard: Granny Yoorleen's name was one that Daisy Bates recorded. She is related to Joobitch and Yellagonga, from the Swan River people. From what I can see, these people feared them [white men] so they left. They wouldn't stay and when you try and probe it, if anybody's killing your family, are you going to hang around there?

Is there anything that you can think of that's south side of the river in Perth that I might not have asked you about?

No, only this part, this is all Yagan's. Everybody is fighting about Yagan being that south side of the river. This is all Yagan's country here. We have always said that this is Yagan and Midgerigoo's country. This is the foundation of Midgerigoo and Yagan's family. They named that park after him over there. He was a rambling man, but he was the kind of warrior who went wherever the mood took him. He was friends with everybody, white men and black men, but this is his country, this is his tribal country right here.

Len Collard: Whose country is this?

I would say Yagan's, and okay, you could say Bennell country too.

Oral history by Sealin Garlett (Uncle)

Nitcha boodjar koonyarn nitcha koorl buranginy boodjar Karluk maya koonyarn wah. Deman demangarmarn wiern kia moort koonyarn. Deman garmarm noonookurt, boodjar koonyarn karla koorliny. Koorlongka boorda gneenunyiny. Those words say that this is my country where I belong.

My grandma comes from a very rich, cultural heritage. As a little boy being with my grandma, who very seldom spoke English, whenever she had the chance to have her grandchildren around her, she'd be feeding us or taking us for walks. She'd often be talking about the birds and speaking about it in her own tongue and allowing us children to sit down and listen to the different birds. You could pick out the different birds by the sounds they made. I remember, as a young boy, this was a very funny situation because, as a young fella, I found it hard to sit down quiet for a little while. When I look back on it, I can hear some of the birds today and identify the language she used to speak.

Len Collard: So when your Nanna Yoorleen was looking after you as a little boy, can you tell me a little bit about who her family was and what their relationship was with the Swan River?

Well, back then, I didn't know, but after talking with my old Uncle Cliff Humphries (his mother was a step-sister to my Grandma Weenie Humphries) and I remember when old Uncle Cliff was eighty-seven years of age, he took me for a ride on a horse and cart in Kings Park. Uncle Cliff was eighty-seven years old, so that would have been close to 1988–89 and he took me for a ride on the back of this horse and cart. We asked the driver to go around the Kings Park area and take his time. He showed me all the *Nyungar* camps. He showed me where my Grandma used to live, where they picked out a camp and where they used to stay. We would pull up and all walk around.

They showed me some of the birds and the trees, and the ashes and the blackboys, and medicine that was in the blackboys. They showed me the roots of the trees and the medicine bushes. I remember when we looked at that camp. He showed me where these people used to get water from. It was a great highlight for me, especially in my young adult years, to absorb all that information at that particular time. To know that I listened to the information he was telling me and that it was a part of me and something that belonged to me. Something that sort of says that this is your heritage and your Grandma is a part of your heritage and a part of Yoorleen's, to keep and respect and to never let it die away. So, that was a privileged event. What they said about creation stories from that area of Kings Park, a creation story that my Grandma used to say was to be passed on to her children and her grannies, and it made sense to me as I moved around there. There are places where you find serenity; where you find a sense of belonging. I was able to allow the birds and the air and the feeling of the breeze of that place, and was a beautiful sense, that this is a part of our place, this is a part of our area, our culture.

Len Collard: So Grandfather, basically, was saying that Kings Park was a camping ground of his/our relations in the earlier days?

Yeah, Lenny, he used to say that (I am a nephew of Uncle Sealin), and that's one of the things that you can say without having any sense of wanting to have people identifying your place here, is that this old gentleman (Deman Cliff Humphries, grandfather) here was able to give us first knowledge, you know? First-hand knowledge of where they camped, where they walked, and some of the places where they would have hunted. He knew of some of the strife that had taken place there, how they had been pushed out and moved along, [white people could not understand] the sacredness of Kings Park to Aboriginal people. It was a very prime piece of real estate at that particular time, and to have Aboriginal people hanging off the fringes, in a sense they sort of degraded the place in their [white people's] sight and so after a while, they would take the children away.

Deman Cliff's mother was Granny Weenie and she's the daughter of Kandianne, and Granny's husband was Bill Humphries. His *Nyungar* name was *Minninul.*

Len Collard: So what you're really saying to me is that old pop (Cliff Humphries) was telling you the camping areas and all these activities that was going on, that's where the ancestors were, before you fellas, in the latter years, had to shift out to live in the wheat belt.

Nitcha boodjar koonyarn nitcha koorl buranginy boodjar
Karluk maya koonyarn wah. Deman demangarmarn wiern
kia moort koonyarn. Deman garmarm noonookurt, boodjar
koonyarn karla koorliny. Koorlongka boorda gneenunyiny.
Those words say that this is my country where I belong.
This is *demangarmarn,* my grandmother and grandfather's
land, this is their land, where their spirits move now. *Boorda*,
or later on, this is going to be the responsibility of my
children and my children's children, their home and this
place will always be linked to their spirit.

***

Our stories are handed down to us from the local Nyungar
oral historians and 'keepers of stories', whether they are
from the Whadjuck, Balardong, Pindjarup or Wiilman
language groups, and extracts from colonial text give
testimony to the Nyungar cosmology, the phenomenon
known as the *Waakal*, the Nyungar Rainbow Serpent,
creator of the trilogy of *boodjar*, *moort* and *katitjin*.

Finally, old Pop Tom Yelakitj Bennell recorded his
thoughts on doing Nyungar history work on his own tape
recorder in 1978. Pop said, 'All the words that I am speaking
now are blackfellas' own words. They're exactly the same.
They are same as white people's words, say yes this and that,
and all this, but Nyungar words are all coming through. All
these tapes that I am doing now, if they'd like to write a
book the same as a white person, what histories they're
writing in they books, well, these tapes I am doing now,
could actually be all the same as anybody's in Australia.'[80]

The Nyungar speakers were active participants in my
research work and I am very grateful to our people and say,

'*Kaya noonar quopadar da un maar wangkiny ngung katitich nitcha,*' or 'Yes, you are very good speakers and writers and I understand this.'

Kaya.

IRENE WATSON

belongs to the Tanganekald and Meintangk peoples of the south-east of South Australia. Irene is well known for her activism and writings against and about the impact of colonialism upon Aboriginal peoples. In 1996, Irene was appointed as one of seven Indigenous judges to the First Nations International Court of Justice, sitting in Ottawa, Canada. She is working as a post-doctoral research fellow in the faculty of law at the University of Sydney.

De-colonising the Space:
Dreaming back to Country

We belong to different nations, languages and peoples who were once in sovereign occupation of traditional lands, seas and waterways which were, at the time of Cook's coming, in pristine ecological condition. Now the land, we call *ruwi*, like the bodies of many Aboriginal people, is fighting for survival against poor health and environmental devastation. In fulfilling our Aboriginal obligations as traditional owners and carers for country, many of us who have been dispossessed or have no power to decide the future of our lands, collectively struggle to occupy, re-connect with and determine their future health and well-being.

To begin, I return to my traditional homelands, the Coorong and the south-east of South Australia, and to my mother, Noeline Casey, who remembers, as a young child in the 1930s, having to leave Kingston SE, on the lands of her people, the Tanganakeld and Meintangk, and travel to Adelaide (on the lands of the Kaurna) with her mother, Irene Gibson. My grandmother moved to avoid the colonial state's child removal policies under the *Aborigines*

Act. And, and, the Prime Minister at the time of writing, John Howard, declared on 21 June a state of emergency in remote Aboriginal communities in the Northern Territory in response to claims of the sexual abuse of Aboriginal children.[81] The purpose of this intervention was to stop the sexual abuse of children, and the response is to bring the Australian military and federal police forces in to communities. I am hearing through the media stories of Aboriginal women fleeing from their communities for fear of their children being removed. My grandmother fled her traditional lands with my mother in the 1930s, when Aboriginal children were being removed for the purpose of assimilation, that is to fit into white society, to stop speaking our languages, and to break our connection to country. Today, Aboriginal children are removed because they are at risk of abuse, abuse whose origins are in the inter-generational trauma of earlier child removal policies. While the reasons for Aboriginal child removal over the years is stated differently, its effect on Aboriginal connections to country is the same: we become dispossessed as traditional owners of our country. During my grandmother's time, and in country areas, Aboriginal families were often more vulnerable and easier targets for child removal, and my grandmother witnessed the removal of children from relatives and feared the removal of her youngest child. The removal of Aboriginal children had been sanctioned by the state under the *Aborigines Act (SA)*. The Act provided the legal framework for the detention of *Nungas*[82] on state Aboriginal reserves, and the appointment of a protector, who held power to control the daily lives of Aboriginal people. As a result Aboriginal people in South Australia (the same legislation applied in similar ways in all other States) became institutionalised, wards of the state known as 'protected persons', rather than citizens of their own Aboriginal nations. It was under these laws that Aboriginal children were removed from family, community and country. In law, we were deemed 'British subjects', but in practice we were treated in accordance with the racist traditions of terra nullius: made invisible, and doomed to annihilation and absorption as assimilated persons. The protector became the legal guardian of all Aboriginal children until they turned twenty-one, and all movement of people onto and off reserves was controlled. Our access to our traditional lands — *ruwi* [83] — was restricted at the same time as pastoralists and farmers were invading them. The colonies established reserves, and rounding up Nungas and putting them in these institutions served to provide enclaves of cheap labour for the local pastoral and agricultural industries. The reserves were essentially concentration camps, where no consideration was given to our clan identity and traditional language was banned. The removal of Aboriginal people from their traditional *ruwi* and their relocation on reserves, sometimes hundreds of kilometres away, became the common practice of the State.

My grandmother wanted to avoid the capture and institutionalisation of my mother, Noeline, and she succeeded in doing this, but it came at a cost and it meant fleeing from country and kin in the early 1940s and living four hundred kilometres away, returning home to Kingston only whenever the opportunity or resources provided for the trip. I inherited this dispossession from my traditional lands and, like my mother; I grew up in Adelaide, country belonging to the Kaurna. I was part of the first generation of my people not to be born on the traditional lands of our ancestors. In moving to the city, my mother had learnt to avoid government officials who had the power to remove children, but once the threat of removal had passed, it had become difficult to return home. The country where you were able to live had become shrunken, titled and consumed by the Crown, and those small pockets of 'Crown' land set aside as Aboriginal reserves were not enough to sustain all the Aboriginal families of the region. Aboriginal families around Kingston were positioned to compete for these little scraps of land and a home for their families, and families who had left due to the effects of the *Aborigines Act* found that returning was impossible. The limited allotments set aside as Aboriginal reserve lands were even further reduced by colonial policies supporting the resumption of Crown land for public purposes. A block of Aboriginal reserve land close to Kingston town was resumed by the Crown as the local council rubbish dump. An ancient site where my ancestors had lived, fished, trapped wild duck and buried their loved ones subsequently buried in the refuse of the local township. When my mother finally returned home to live in Kingston permanently, she became active in the protection of her mother's country and looked to take care of her grandmother's burial site. This had been fenced off (an effort of the local school) but was still surrounded by the town dump.

Caring for country can evoke romantic images of Aboriginal people and the land, and it can be all of those images, but it can also be a lot of worry, sadness and hopelessness over our dealings with a dominant culture that doesn't care in the same way that many Aboriginal people care for the land.

'They covered our country with their rubbish but I have returned home and have taken it away and covered the land with trees which in turn have brought home our ngaitje-*bird.* Ngaitje *means spirit being or totem.'*

Courtesy Irene Watson

Protection of the burial site was always a concern of our family and the Elders and was a project to which Mum solidly committed herself. In 1988 she was instrumental in starting the Kungari Aboriginal Heritage Association. She was the chairwoman of a group of Elders, including Janet Watson, Fred Ahang, Lola Bonney and Ronnie Bonney. The group worked voluntarily to restore the land by getting the council to close the dump and remove the rubbish while Kungari members helped and planted thousands of trees, shrubs and groundcovers. Kungari also concerns itself with the protection and restoration of other important sites throughout our *ruwi*.

Mum spent most of her life growing up in the city, where she had had her own family, but throughout those years we often returned home. In my mother's words:

I went back home permanently when I was over fifty years old. It was then that I got involved in [Aboriginal] *Heritage. The Aboriginal Heritage* [state government officers] *come into town one day and said is there any Aboriginal sites here that need protection? And I said, 'Yes, there are heaps around here all along the coastline and we have a special Aboriginal burial ground here that could be*

86

upgraded and could be saved.' And they said, 'Well, that can be done.' So there we are, we put the unemployment team on to do it all up and that was in 1988. We done it all up and got rid of all the rubbish, but see there was still a dump there, so we got the dump cleared up and got the local council to move their dump away from our burial and camping sites. That was done by four young Aboriginal men and my son was there and he led the way to clean it all up. They did a pretty good job in planting all the trees. In the beginning we had no resources, no office, and we worked from my house. We had meetings and the Elders, we all agreed, but unfortunately they are all gone; we had a good team and they were supportive then. It was important to do [protecting the burial grounds], *because a lot of the old people are buried there; my great-grandmother, Catherine Gibson, is buried there. All along that coastline you will find* [human] *remains around there. A couple of years ago we found remains just alongside the burial ground, so that was buried back. All the developing that is going on now is just disturbing everything. Aboriginal site protection is important to me and I think the sites should be left alone. They are put there for a purpose, and that's to rest; it's a resting place. And it doesn't seem to sink into some of these developers. They just want to go in and dig up. But we did re-bury back a few remains, and hopefully we can still go on doing that, and if they do get dug up, we bury them back again. We haven't always been successful at protecting sites — at Robe, in the south-east, an important fishing cave was destroyed — but we are still trying to hang onto what's left. The coastal cliff, it was a beautiful spot there, with all the natural shrubs and trees the native plants, they need to be protected. We were negotiating with*

*the Robe Council for nearly twenty years, and we thought
they would agree to protect that site, but we lost the battle
and they went ahead and built the yacht club anyway. It
was pretty sad really, we tried all those years to stop it and
they went ahead and done it anyway. I think they will be
in trouble later on, because the tides are rising and that
yacht club could get washed away. But as I said, people
with money can get their way. The land is important
because that's where we come from, that's our mother earth.
That's why it's important, but it is slowly deteriorating, the
planet is slowly getting hurt and hurt. But the land, it
made us real strong, the land.*

If not for the strength we gain from the land, it would be
difficult to continue the struggle to care for it, particularly
when we mostly lose the battles. If not for the strength
gained from the land as sovereign peoples, we might
surrender and walk away. But country calls us to act and for
the few Aboriginal warriors left standing, it is an
imperative. Saving the land from environmental vandalism
is often difficult, particularly when Australian and
international law provides no real way to help protect
Aboriginal interests in land. Its main interest is in
assimilating Aboriginal peoples into the business-as-usual
paradigm. The South Australian *Aboriginal Heritage Act
1988* purports to provide protection similar to other State
and Federal legislation, but it has proved to be weak and
next to useless in looking after Aboriginal culture and sites.
The power and interests of Aboriginal people are
outweighed by the power of interests like farming, mining,
tourism, roads and towns. It is hard to just sit on the beach
and enjoy the sunset when many of our people worry about

country and the damage and destruction of important sites. The worry and concern are extended by limits on our power to act. All we have are the powers to say no and to remember that it is the *land that made us real strong.*

The Wave sings me home every time
Courtesy Irene Watson

Our connection to country hasn't always been one of struggle. In the past there were peaceful times, as Eileen Brown Kampakuta, Elder and founding and continuing member of the Kupa Pita Kungkas[84] remembers:

> *As a young girl I used to camp with my mother and grandmother and I used to ask a lot of questions about stories from a long time ago, about how they learned and how they teach young people, so I used to go and lay down with my grandmother and ask questions. She used to look up to the sky and tell the story about the creek, you know, up in the sky and the stars mean something. And a lot of stories she used to tell, and later I would go to sleep and my grandmother would call out to my mother, 'Oh, you can come and pick her up now, she's gone to sleep.' The old people taught us how to hunt bush tucker, and when we grew up we used to go and hunt for the bush tucker ourselves, and they taught us the ways and we learned how to find things. You feel at home when you are learning about our Aboriginal culture and you should be out there, on the land, and don't bring into the big city. But it's a real thing when*

you are outside with the trees and the fire going and you are
sitting down with the people. But down there [in the city]
is good, but our people should ask them to come up and come
to the land and sit down with us here. But sometimes they
like going down there.

But such peaceful times have become rare for Nungas.
We have become preoccupied with worry for country and
the weight of resisting historical pressures to assimilate and
to heal from the inter-generational traumas of colonialism.
It is the memories held by Elders that remind us of who we
are and the importance of our connections to country. But
we are still afflicted in many ways. Some of our lands were
considered to be so remote and of such little productive
benefit that the Federal and State governments viewed
them as suitable sites for testing nuclear weapons in the
1950s. Today they are the site of an expanding uranium
mine.[85] Other lands are earmarked for the storage of
nuclear waste.[86] But these lands are occupied and travelled
over. The Kupa Pita Kungka Tjutja struggled to keep their
spaces safe from nuclear waste for the future survival of
their grandchildren. Emily Austin talks about travelling
over and connecting to country for her future
grandchildren:

I was born in — they call that place Amata now, but it was
Apara ... I am Yangkuntjara. I live a good life now; it's like
in the old time we used to live a good life. Travel around,
we used to walk and our mother used to make a road with
a foot track, you know, we had no shoes. We travel around
and you know we used to have a good life. But today is you
know they on the smoking all those things, drink; I think

that's why today's life is a bit weak today. But long time ago,
we grow up good way, you know, and bush tucker. They
used to live on a bush tucker, say like a kangaroo, emu,
goanna, all those things you know and witchetty grub, that's
the main good food they used to eat, you know, and that's
how they lived strong! You need the culture, and you know
when we used to going out to stop that waste dump [87] ... *It*
was for our children, their future, you know. Because we'll
all be gone soon, and what they gunna see and learn? You
know, so all the grandmothers got together and we talk
about it. And then, when we heard they gunna bring it
[nuclear waste from the Lucas Heights reactor] *and put*
it in our country and it was really close, you know — they
had it over here first on station, I forgot the name of the
station — anyway, we stopped that one. We used to go up
and down talking ... we used to try and talk, but they
wasn't listening to us, but we didn't stop we kept on going,
because we was thinking of our children's future, you know,
little ones coming up, great-grandkids gunna come so they
gunna have a good life too. And we knew it was strong
poison too, you know, if they buried around our country,
it'll go down to the water. Because out in the desert we got
underground water, so the poison would've went down
there.

The health of the land will sustain future generations, but
contemporary Australian law is impotent to protect the land
for the future. Both State and federal laws fail to provide the
power to protect country beyond sites where there is
development. Site protection only occurs where it can be
accommodated by development. Australian law and policy
have failed to provide adequate protection and guarantees to

both Aboriginal and non-Aboriginal people that their lives will not be affected by environmental disasters, such as the pollution of underground water bytoxic waste run-off. Historically Australian governments have treated Aboriginal lands as vacant, but theyhave always been intimately known to us. Every part of the continent comes under the jurisdiction of Aboriginal peoples and their distinct laws, and every part has an Aboriginal language name. Ivy Stewart, another founding member of the Kupa Pita Kungkas, travelled country thought of as an empty landscape, but for her it is far from empty; it has been known, nurtured and loved by generations, and it is hoped that it will be known and cared for by many succeeding generations:

I'm a Yankungtjatjara woman, and I was born at Yuintja, and our family took us away east from there. They never took us back to their own area to show us their country but we always been out east and that's where we grew up, near Macumba way. We walked around there — Macumba, Pitjiri, Oodnadatta; we hunt around there, we lived around there, we moved around. A place called Alpainta, that's our area. I worked at Macumba, then I used to go down to Oodnadatta and moved around Anna Creek Station; I worked there. We still got our Laws, wangka *religion, you know, we have that knowledge. I am going to talk about myself, and my grandmother taught me lot of things and they showed us all how to hunt, how to dig, get the rabbits out, cooking and all that, and they used to take us out and teach us* inma[88], kungka inma *and I know all that. They taught us how to hunt and* inma, *I got it. I travel around everywhere, I know the country when I was young, but I am slowing down now, because I am getting ageing, but I know the country.*

Eileen Crombie, a fellow founding member of Kupa Pita Kungka Tjuta, spoke about travelling over country and the hardships of day-to-day living. It is culture that makes us strong with the knowledge that culture is still alive in the land:

I been born in Sailors Well, and I'm a Yankungtjatjara woman. My father been taken from there, his woman's from Sailors Well and he's been married and we been start travelling from there … I grew up and we been come this way, Coober Pedy … That big Maralinga test [89], *they been shift us from Boolgunya station, policeman took us away to Yalata … After that I been live here* [Coober Pedy] *for a long time, till kids grow up they can all get married and make a home here.*

Culture make me strong, and I know; I just wake up, from just like a sleep, you know, like that story I been telling 'em this morning, I been wake and you know, 'Ha this one's all right,' and I can fight for my country. Story still in the land, today, today, not from book: we singing, we from here [points to her heart] *and bring 'em out from heart, we know. Grandmother's* inma, tjamus inma, *grandfather's knowledge we got. And we can tell 'em. We telling 'em young people, and they don't listen, they go, 'That's you fellers.' See, how they going to learn?*

We telling them, 'Story, you got to keep 'em, you know, for the kids, so you can learn your kids.' And they say, 'No, that's all rubbish'. But rubbish wiya. *We been fight over that dump, that's through culture. That culture we been*

showing 'em, this culture still in the land, never die, we still
… and you fellers got to learn too. See, big story. Tryin' to
tell young fellers, tell kungkas, *they go other way, white*
man's way. They don't worry about old culture. They worry
about white man's culture: drink, marijuana, breaking in,
going to gaol. They lose everything. But some of them, we
helping 'em, everything, culture. They said, 'No. We don't
want to go culture, no good. We want this way, white man's
way.' How they gunna keep their story, tell their children,
grandchildren, great-great-grandchildren? Grandchildren
take it on. We said, 'You fellers got to take it on. When we
going, you fellers got to take it on, show all the families.'

Some of our people have been taken away from culture
and though, as Eileen Crombie States, many of her younger
generation refer to culture as 'rubbish', she responds by
stating that *wiya*, culture, is not rubbish; culture is still
strong in the land. Our biggest struggle is against the
demonisation of Aboriginal culture, and towards its
restoration as a central source of our survivalas distinct
Aboriginal peoples. The Howard government's emergency
measures, which I refer to above, have the potential to do
more harm than good and further isolate Aboriginal
children from their culture.

While there is cause for concern about future generations
when it comes to handing down cultural knowledge, it is
not just the older people who care about such issues.
Kokatha woman Dylan Coleman is two generations
younger than the grandmothers who have spoken above, yet
she, too, talks about identity, culture and land, and of the
desire to care and nurture country for the benefit of her son.

Probably since I have gone back to Ceduna, since I have had my little boy, I have learnt a lot more about our Dreaming and ask a lot more questions of the old ones. I feel that when I drive back to Ceduna, and knowing the places and the different things that happened along that Dreaming track, even though that's not our country there, but it's knowing the story. When I see and drive past Iron Knob and see that there, I throw my energy down there into the manta, *and I send my energy down and I think about the Seven Sisters, and I think about the country that has been damaged, and I think about our women and the struggle we have and the need for us to come together. I think about that Dreaming story and I always think about our women and the struggles we have, the strong ones and the weak ones … I think our Dreaming has brought a lot of understanding back to me.*

Dylan's mother, Mercy Glastonbury, also of the Kokatha people, was born at Kooniba Aboriginal mission on the west coast of South Australia. She spoke about the contemporary struggle for traditional owners to speak for country and to keep culture going, particularly during the competitive and soul-destroying era of the federal government's Native Title Tribunal, investigating claims and rights to country:

I have seen myself as a strong Aboriginal woman, but the struggles with Native Title have pulled me down. But I do believe I still have enough strength because my kids, my grandchildren, they look on me as someone with strength. The Native Title business has tested all women, because the men, in our area anyway, have said the women are not to have any say over the land, that's the men's business. But us women, we know we have got very sacred sites and we've been told by Aboriginal women all over in South Australia, as far as Blackstone in WA, that we have to look after those sites that we've got in our area, and don't let the men go there because the men can become very ill. And we have been struggling for our sites. The Dreaming has got to do with the Seven Sisters, and it is all there in stone and in the land ... Native Title has caused dispossession of tribal clans and tribal groups, and the loss of identity through the wrong groups claiming land that don't belong to them; claiming language, as well, that don't belong to them. And it's like some groups are losing their identity. This has broken my heart. But within myself I still feel strong, but what strength I feel now is for my children, and to teach them and to give them support. I don't want to be out in the political arena struggling anymore, I've spent my whole life out there and I feel like I have done enough, and now I am pulling in.

We've got a very strong history, through our forefathers and where we have stood in society, and just the knowledge of having forefathers who have been bosses in the tribal ways before, that knowledge, that strength. I think about them. I think about what my grandmother used to teach me, and my standing, my place, even though two hundred years has changed it now and we've been robbed of a lot of things. A lot of our people don't speak fluently our language anymore, particularly the younger ones, because we were dumped on the mission and told not to speak our language and not to practise our culture. But my grandparents used to take me to different waterholes to clean them out, and I can remember, as a little girl, those kind of things. My times in the bush and *the bush tucker we lived on and my relationship with my extended family, you know, and that was really warm, and even though now it is drifting apart, especially with the younger ones coming along, you lose contact with them. But you just know where you stood in this society, and that's what gives me a lot of strength.*

Many of our families have travelled large distances. Roslyn Weetra tells her story of journeys across family lands, crossing both the north and the south, and of the many obligations these crossings hold for her.

My mother's Narunga, my father's eastern Arrernte, my grandparents are Nadjuri, Kaurna and Ngarrindjeri. I was born in Alice Springs, and Mum moved down from there when I was about six months old. Then we moved and lived on Pine Point, which is in the Narunga country, on York Peninsula, and we lived most of our early childhood there.

In my life, I think it is the culture that has kept me strong, whatever that culture is, as I have developed over the years. It's been my culture, and sometimes back then, we weren't allowed to talk about it, we didn't even know our language groups, we didn't talk the language. Going through in the fifties, going through primary school, it wasn't a pleasant place to be. But the culture was there and we are born into it. But we have got no way to express it, or to use it, or to be a part of it, while we are growing up in the city, because city life, urban life — even country life — doesn't allow you to be and to shape and develop and grow with your culture. You've got to earn a quid; you've got to depend on the government, they make us into a welfare people and we think that is the way to survive. But now I am here, I know the way I survived was hanging onto that very slim thread of my culture. When I had my back up against the wall, instinctively my culture said to me, 'Roslyn, this is the way to go, depend on your culture.' It's there; it's in us, all of us;, it's not up here [pointing to her head], *it's in here and it's in here, and it's in your body. But when you are young and you are not taught this continuously, you're picking up what you can from the black and the white culture just so you can survive, so you can be whoever you want to be. And you're teaching those same things to your children, that the white stuff is what you need to survive, which is the wrong teaching. It's the black stuff. It's the culture, but we can't see it, we can't hold it. We can see the white culture, you can get your pension cheque, you can go to school, you can do all those things. They're visible, they're acceptable. But what's hidden inside of us and comes with us everywhere is our black spirits and our black culture. So that was the biggest learning curve for me in my whole life when I was diagnosed with cancer, and it just came up. And I had it here, in the* mankari, *and it just came up from nowhere and to me that was a turning point for me in my whole life, not ever, ever before. I am still experiencing that. When it comes, you have to be obligated in a whole new different way. It's not just about looking after your people; it's about giving strong obligation.*

In concluding, I return as always to my traditional country, my spirit home, a place my mother worries and cares for, a place that I, too, worry and care for with her. It is the land which makes us strong but also makes me cry, just like when I cry for the many losses of so many of our people who were too young to pass from us. Our bodies and the land are connected. Our health and wellbeing are tied together. That is what I have grown up to believe. The modern world sees ideas of belonging to land as antiquated, but why do they see disconnection from country as progress? In the current climate, with the Howard government's state-of-emergency intervention in Aboriginal communities in the Northern Territory, the Aboriginal idea of caring for and belonging to country is under attack from people we might have thought were aware and sensitive of the Indigenous position. As the keynote speaker at the Cape York Institute conference, 'Strong Foundations — Rebuilding Social Norms in Indigenous Communities'[90], Michael Meyers, president of the New York Civil Rights Coalition, was quoted as saying: '... Indigenous cultures are an antiquated concept in the twenty-first century: People have to move out of their ghettoised attitudes, get away from the idea that people belong in certain lands.'[91] These comments could be construed as in support of the Howard agenda to remove Aboriginal people from remote areas. Colonialism stole everything from us. It stole from us the entire Australian landscape, our ability to govern our lives, and our relationships to our country. Many Aboriginal people, just like my mother, were removed from their country by *Aborigines Acts* policies. That was my inheritance:dispossession and assimilation. But though I am dispossessed and assimilated, I am still a resisting Tanganekald Meintangk *mimini*. I still belong to country. It is bred into me and it is an old idea and it is one that still lives. It may not survive in the landscapes of Wall Street, but it lives in my life, in my backyard, as it does with my mother and all of the nieces, sisters, aunties and grandmothers I have spoken with. Belonging to country is an old idea that keeps us alive and in which we live to pass onto our children and theirs to come.

NOEL NANNUP

is a Nyungar/Indjarbandi man who works tirelessly to promote public awareness of the importance of caring for the world we all share.

Caring for Everything

As an Aboriginal person, I am connected to the South-West and the North-West, two very different very areas of country in Western Australia. This is because my father came from the south and my mother from the north. My dad, Charles William Nannup, was born in 1910 near Mundaring Weir, in the hills on the Darling escarpment just east of Perth. He had links to the Whadjuk people, the Wadandi people who are down near Busselton, and the Balladong. They are all, of course, Nyungar people. My mum, Alice Isabel Basset, was also born in 1910; but she was born on Abydos Station, which is just south of Port Hedland in the Pilbara. And she is a Karriarra person. Mum's mum, though, was an Indjibarndji woman from Roebourne, so Mum had connections to country through those groups as well. There are many ways in which Aboriginal people connect to country, and what I mainly want to share in this essay is how the stars and the waterways connect different people to different countries and different countries to each other.

I will begin with the stars, which are very important to Aboriginal people. Mum told me stories about the stars for as long as I can remember, but one story used to really fascinate me. It was a true story about how three young girls left New Norcia mission and followed the stars all the way back home. This story impressed me because I thought it was so wonderful that the stars in the sky could actually tell you things. It made me understand very early on that there were a lot of useful things in the sky and I should learn about them. As I got older, I heard more star stories; and I began to realise that as the world turns, the star patterns pass overhead all the time, too. I used to sit outside at night and watch them, because by looking at the stars you can actually tell what time of the year it is. There is a pattern that the different seasons follow. Nyungar people have a six-season cycle that allows you to know exactly what is in the sky and when. Each season lasts roughly eight weeks. Our lives used to be guided by the seasons in the old times.

It was my dad's brother, Uncle Thomas, who taught me about the Nyungar side of culture. He liked to tell the story that I call 'The Carers of Everything'. When he told that story, he liked to point to the sky and to what he called 'the star pot', which he referred to as *comal*; the possum's skin pegged out with the tail still attached. *Comal* is the possum shape in the sky that the stars make. There are many shapes in the sky that we know to look for. For example, the Southern Cross and the stars around it are really the head of a kangaroo. You can see the ears and the teeth, you can see the kangaroo's back coming down and the tail going off. Then there is the very important story of the Seven Sisters, which some call the Pleiades, and how they came to be in the sky. Many different groups across Australia have stories about the Seven Sisters because it is an important Dreaming. You see, certain stars are connected to certain Dreaming tracks and stories. When it comes to the story of the Seven Sisters, there are really only six, as the seventh is one of the planets, and the planets go the opposite way. This is why you will always hear the desert people saying the seventh sister is coming home. You can see what they mean by sitting outside at night and just observing the sky. You will see the seventh sister getting closer and closer, but then she will go past and continue her journey. And when that happens, the people will say she has visited her sisters. That is the Dreaming of the desert people, the Wongi people. Their Seven Sisters Dreaming starts at a place called Weibo, north of Kalgoorlie in the Goldfields, at a very special spot where the sisters came down from the sky. It's a spot that needs to be protected because of its significance.

The Milky Way, the home of our solar system, is the main feature of our sky; and the whole of the Milky Way is represented by a spirit woman from the Dreaming who had long silvery white hair with a real sheen to it. *Djindalade* they called it. *Dyoondal* was the colour and *djumbar* was the hair. This spirit woman once walked on the earth and *dyoondal djumbar* was where she put the little spirit children that she collected from the landscape before she became the Milky Way. One of the stories tells how the spirit woman was waiting at a place where a large gathering was happening to determine who would be the Carers of Everything across the land. There was a process of elimination going on, and all the birds, plants, trees and the animals were eager for a chance to be picked as a carer. But slowly, as each one realised they couldn't do the job well enough, they left the gathering. The *wetj*, though, the emu, he ran off after the others trying to gather support for himself. The *yonga*, the kangaroo, thought the *wetj* was *karta warra*, which means thick in the head, and before he left he made it clear he didn't want *wetj* in charge of everything because he didn't think he would do a good job.

Finally, there were only two people still at the gathering, a spirit man and a spirit woman. While they sat there waiting to see what would happen, they showed three qualities and these three qualities we show every single day of our lives as human beings: impatience, inquisitiveness and emotion. They grew impatient for the *wetj* to come back, so they stood up and looked around, and when they stood up they were taller than the giant karri trees and towered over the landscape. Then they saw all these little eyes blinking at them and they wondered what they were: that was when inquisitiveness came into being. The spirit woman bent down and picked up a pair of eyes, and when she did so she began to tremble and shake with emotion. These were little children and this really affected her. The child she was looking at was so beautiful she couldn't bear to put it down, so she tucked it into her hair. Then she wandered around collecting one little spirit child after another, putting them in her hair so she could carry them with her as she walked. Soon she had thousands of them. When she looked over her shoulder, though, she saw the spirit man following behind her eating the children he found. She continued to walk across the land collecting children from here and there and using her hair as a big net, but finally she stopped and began to think. 'What have I done?' she asked herself. 'These little children have been placed in the landscape because they are the future generations. It is people who will win the right to be the Carers of Everything, I will have to put them back and I will have to tell the spirit man to stop eating them.'

Meanwhile, the spirit man had hidden himself in the

Noel appreciating a rare species of eucalypt, Salmon Gum, in a patch of remnant vegetation near Quairading, 2007
Courtesy David Deeley

darkness to make it difficult for her to find him, but still she searched. As she travelled around, some of the children fell from her hair to the ground and turned into stones. The stones grew higher and higher around her, so it was hard for her to look. But she broke through the stone and kept on looking. By then however, some of the children had also turned themselves into birds, and were swooping and pecking around her as birds sometimes do. Because of that, she stepped away from them and on to one great big stone, but it toppled over; and when it hit the ground it splashed across the southern part of the land and formed the great outcrops of stone that you see all through the south. Nyungar people know these stones as *bibi*, which means breast. So Bibbelman is the land of many breasts. That is what it means; and the people in the south, all fourteen groups, belong to the Bibbelman Nation.

Later, the spirit woman was standing on some soft stone, which oozed into a great big wave, which these days is called Wave Rock. When she was standing on Wave Rock, it felt just like a trampoline under her feet. And as it sprang up, it lifted this great spirit woman into the sky. Higher and higher she went, until she knew she could never walk on the earth again. She would live in the sky now. This made her feel sad, because she still had some of the spirit children with her in her hair. She kept wondering what she had done. She felt upset and worried because she had taken them away from the earth when they were supposed to one day be the Carers of Everything. Suddenly, she turned into the Milky Way and all the little children with her turned into twinkling stars. Then as she looked at them she realised how she could send them back to earth: she was the Milky Way, she could send them back as shooting stars. That is why we always say *bwaay coolarnngger* when we see a shooting star, because a shooting star is a little child coming back to earth. So in this way the stars really do connect to the earth and to different parts of our countries.

The other things that connect us in ways that people often don't think of are the waterways, especially the underground waterways. Believe it or not, waterways connect my mother's country in the north with my father's country in the south. There is an aquifer that runs deep down under the ground through the Hamersley Ranges and Millstream. Millstream is a tropical oasis that forms part of a national park in the Pilbara. My mother has family connections to Millstream, and the water runs under there as that place sits on the rim of the aquifer. There is a spot, I have been told, where the water travels under the ground and comes out down near Dongara, at a place called Yardareno. That same water also comes out in Mardu country, at Lake Way, near Wiluna, where there is a big aquifer of warm, saline water. Some of the water also leeches back in through the eleven soaks in Yamatji country on Ningin Station, where there are eleven springs. So that water is connecting different peoples and different countries through the way it flows underground.

My mum was taken away from her own country when

she was twelve years old and that was a very sad thing for her. But in 1987, mum and I and some other members of our family went back to her country, to Millstream. Mum said she had to go out to this pool and when she described it I knew exactly where it was. A great serpent lived there and she knew the right protocol that she had to do when she returned there. She had to get the water in her hands, then put it in her mouth and spray it out. 'I am a child from this country,' she told us, that's why I have to do that. She said that we had to see a rainbow and if we didn't see a rainbow, then we all had to leave because we were not supposed to be there. Mum was in a wheelchair at the time and as she couldn't get out of her wheelchair to get the water, I went over and got a handful for her then put it in her hands. 'Sssh!' she said, then the next minute she was talking out in a language I had never heard before in my life. Magically, a magnificent rainbow appeared in the sky and we were all so overcome we were shaking and there were tears in our eyes. Mum was very happy, so pleased to be back in her country after nearly seventy years. It gave us all a great feeling of belonging. I am sharing this with you because it shows how strong our connections to country are and how those connections aren't broken when people are taken away.

In the south, as in the north, people are connected to the waterways, most of them through having been born in catchment areas. Within each catchment they needed to know where the water came from because water is the giver of life and everything in that catchment is a part of you and you are a part of it

Now, if I return to talking specifically about Nyungar country, then let's look at the City of Perth. Nyungar people call that area Boorloo, that is our name for it. Boorloo, not

Perth. Boorloo had a series of lakes and big mobs of *kwulla*, the mullet, would come up from the sea around March to lay their eggs in the shallows where they wouldn't be disturbed. Also, the Swan River, we call it the *Derbal Yerrigan*. Now the word *derbal*, to my knowledge, means mixing; because it is where you have the sweet water and the salt water coming together, especially near the islands at Burswood. That is where you have got your tidal movement. Water flows under there too. It flows in from inland from Perth and it flows from out east of here, from the Avon District.

The water connects places most people don't know about. For example, if you go out to Wave Rock, which is about four hours' drive inland from Perth, you will see that the water comes from there as well, making its way via little tributaries to join up with water in other places. There, you have got it going two ways at Yearlamining Lake, because it is in balance. It also happens to be the border of two different peoples' country. They are the Wilmen and the Ballardong; and the water that comes into Ballardong country is the water that runs into the Avon. The water that flows the other way, into Wilmen, goes into the Goreng people's country and then on to the Wadandi and the Bibbelman people's land before it reaches the sea down near the town of Augusta. So the water that comes this way then runs into what they call the Avon River, but in the old way it is called *gugleyar*, which means laughing water. This is because when it runs over the rocks it celebrates; it wants you to hear it, so you hear it laughing. It also wants you to see it, that's why you see all the little bubbles coming up; and by that time it is coming down past Bullong Pool. Bullong is like the crane, you know, the long-necked bird. That place is just between York and Northam. Sadly, some people interfered with the river. They tried to make it flow quicker by clearing it out and in the process buggered up Bullong Pool. A lot of sand flowed into it and the spirits were not happy. The water flows through York, Northam, Toodyay and then through the Hills to Walyunga National Park, which is a very important place. It turns into the *Derbal Yerrigan* where the rocks finish, so now it is on the coastal plain, where it runs deeper and narrower. Oh it's just magic really, the way the waters flow and mix and connect up with each other.

There was a time, long ago, when the old river used to run from Walyunga, slightly to the north-east. Then it would build up and flow back through there and into the coastal plain that way, coming out at Success Hill. But there is a Dreaming story that thousands of years ago, the *djidi djidi*, which is our name for the little willy wagtail, was responsible for puncturing the rock that allowed the river to go the other way; so now it runs down through Herne Hill, Henley Brook, on to Middle Swan, then to Guildford and from Guildford on to the city of Perth as we know it, and down to Fremantle. All that river along there has some really important sites for Nyungar people, and thankfully a lot of them are still known and understood. But what they are doing, with all this development, is putting that wonderful heritage under pressure. That is very worrying because those places should be protected and looked after for future generations. People don't realise it, but there is some very strong country here around the City of Perth. Take a place like Kings Park for example. It's an important place now, but it was important in the old times too. The spirit in that land is so strong that it has saved itself from development. That happens sometimes: the land protects itself.

Now, if you approach the *Derbal Yerrigan* from the ocean

side, then you need to understand that the sea used to be further out than it is now. The mainland used to take in Wadjemup, Rottnest Island as its known these days. Thousands of years ago, the river used to run out north of Wadjemup; and the old river system is there, but then the sea rose, and as it rose it created a whole new set of stories in relation to the coast and sea. The spirit woman, the one who collected the little children, the one who couldn't walk on the earth again because she became the Milky Way, came back to earth as a powerful serpent. I am talking about the *Waugal* now. The first *Waugal* was a male, and he was here all the time, but then the spirit woman came down as a female *Waugal* to make sure that all the colours were right. She was very powerful and she lived in the sea. Sometimes she tried to come in to get into the sweet water, but two male snakes had been posted to guard the spot where she tried to get through. Now that female Waugal could change shape, so she turned herself into this weird-looking thing, which the male snakes hadn't seen before, which was the seahorse. That is why the seahorse is part of our story for the river. There she was, swimming along like a seahorse in this weird shape with her long silvery white hair floating in the water, and of course the guards couldn't help staring at her. They forgot what they were meant to be doing. They forgot they were supposed to stop anyone from getting through. By the time they realised what was happening, she was almost past them. They remembered just in time. The female *Waugal* realised they had caught on, so she dropped the disguise and left it in the deepest part of the river, where the water is over sixteen metres deep. It is called *Djenalup*, the footprint. She dropped the shape change, turned back into herself as a serpent, and took off with the male guards chasing her, trying to catch

Noel at a major Nyungar site — Djenalup in the Derbal Yerrigan (Swan River) 2007
Courtesy David Deeley

her. They didn't have a hope because she went in under Blackwall Reach and headed inland. She created Perth Water and Melville Water. She went under what is now called North Lake Road and she came up in a few places along there. But she also came back looking for the male and couldn't find him, and she lent gently against a hill and that is the area where the women's fountain is in Kings Park and she looked for him, but when she realised he was gone she came down the Canning River and made what they call Pioneer Lakes. Then she came up and looked around near Murdoch University and then North Lake, then Bibra Lake, South Lake and so on; right the way through to the Murray River. She formed all those lakes all the way along.

She went straight in under the rock and there are three big caverns there. That is the beginning of another story, which the desert people can tell you. Because she went travelling straight out into the desert country and when she came out the other end she was caught in that country. That female one would eventually be the link to all Law, all the way across. They chased her across the land, went in a big storm right through Uluru to Queensland. There is an important pool there where she surfaced and then she turned back and went into what is known as the Dorrigo River. You will see three things wherever she went. There can be two hills and a valley; or two valleys and a hill; two white cockies and a crow; an eagle and two crows — everything is in threes. You will see that over and over again. And everyone who followed the trails knew that story and the songs and dances. And of course, while she was making all those places, the males were making their places too. The male *Waugal* is still here, living sometimes under what is now called Mt Eliza, or Kings Park. Our stories tell us how the Dreaming ancestors made the land. So where they traveled, that is where you get the songlines, the Dreaming tracks; you get the connections, you get different country, different people, different language, but they are all connected to each other.

Unfortunately, it has taken a long time for people to recognise the importance of our waterways, and in the meantime a lot of harm has been done. Felling trees and fertiliser over-use have damaged our river systems. The *Derbal* looks *mindytch*, which means sick in Nyungar language. It just lies there, asleep. It has been doing that for a long time because it is sick and needs help, but the help is slow in coming. Effluent and pollutants still find their way into the river. It is pretty clear that some has come from the Belmont and Ascot racecourses, but there are also companies near the river that make bricks, tiles, cement, all those things. What we need is a group of Aboriginal people trained up as river rangers, with direct responsibility for going to companies along the river, monitoring the water, and finding out where this dreadful stuff is coming from. Polluting the river needs to be policed, which means the river rangers would need the clout to stop it when they find it. Nobody should be allowed to continue to pump waste into the *Derbal*.

We have got to stop it because of our spirit. When the river is healthy, we are healthy. We have to make sure nothing is overlooked and that the right thing is done. Pollution in the river is like toxic waste, which can stay in the environment for thousands of years, even if you can't see it or the damage it is doing. Often you can't see the effluent in the river, and everyone thinks that if you can't see it, the river is okay. People think it is clean because it is exposed to sea water and most of the sea water is clean; dolphins swim in it, so everyone thinks it's all right. But the bottom of the river is just all black sludge. The mussels, which are the cleaners, the filter feeders in the river that clean and keep it tidy, are not there anymore. And every year, fish die. The toxicity shows up in tests, whether you can see it or not, it's right there. The river is sick and it is really, really sad and needs us to help it get better. But even if we make a great effort now, it will be decades before anything we do has a proper impact. Also, the rainfall patterns seem to be changing. The rain is important because it flushes the river, but we don't always gat a decent rainfall every year. The outlook for the *Derbal* is pretty bleak, yet it is such a beautiful thing in the middle of the city. If it weren't for the sea and the salt water that is deposited in it, it would be a cesspool.

I often think about what my Uncle Thomas taught me, what my mum taught me and what I have learned in my work in different places around the state as a national park ranger. There is a deep beauty in the land and the people, but there are many places that are sick and need help. If people are meant to be the Carers of Everything, then we have to accept that we are all responsible for helping to look after this country in an honest and caring way.

BERYL DIXON

*is a Nyungar Elder from the Great Southern region
of Western Australia. Her bloodline links to country
are through the Minang and Goreng peoples.*

Back Home to Country

I'm nearing my eighty-second birthday, so I am in my twilight years really, but I'm still as sharp as a tack. I know what's what in the present, and I can just as clearly recall my younger years growing up in the bush and living in small towns when my mum and dad followed the work, as Nyungar people had to in those days. Though I have lived in the city most of my adult life, I have made it my business to go back to my country, whether to live for a while or visit family or to put my feet again on the land where I was born all those years ago. When I walk in the footprints of my childhood, the years just fade away and I feel like I am there again as a young girl. I am flooded with wonderful memories of the sounds and smells of the bush, the joy and laughter of my sisters and me, and the connectedness and security from the voices and words shared with us kids from our Elders. Going bush was something we did all the time when I was young and it kept us grounded in culture and closely connected to our land.

I was born in the bush in the South-West of Western Australia in 1926. My name is Beryl Dixon, nee Keen, and I am the oldest of twelve children born to Emily Keen, nee Farmer, and Lennard George Keen. Both my parents were Nyungar, which makes me Nyungar, as it does my children, grandchildren and great-grandchildren. Our bloodline links to country are through the Minang and Goreng peoples of the Great Southern region. I like to think of myself as being born in the bush, and though I am not a true bush baby, I was not born in a hospital. This is because my mum was *boodjarri* with me when she was on the job, living with and keeping camp for my dad and uncles when they were contracted to clear land for several farmers out of Broomehill. The story of my birth is a funny one, and because of that my Aunty Ednah, Dad's sister, has retold it many times over the years. Her skill of sharing a yarn, as we Nyungars call it, was so good she had everyone in stitches of laughter over what happened.

My mum was nervous about my coming birth because I was her first baby. Also, things could go wrong in childbirth and with medical assistance a long way away, it was a worrying time. On the day of my birth, my dad and my uncles were in the bush cutting down trees and my mum was at the camp with Dad's younger sister, Aunty Ednah. They had a whistle to blow to bring the men in for their smoko, lunch and dinner at the end of the day. The whistle was also for emergencies, or in case mum went into labour. The men had just finished lunch and were well into their job again when they heard the whistle. At first they ignored it, after all they had just been at the camp and everything was fine. But the noise of that whistle kept on and on, bouncing off the gum trees that surrounded them and making a hell of a racket. Then it finally hit Dad that it might be the baby. Forgetting to bring the horse and cart, he ran full pelt back to camp, only to find that Aunty Ednah had practically winded herself from blowing the whistle so hard to get their attention. Gasping for breath, she quickly explained that Mum was ready to have the baby and needed help.

'I'll get the horse and cart!' he told them 'Be ready to hop on board as soon as I pull in!'

Katanning hospital was around fifteen miles away, so it was going to be quite a long ride.

Well, Mum and Aunty Ednah heard him coming, all right! Dad flogged that horse and cart so hard he couldn't stop in time and galloped straight past them. They just stood there in shock, watching the tail end of Dad and the horse and cart go flying past. They didn't know what was happening, and they didn't think Dad knew either. He disappeared into the bush again and though they couldn't see him, they could hear the horse neighing and Dad cussing and fumbling around.

'It's all right!' they heard him yell 'Just get ready, I'm coming around again!'

By then panic had gripped them all. Mum and Aunty Ednah didn't know what to expect, with Dad in the frame of mind he was in. Aunty Ednah went into hysterics laughing and Mum went into labour and started crying.

Eventually, they were headed off at a quick trot for Katanning, but it soon became obvious that I was determined to come into the world there and then, so they detoured to old Grannie Finn's farmhouse, where I was born on the kitchen table. Later that day, we were taken to Katanning hospital in Grannie Finn's car. I was fine, but mum needed some medical attention from Dr Loftus. Personally, I don't think being bounced around in the back of the cart by Dad had helped her any! So my life began with a funny story, which was just as well, because it would be humour that would keep me going through some of the hard times in the future.

On a more serious note, though, even though as Nyungar people we have learned to laugh at just about anything, there is always a sad side to our lives. One of the things that saddens me is what has happened to our country. Nyungar people cleared a lot of land for the farmers back then. Unfortunately, the oppressive laws of the day made it impossible for us to live as ordinary people might. It also made it impossible for us to look after the land the way our old people would have done in the times before the white people came. Our lives were hard. We had no opportunity and little access to a proper education or regular jobs with decent pay. The farmers employed us because they couldn't get anyone else to do the work cheaper. They also took advantage of our situation, because they knew that we needed the work to survive. It was the only way we could put food on the table for our families. There were no handouts to talk of in those days, only the rations the Native Welfare Department gave to Nyungars, but this didn't amount to enough to survive on. Our families were forced to scratch out a living in whatever way they could and because of that we also learnt to stick together like glue.

Most of the work was seasonal, so in the lean times families stayed close at hand because if one was out of work, others wouldn't be, so this was a way of providing for each other. Everyone shared what they had, it might not have been much but it was shared nonetheless. Looking back now at some of the jobs our people did, especially labouring to clear the land for farmers in the South-West, I think sadly of some of the consequences. Felling all those trees has degraded the land and caused the water to become salty. Also, there are fewer places for the birds and animals to live. This could have all been avoided if, when white people first came to Nyungar country, they had listened to the wisdom of our Elders. That's the reality of it. The truth is the truth, you can't change it, but we have to learn from the mistakes of the past and try to put things right as best we can. To do that, though, we all have to work together in a different way.

The other thing that saddens me is that a lot of our people died in those days: babies, young children and young adults, as well as many of our oldies. I nearly died from diphtheria when I was nine years old, and I was between six and eight years old when I lost my little brother, Lennard George Keen, who was named after my dad. He was under twelve months old when he passed away with gastroenteritis, which was a real killer for a lot of Nyungar kids then. There was not much that could be done if it got a hold of you. I think one of the reasons so many of our people died was the dramatic change in our lifestyles. We went from being a healthy people to unhealthy. We never had enough of our traditional foods in our diet. Our people weren't allowed to hunt and gather anymore because the ownership of the land was taken away from us. You had to get permission to hunt kangaroo and possum, gather berries, carrots, potatoes, roots and seeds. These were the foods that had kept us healthy, but we didn't have access to them anymore. Some farmers were tolerant of Nyungars who worked their land for them and let them hunt for food, but others were not. You got into big trouble if you got caught on someone's land hunting without permission. Nyungars were caught between two worlds and we suffered for it in many ways. To provide for our families we were forced to do jobs that destroyed the very same country that had once sustained our old people. That's the truth of it.

Like most Nyungar families, in order to survive my parents had to follow the work. And as much of their work was on farms, they often had to camp out in the bush in difficult conditions. Though they did their very best to make things comfortable, it was still hard if you had a big mob of kids with you. I am the eldest of twelve children, so you can imagine how hard it was for them. This meant that for some of my childhood I lived with my Grandma Farmer, who was a stoic, no-nonsense person. She was also a very loving woman and blessed with a little house in the town of Katanning. She protected us from being removed from our family, like many Nyungar children were at that time, because she was always one jump ahead of the authorities. When she was only eight years old, the Native Welfare Department had placed Grandma Farmer with a white family so she could be trained as a domestic servant. This didn't mean she was adopted: that didn't happen in those days. Even if a child's father was white, Nyungar children were seldom claimed by their white relations. Instead, she was trained to be a housekeeper, so that while she was doing all the hard work, the lady of the house could be just that. A lady. Grandma Farmer was well thought of and this gave us a bit of extra protection. She often worked with Dr Pope delivering babies, and four of her sons even fought in the First World War, with two of them losing their lives and being buried in France. Grandma Farmer was pretty good at working out how things stood, so she kept an eagle eye on us kids.

As a family, we would go bush most Sundays. Grandma Farmer would take a sugar bag with everything we needed for the day like flour, baking powder, tea, sugar, salt and water. She also had two old tins, one to make the damper in and the other to wash up in. She'd bring a few medicines along too, just in case. Gran would collect the right-size leaves from the flood gums, heat them up and then use them to rub on bites and stings. The leaves were hot and they'd burn a little, but they certainly took the sting away, even a bee sting. I know, because I was treated many times with this medicine. Grandma Farmer had a lot of bush remedies.

We also went to visit the cemetery regularly to clean up the graves of family members and to let them know that they weren't forgotten. There were strict rules we kids had to follow: no running wild, talk in a soft voice, and show the utmost respect to the graves and where we were. After our visit, the Elders would take us up into the bush behind the cemetery, where we'd make a camp fire and have a feed. The Elders would oversee our jobs because of the scorpions, snakes and spiders that could be in the wood we were collecting. We'd also gather rocks to put around the fire so it didn't get away from us and cause unwanted damage. When everything was ready, we'd drag some logs over and place them around the fire so we all had somewhere to sit and enjoy our bush tucker picnic. We'd have foods like *cumuuk*, quondongs and bardi grubs and a *karrdar*, which is a goanna, to throw on the coals. Grandma Farmer and her eldest son, Uncle Harry, showed us where to get the food. The women in the group used to take us girls to find *cumuuk*, which didn't need to be cooked. They grew on a bushy vine about two feet high. The fruit was ripe when it changed from an inch-long hard green berry to a soft mauve colour with sticky plum flesh. You could eat every part of this bush berry, it was very sweet and we kids loved it, so of course we ate as we gathered. There were so many in those days that there were still plenty to take back to camp and share with the rest of the family.

Quondong trees were everywhere then, too. They grew to around six foot high and had a thin bark layered close to the trunk. The branches were few, but they had quite a bit of foliage on them. You couldn't miss them because in season they were loaded with bush peaches, which were bright red when ripe. The women used to make quondong jam when the fruit was in season, so we had jam all year round, and it tasted wonderful on damper. The seeds didn't go to waste either; they were about the size of a large marble and the women used to make necklaces out of them. Some women still make necklaces today out of them. We kids also liked the manna and jam tree gums. When you cook it up in a little pot with sugar and water it makes a great toffee. We got bardi grubs from the smaller jam gum trees that had protruding lumps on their trunks. We'd chop the lump off with a small tomahawk in a way that didn't damage the tree. There was usually only one grub in a lump, but it would be big and fat, about two inches long, and they were juicy and delicious. Sometimes we ate them raw, other times we cooked them on the coals. They had a sweet woody taste.

Now and then, when Dad was in town from working in the bush, he came with us and he always bought his .22 rifle along. Dad and Uncle Harry would go off together and bring a rabbit or a *karrdar*, which was usually killed with a *dowick*, to add to our picnic. They would be prepared by the women and cooked on the coals. *Karrdar* meat is white and looks and tastes similar to fish. We'd always have damper, too, so it was a really *mooditj* feed.

Like our behaviour at the cemetery, there were rules we had to follow in the bush, too. We weren't allowed to wander too far from the camp on our own. Snakebite was a big thing in those days, because there was no antivenom to speak of. We were taught that if you left the snakes alone, then they would leave you alone, and this seemed to work pretty well for us.

The Elders also warned us of other things: there are creatures in the bush, and if they get their hands on you, you might never return to your family. The Elders told us about the *baalups*, who were little hairy men with red eyes. 'Don't wave red-tipped glowing sticks around the campfire,' they warned us, 'because you will attract the attention of the *baalups*. They will get curious and come into the camp, especially when everyone is asleep. Then one of you kids could go missing. Also, if you are in the bush and hear someone calling your name, if you don't know that voice, then be wary of walking towards it. You might not come back.' Then there was the *jaanark*, a night spirit devil bird. 'Don't whistle at night,' they instructed us. 'If you whistle at night, you might attract the *jaanark* bird, who will bring danger and bad luck to everyone.' And, of course, there was also the W*weerlo*, a bird that is also called a curlew. 'Don't talk too loudly at night,' the Elders used to tell us, 'especially if you hear that *weerlo*. If you hear them, don't talk loud, because if you attract their attention with your voices then they will screech over our camp all night. And you know the *weerlo* is a messenger of doom and danger.' All this kind of knowledge was important cultural learning for us because it helped us to know how to behave in the bush so we kept ourselves safe and didn't endanger anyone else either.

When we were in the bush, the spirit world was very close to us, especially at night. I would like to share a story involving my Uncle Alf, whom we kids called Uncle Tommy, and his brothers, Uncles Ken and Lou Farmer, the two sons of my Grandma Farmer who had survived the First World War and come home. Uncle Tommy was camping on the job, cutting fence posts out of jam trees in dense bush between Broomehill and Kojonup. He needed to move camp, so Uncle Ken and Uncle Lou decided to go out and help him shift. I was allowed to go along too, and so was a smaller cousin of mine. The trip out to Uncle Tommy's camp was great, but not that eventful, though this changed once we got there With everything packed to the hilt on the back of the truck, the truck got bogged in the sand and no matter what they did, the uncles couldn't budge it an inch. In those days, there were no real roads to talk of, except for the few main roads that the Main Roads Board laid down between towns. The rest were just sandy tracks, so if you drove off the main roads, then things could get pretty tricky.

Anyway, by the time night fell, they still hadn't got the truck clear. So the uncles built a big fire and very firmly told me and my little cousin to sit still by the fire, be very quiet and not move. It was pitch black and, besides the fire, there were only the stars for light, plus the truck's headlights. So there we were, sitting and looking at each other and wondering how long it would take our uncles to free the truck. The night was very still and an eerie feeling descended on us. I remember having a sense that something was about to happen, only I didn't know what. My little cousin felt it, too, and he got so anxious he started to shake and cry.

All of a sudden, this bloodcurdling scream erupted from the bush. It sounded like a woman in terrible pain, like she was getting belted or something, but there was no other camp near us: no people, no farms, no other light from anyones camp fire, nothing within cooee of us. We were alone, surrounded by dense bush. My little cousin started to cry really loudly in fear and I felt like crying too. I could see that though the uncles were acting brave, they were just as nervous. The screaming didn't stop; it went on and on like it was never going to end. I have never seen my uncles move so fast in all their lives! They got that truck out of that bog as quick as you could say Jack Flash and had us speeding down the track in seconds. We were thirty miles from Katanning, but before we knew it, we were home. It was like we flew!

A couple of days later, when my dad and Uncle Tommy were having a bit of a yarn, my uncle told Dad what had happened that night. I know I shouldn't have been listening to the Elders talk, this was a rule of Grandma Farmer's, but I did anyhow and I was shocked to hear them burst out laughing about that night. I didn't understand how they could laugh when it had been so terribly frightening. But as I grew older, I began to have some experiences like this myself. This led me to appreciate the role Nyungar humour played in our lives. Dad and Uncle Tommy hadn't focused on the frightening spiritual experience so much, but on the humorous human element: three grown men had busted themselves to get that truck out of that bog and away from that area as fast as they could. Spiritual things like this happened then and still happen today; these are the things we know about and experience, but we don't talk too much about them because they are just a part of our country and our culture. My Elders understood it back then and I understand it now. These things are experienced by all Aboriginal people, right across the country, and we acknowledge and respect them.

Another place we used to go a lot, especially when it was hot, was Police Pools. This was where the police troopers used to water their horses in the early days, and it had always been an important source of fresh water for Nyungar people. I remember that everything was so alive in the bush then. The sounds of the birds and the smells of the eucalyptus and sheoak trees were magnified to the point that they were intoxicating. And the frogs — there were many of them, but there was one in particular that the Elders told us not to go near or touch because it was special. This was a very strict rule and they expected us to take notice of it. The frog they were talking about was green and had its own special croak. When we heard it we were happy because Grandma had told us that it was the protector of that pool and it watched over us when we were splashing around in the water. We began to understand then that frogs were very important because the waterways needed them and they played a major role in keeping everything as it should be.

One of our other favourite places was Lake Ewelamaartup, which is a freshwater lake east of Katanning, surrounded by sheoak and eucalyptus trees. There was also a broom bush that the old people used to make brooms out of, to sweep their bush camps and also to sell to white people to make a little money. The lake was a favourite watering hole for all the animals and the birdlife there was very rich. We loved swimming and having picnics there because there was so much to see. The oldies usually rode in the horse and buggy when we went to Lake Ewelamaartup and we kids liked to run alongside the buggy, jumping on it every now and again for a ride as we made our way to the lake. We walked for miles and miles in those days and thought nothing of it. It's probably one of the reasons we were so healthy and fit. The lake was always a special place to us as a family and I think this was also because of its cultural significance. Nyungars used to gather there, and I am talking about many, many, many years before I was even thought of, let alone born. It's a big freshwater area with lots of bush food, so they would have had corroborees and other large gatherings there. Nyungars keep doing the same things and going to the same places year in and year out, especially if they live in their own country. So when we went to Lake Ewelamaartup we were following in the footsteps of the Nyungars who'd been before us. We were even doing similar things, like sharing food, yarning and enjoying our family's company. Where there are fresh water and food to do social things with family, then these places are culturally important. My old people knew just where to go and what each place could provide. They would have been taught this by their old people, because this kind of knowledge was passed down from generation to generation. So, as it had done for the people who had gone before me, Lake Ewelamaartup played a major part in my growing up, and after I came to live in Perth memories of it often floated fondly through my thoughts over the passing years.

In 2005, I made a trip with other family members back to country, to a Nyungar celebration reunion in Katanning. This meant a lot to me and my sisters and cousins, because we'd all grown up in this town. There was a part in the reunion programme where I was asked to speak, as one of the Elders, to a large gathering of Nyungar people who were also from Katanning and surrounding districts, which made me realise a lot of Nyungar people still called Katanning home. While I was speaking, someone asked me where I'd lived in town as a young child, and that was easy to answer because all I had to do was turn around and point at the house we'd lived in as a family. The reunion was held at the Katanning Aboriginal Community Centre, and our house was just across the road. It's amazing it's still standing, really.

The reunion organisers also asked me to go along on a tour of various places where Nyungar people often used to gather in my early years, places of significance to our people. We set off in a small bus with quite a few younger family members. Everyone was excited to be going on this trip, because one of my cousins and I, Elders in our family, were going to take them down memory lane, sharing aspects of our childhood in Katanning and Broomehill, as well as taking in Police Pools, Etticup, Broomehill Cemetery and Lake Ewelamaartup.

Our drive from Broomehill to Lake Ewelamaartup was just

wonderful because we were travelling along the childhood tracks we had once travelled with our Elders so many years ago. It began to rain as we were driving, but it wasn't so heavy that it distorted our view of the lake. When we arrived, we could see it

Beryl with her sisters Shirley, Marie and Kathy — Back to Katanning Nyungar Reunion 2005

Courtesy Beryl Dixon

very clearly and it was so beautiful. As we disembarked from the bus, an amazing thing happened. The rain stopped, the sun started to shine and there was no wind at all. A stillness descended over us. We all noticed it, but didn't say anything to each other, instead we were all just quiet, looking at the lake. Then, on the bank at the edge of the lake, a vivid rainbow began to form right where we were. It was small at first and hovered at the lake's edge for a while. It was so close that it seemed as if any one of us could have reached out and touched it. After lingering there for about ten minutes or so, it started to move, shimmering across the lake and growing in size. On and on it went until it was on the other side of the lake, where my dad, Mum and we kids had lived all those years ago when Dad was first working on the railways at Nyabing. It was a glorious thing to see and we were all shocked because that type of thing rarely happens in the city. Then my cousin turned to me and asked, 'What do you reckon about that Beryl?'

'What do I reckon?' I replied, 'I reckon that rainbow is here to show us the significance of the spiritual side of our

Lake Ewelamaartup — a rainbow appears at the start of a visit which is seen as a spiritual sign by family members, 2005

Courtesy Eric Hayward

Nyungar culture. It's a sign from our dead ancestors, who spent time here with us when we were kids. I think they are very happy that we have all come back home to country.'

As I said before, I hadn't exactly been born out in the bush, in country, so this doesn't make me a bush baby in the proper sense, but I certainly wasn't born in a white man's hospital either, so perhaps this puts me somewhere in the middle of it all. And that is how my life has been really, because I have worked hard to do well and I have done my best to help my family do well too. At the same time, I have kept all my cultural connections with my large extended family and my country, and when I think of all my old people who have passed away now, this makes me happy. I have decided that when it's my time to go, I want to be laid to rest not too far from where my mum, dad and siblings are buried. It's not in my country exactly, but it's still in Nyungar country. Up on the hill, in the jarrah walk that is surrounded with eucalypts, kangaroo paws and spider and donkey orchids. I wish for the people who meant a lot to me, as well as the things in the natural world that gave me many wonderful memories, to be near me. It would make me very happy to think that these people and those things are close to me, even when I have departed this life.

GREG LEHMAN

is a Palawa man descended from the Trawulwuy people of north-east Tasmania. He has worked in Aboriginal education and heritage management for over twenty years. Greg is manager of Aboriginal education for the Tasmanian Department of Education. His essays and poems have been published widely.

A Snake and a Seal

The rolling waters of Bass's Strait swirl and boil.
Hardly an island,
a few stark boulders are just enough
to part the current's run and churn its blue embrace.
If not for their foaming wake, these rocks would be missed
by all but the best of a schooner's watch.
But one tired eye knows them well.

The rounded shape would bring to a sailor's mind
the bursting breasts of a nursing wife
that he has left behind.
In a heavy sea, they slip from view behind marching crests
and rise again.
None too rare in these waters,
a rogue wave will break clear over the top.
The hard granite rock, stained orange and black,
is scoured smooth by driven brine.

Deep in the islet's bosom where the wind cannot reach,
lies a quiet shelter.
And in it,
motionless,

a silent form.
Crouched with her back to the cold stone,
wrapped tightly in a cloak of wallaby skin
to hold the damp at bay,
a young woman waits.

There is a snake moving along the river this morning. He is
a big one. White. Slow. Very cold. I can feel the chill of him.
As he makes his way, it is the banks of the river that guide
him — mostly. Maybe he is impatient to get to where he is
going, or perhaps it is because he is just afraid of nothing.
But he will sometimes move straight ahead, past factories
and bridges. At a bend in the river he will climb straight up
and over any hill that gets in the way. If the river widens into
a bay, this snake swims straight across. He is very
determined — like an old man who has seen everything
there is to see — he has no inclination to stop and wonder
about what he doesn't know. And there is so much to
understand on the banks of *Nipaluna* these days.

I have watched him. Ever since I came to this cold
country in the south of the island. I see him every winter,
moving down the valley toward the sea. Do you wonder
what he does when he gets to the coast? Once, maybe ten
years ago, I found out. I was watching the news on
television. After the stories had finished about war and
money, they moved on to the weather. Snow had been
falling in the mountains and was finished for now. The wind
had swung to the north and everything was peaceful. The
satellite photo showed no cloud, so the river's mouth was
clear to see. Can you believe it? The snake was there on the
screen!

The people who have lived along the river in recent times

The Jerry Snake
Courtesy Greg Lehman

know him too. They call him 'the Bridgewater jerry' and wake to see him in the morning — already among them — because he comes in the early hours. 'Oh, there's the jerry. It's big today. You'll need a coat for sure!' I also used to think of him like they did. The jerry. A fog. Something to keep out of if you could. Cold, damp and chilling to the bone. But when I saw it on my TV, I held my breath. As it was gliding out of the mouth of the river and across Storm Bay like a giant rope slung over the waters, I knew there was more to this 'fog' than just mist and science.

Here on *Trowuna*, the island that is now called Tasmania, we have some problems. Not that long ago, the British arrived to bring grief to my Ancestors. This wasn't simply due to their being European: the French had been here before them and their visit had gone well. We met and ate with them, showed them our dances and taught them many things. They were quick to learn and showed us a thing or to as well. Some of it fascinated the young ones (flutes, and axes) and some was not worth the bother (mirrors, beads and coins). Before them, the Dutch had come. They had been nervous and sailed by without meeting us. Maori had come long before this and left their flax behind. There had been others, too, but those are different stories.

These problems began when the British decided to stay. Killing began. Not just of *cartela*, the seal, but us *Palawa* mob too. That's the simple truth. Lots of killing. All this happened because of one thing: the sons of England did not know *tunapri manta*. This is our knowing that comes from the old stories, handed down for a thousand generations. It gives us our Law and a way to know the world that works for everyone. But the sealers and soldiers would not learn! If it is true what the Old Man *Woreddy* said, that they were *num* — the ghosts of our own ancestors — then this is hard to understand. Because *num* are part of *tunapri manta*. Something was not right. Something had changed. The story of their arrival, of *numlaggar,* could be a long one with much crying and sadness. But there is something more important to tell. To understand my story about the White Snake, you need to know how my people are today. And that is more than a simple matter of recounting history.

Her face is soft with youth,
her russet skin laced with scars.
One of her deep-set eyes is large and dark.
The cornea tinged with blue.
The iris and pupil merge as one.
Her other eye is gone.

An emptiness gnaws at her heart,
as cold as her rocky home.
She has not heard her own name spoken for months.
Instead, it is snarled by the wind.
With a scorn that cuts her deep
tunapri manta is broken.

Whether it is to the living or the dead
that the wind gives voice, there is no telling.
But always, amidst the din,

her own name is screamed,
'*bunga!*'
A mother pleads as her child is dragged
across the sand to a longboat full with stinking *num*.
They dip their oars and pull away.
Beyond the breakers.
On *rowra's* evil toil.

Existence for us today is confusing. We live in two worlds — or many more if you consider *tunapri manta*. But the world of the *num* is very different from our *Palawa* worlds. We survive in this because all of us can count *num* among our ancestors. Think of it! We come from the people of the land, made from *tarner* the kangaroo by the creation spirits, *dromedeener* and *moinee*. And there, two lifetimes ago, comes a *num* grandfather for each of us. So, we are descended from ghosts of our own dead! Even after two hundred years, none of our Elders has created a story from this that gives us peace.

Or perhaps this is not quite right. We do sing songs of our survival in the face of a long hard struggle. Songs to bring the children home to have our land returned. But all of these are tinged with pain and have a demon as the boss. *Numlagger*, 'the white man comes'. Not only were we chased from our country and family, but perhaps worse than this, we left the world of *tunapri manta*. I often wonder what all the spirits of the land have been doing since the time we last sang their songs and performed their ceremonies — since we forgot their names. They were kept in our minds by the stories and dances of the Old People like *Woreddy* and my own tribal grandmother, *Woretemoeteyenner*. Do they just disappear when the Old Ones die? Do they fade away like a fiction? It certainly seems that way; they are hardly mentioned anymore. And for most of the people who live here today, they have never existed at all. Or so they think.

Seal Shooting in Bass's Straits, 1881
Courtesy State Library of Victoria

Maybe those spirits are just hidden today — obscured by the language we speak. Words like 'mountain', 'tree' and 'wind' are no invitation for them to show us their presence. My own people have been too clever at learning the language of science. We now live in a *num* world where a rock is just a rock and the wind is just the wind. We no longer speak about how *Kunanyi* breathes out rain to fill the streams that run down her slopes. We do not hear the words that are carried in the screeching cry of *moingana* as he flies down from *Kunanyi* to warn us of coming storms. Worst of all, we hardly pause to heed the voices of our own Ancestors as they sing to us in the wind that blows through the trees — the trees we once knew as countrymen.

It is not that long since we were surrounded by all of this. We didn't have to think about what we had lost, or yearn for understanding of things past. *Tunapri* was everywhere; in everything we did. The law was our life. Not just *Palawa*, but all things in the world followed this. The birds gave us notice of what was to come. The bush would call us when it was time to burn. The rain would punish our lazy ways. And always, the great ancestor spirits would watch us as they lay sleeping — their bodies forming the ridges, peaks and valleys of the country all around.

A seal barks from a ledge below:
'Bunga, are you there?'
She inhales a breath of grey salted skins at her side,
'Cartela.'
The *num* will come back soon, to take the skins away.
They will leave her bleeding. And colder still.
If only her sisters were with her.
They will know the *num* by now.
Spirit children will grow inside them too.
They could tell her how to back home.
'Tyerlore' she spits. Island Wife.
Married to stone and sea.
A wooden club, a steel knife
and a pile of stinking skins.

There is an island near the mouth of *Nipaluna,* called *Lupaylana.* This name tells of the place before *rowra,* the powerful devil spirit who lives in the deep, raised up the waters to cut off the land and make an island of it. It is a place close to a big lagoon that in good years is full of eggs and fat ducks. The story of this place is also of a young girl who was being chased by a group of men. They were from a tribe that had no rightful business with her. She ran away fast, because she knew she must. For them to catch her would be for her to carry the blame of their crime. This is *tunapri.* She knew it was right because without the law, she might weaken and slow her flight. To be caught by them would maybe lead to war, because the men of her tribe would not rest until they had caused the deaths of these men. And that would be only the beginning. In this way, each *Palawa* carried responsibilities; for themselves and for *tunapri manta*. The men of her tribe too would have consequences to face — but that was their business and her tribe would see to this or perish.

So the girl ran until she reached the beach. The waves here pound and churn with all the power of an ocean that stretches without end. She had dived here for shellfish and lobster many times, and the familiar water called her to safety. Blind to the chaos of pounding surf, she dove into the cold, exploding waters and began to swim. Slipping under the breakers, she soon cleared the waves and looked back to where she expected to see her tormentors standing on the beach waving their spears and shaking their heads in fury. What she saw shocked her. Like so many children, too young to have heard of *rowra* — who dragged men who invaded his domain to certain death — they too had entered the water.

Bunga stretches her slender arms and legs.
She arches her supple back and rubs her leathery feet.
The day begins.
A penguin track of hard packed sand
leads through sharp tussocks to a humble rise.
The wind slaps her face,
blowing hard from a sky that gushes flesh and blood.
Every morning *Bunga* looks for a sign of what the day
    will bring.
Today there is flash of green ahead of the rising sun.
Away on the horizon,
in the heart of a stiffening breeze, a sail.
They come.

As long as the seals will call.
They come.
And she answers with her club.
Flensing fur from flesh
to hoard their bloody prize.

Rafts of *yula* skim the swell and
hurry by to fatten hungry chicks.
Along the surging water's edge tangled kelp writhes and
    foams.
Bunga picks her way across the broken shore.
She advances to where the seals have hauled up on
    sloping shelves
and slumber in the building sun.
Closing in on hands and knees
she slides, head down.

Her heavy club behind, she inches forward.
Silent.
Watchful.
The seals will sense her soon.
They know her business well.
The stone beneath her hands is limpet-flecked and tears
    her flesh.
Her lips part. She whispers low.
An ancient song to calm the sea and quiet her racing
    heart.
The words meld with surging foam
and dripping fur that now smells close.
Bunga gradually raises her head.
A single seal has fixed her in his gaze.
Liquid.

Soft.
His fur not dark, but white.

When *Bunga* wakes, the sun is high.
To the south a distant coast is ripe with trailing smoke.
Fires lit and easing winds.
Her Mother's voice feel close.

Beside the glowing hearth, an old woman
begins her daily chant.
Intones her daughter's name
to call her home.
To call her home.

A raft of skins at her feet,
bundled close with strings of grass,
is sealed tight with fat and clay.
Bunga wades out to a welcoming swell.
She kicks to where the current runs and smiles.
The wind is at her back.
Her arms and legs feel strong and married days are
    done.

Today, if you look at *Lupaylana*, you will notice that
beyond the large main island — out toward the open waters
— is a smaller one. You see, *Rowra* took pity on the girl. As
the men waded out into the surf, each clung to the other in
fear — and this is where they stayed. To save the girl and
punish the men, *Rowra* turned them all into stone.

When I saw that snake on TV, he was sliding close by
Lupaylana. The story I already knew of those islands
mingled with the one unfolding. I saw then how the world

keeps itself. The white snake watches over *Lupaylana* to hold *tunapri* strong. And for all who see the snake, as he makes his long journey down the valley, there is a reminder of what is learned from this and every other place along his path.

Our life since *numlaggar* has distracted us from the teachings that the country still keeps. It's not that the wisdom has been lost. Some stories may have ceased to be told, some dances may have been forgotten, or some songs left quiet. All of these are like fruit that has grown on a tree and, without harvest, falls to rot back into the earth. We are now too busy to stop and fill our bellies. Our appetites are spoiled by the rubbish we eat. And we grow lazy with the fine things that money brings to our *num* lives. If we spend our time living in a *num* world, it is not because of that ghost ancestor. It is because we, too, have closed our eyes to *tunapri manta*. So I say — when the news comes on TV — don't be distracted by the stories of politics and greed. Take careful notice of the weather. It is the best show around!

The conversations we have with our world have become like those of children. We need to stop thinking about ourselves and the things we can't have. So, I will make more time for listening to the wind. The birds aren't worried that I don't hear them much these days. They still call to me because they have never stopped believing. And the White Snake will slide just as well through the office blocks of the city as he does through the trees of the forest. That big snake has taught me something. Even if I don't know all the old stories, there is no excuse for not knowing the country. And a few generations of *num* life don't mean I can't go back to believing. If I cannot find the old stories for a place, then I should listen and learn — and take my time to create some new ones.

PAT DUDGEON

belongs to the Bardi people near Broome in the Kimberley. For many years she was head of the Centre for Aboriginal Studies at Curtin University. Pat, who is completing her doctoral thesis, has national recognition for her leading role in psychology and Indigenous people.

The Sinking of the Enid

The Enid, *a two-masted schooner, 12.15 tons. Dimensions: 36.5 x 11.1 x 4.9 feet. Built at Fremantle by W Chamberlain during 1903.*

Owners: John Sydney Hicks, Doctor, of Fremantle, D N McLeod, Pastoralist, of Carnarvon, Victor Ralph Kepert, Pearler, of Broome, Thomas Clarke, Pearler of Broome and Albert Barnett Saunders, Pearler of Broome.

The vessel left Broome for Fremantle under C Kruger, Master, on the 22nd of May 1928 and was not heard from again. Three lives were lost.[92]

Some years ago I found out that my great-grandfather, William Munget, had died in a shipwreck. I was surprised at this information. Though I had discussed our family history with my grandmother on many occasions, she had never once told me about her father's death and the circumstances surrounding this. Fortunately, my *lulu* (great uncle) Mathew had told me the story before he passed on. I searched through the State library maritime records and found the entries about a schooner called the *Enid*. Three crew had been lost at sea, presumed dead. Only the master's name was mentioned. The other two people remained nameless and unknown. I wondered whether this had been the convention of the time, as the other recordings mentioned only the captain's name and not those of the other crew members. I wondered whether this was because they might have been Aboriginal, like Grandfather Willy, or Asian. I wondered whether that had been William's first trip to Fremantle or whether it was one of many he had been part of. The ghost of the *Enid* haunted my thoughts. How could a pearling lugger disappear like that, never to be heard of or seen again? But I was thinking about the *Enid* in the context of modern technology, when seagoing vessels rarely disappear or are wrecked. Eighty years ago, the situation was very different. Sometimes debris might wash up to identify that something terrible has happened, but more often than not ships just simply disappeared.

The north-western Australian coast is a very remote area. Survivors of shipwrecks there during the nineteenth and even the twentieth centuries would have found it difficult to last even if they had made it ashore. Further, the region is within the cyclone belt, which extends from the northern part of the continent to about halfway down the coast of Western Australia. Whole pearling fleets have been wiped out by cyclones. It was not uncommon to assume that if a vessel went missing, it had been wrecked in a cyclone. The *Enid* was going to Fremantle on a postal run and for refitting. She might have been caught in a cyclone around the Exmouth area and sank, all hands lost.

In 1928, William Munget left Broome on a lugger, the *Enid*. He was part of a three-man crew going to Fremantle to have the *Enid* refitted. The *Enid* also carried post and other cargo for Perth. Sea transport was common between towns along the west coast in those days. Though the report quoted at the start of this chapter says the *Enid* left in May, two other reports say it left in February, which was more likely. It is not very important, dates get mixed up in history, but February is in cyclone season, unlike May. Australia's tropical cyclone season extends from November to April. The pearling season is during the dry season, from April to October, and 'lay-up' is during the wet season, November to March. William Munget was thirty-four years old, in the prime of his manhood; too young to die and too young to leave a dependent family behind, alone and unprotected.

Family legends whisper that maybe they mutinied on the *Enid*, capturing the lugger and sailing to Asia, where the men might have started new families. William Munget was a Bardi man who would not have left his family and home country. (Family legends whisper that it was really Jurud, William's mother, who found the famed Southern Cross Pearl, and she traded it for tea and tobacco to the white pearler who is famous for the find. The dates of the find and Jurud's age match up, but that is another story.)

Some weeks after seeking this information about William Munget and the *Enid*, I had a dream in which I was a man drowning in a violent storm out at sea. Amid the terror and desperation of the situation, I knew that I wanted to live, I wanted to grow old with my family, and my last thought was that I would die far away from my country, and they would not know that I died, would not know where my body was and would not mourn me properly. I woke up shivering and terrified. I wondered whether my curiosity about the *Enid* had made me dream of dying like William, my great-grandfather, must have done on that night, stranded and alone in the middle of the Indian Ocean. The crew would have seen the cyclone coming in; the black thunderclouds before sunset. The barometer would have dropped and the wind would have been gusting in from the east. The skipper might have thought they could ride it out, dropping the sails in preparation. Or did they try and run for shore and shelter, only to be immobilised by the eerie dead calm before the storm, the schooner drifting helplessly in that strange vacuum? She might have capsized; turned over and over until she filled with water. Her timbers might have been shattered in the battering waves out in deep ocean or splintered by the power of the monstrous surf close to shore. In this story, the *Enid* is caught in a hurricane out at sea and this is the dream that woke me, choking for air, my heart beating like a fast drum.

The water surged all around him; the world was grey water and darkness. For a brief second he was hurled out of the water and in the seething dull foam he saw the cat, a momentary beacon of white and orange, desperately scrabbling onto the tossing wood and sailcloth, front and back legs working wildly; but already the debris was sinking. A mountain of water smashed down on him, would he ever surface again? Clinging to the pitiful lifesaver, he tumbled over and over. He tried to force himself to think calmly, measure the time he would need to suck in air if he came up again, hoping for another surfacing and another breath of air. He was a helpless doll swirling and buffeted in the wild ocean. With absolute certainty, he realised he was going to die, like the cat. It was his time to die. His thoughts ran full of terror and despair; he was going to die. It wasn't right to die like this. A man in his prime. He was too young to die. He had too much to do. His family was too young to be left alone. All alone and with no-one. No-one would know he had died. So far away from his home country. His spirit would be lost. In desperation, he struggled against the pounding water and opened his mouth to scream, sucking in water where there should have been air.

Fathoms under the raging sea, all was calm. With other bits and parts of the lugger, his broken body sank slowly down to the seabed to finally rest, far away from home.

Jurud woke up in middle of the night. She sat straight up from her bed, her mind clear with sharp waiting. There was a tingling in the air, she wrapped the blanket around her shoulders and crawled out of her hut. The night was bright and crisp, no moon but bright stars lit the trees. She breathed deeply, drawing in the brittle air, tasting it to find what was wrong. She went to her camp fire and pushed the dull red embers around, placing a few small sticks there. She checked her dogs but they were fast asleep; one near the fire and one curled in the opening of the hut.

'Jurud!'

She heard her name called clearly. That must have been what woke her. The call came from both inside her head and from the clearing in the trees away from the camp. She pulled the blanket closer around her thin body, clutching the folds with one hand to her chest feeling her heart beating loud and fast. She knew what it was, but was terrified to have it confirmed. Her dogs whimpered, one twitching and the other pawing restlessly at the ground, but still asleep. The camp fire slowly flared, shedding more light, but everything remained still and crisp like the night had frozen and she was the only thing able to move. She walked slowly away from the camp to the clearing in the trees. She looked up a slope on the side and saw the outline of a figure, pitch black against the cold white starlight. Black and void of light. She realised she was sobbing in terror and grief, clutching her blanket. She knew who it was.

'Willy,' she said harshly, 'my boy, you have to go now. Good job you come back to tell me, but you have to go now. Go, go on. Go!'

She hissed, waving her free hand at him. The shadow figure stood watching her and then, gradually, it inclined its head and in the slowest motion drifted down behind the slope, not turning away, watching her still as it sank out of sight.

It was gone.

Her grief bust from her, and she keened under the cold stars for her son, who had passed away in strange country but found his way home.

Thirty years before, Jurud had thrown Willy up onto her straight, hard shoulders, his sturdy legs wrapping around her neck. He was about five years old and the centre of her life, this beautiful black child with white flashing teeth and sunlight in his heart. Jurud carried him easily down the dunes to the beach. They stepped out of the shady bushes and the beach opened out before them, endless, edged by blue sea, all sparkling with white stars from the sun.

'See over there, little man?' Jurud pointed with her lips across the sand to where the mud began. 'Cockles.'

Willy nodded yes, vigorously, as he scrambled impatiently down her body.

His aunty laughed as she walked out from the shade. 'Eh, boy, you are just like a little goanna running down your mother like a tree!'

Willy stuck his tongue out at them and turned to run down to the sea, laughing and yelling, 'Old dugongs! Slow old dugongs, try and catch me then!'

Later he brought them cockles — too small for them to bother cooking — as a peace offering, mischievously giggling behind his sand glittered hands after his olive branch had been sombrely accepted. Now, when Jurud thought about him, the most vivid image was of that five-year-old boy, the pride and love of him, the first born of her and her sisters; his bright teeth in his laughing mouth, those dark eyes flashing in glee as he ran down that white beach to the sea, while they yelled back to him and shook their sticks at him, pretending offence but laughing with him, on that warm spring morning.

Willy had grown up in the mission. Jurud didn't mind that Willy had been taken into the mission. She was sometimes sad that he would not be taught the old ways properly, but times had changed so much since she was a girl and the first *gardiyas* came. He was special, born when not many children had been born. He was special to her and her sisters and to the missionaries, too. They took him in and put the three powerful spirit beings into him. That old man, very powerful father one; and his son whose totem was the cross that they put everywhere; and that third one who was hard so see, but whose totem was the white bird. New spirits from another country but good ones, very strong, to keep away all the pearlers and sailors who came to make humbug for the women. Frightened them right away from the mission. Everybody fell down on their knees when they saw the totem for the son one. Ceremonies all the time for these spirit ones. Jurud had hoped these new spirits would help protect him and make him even stronger. But they weren't any help now. Nothing was any help.

She knew he was dead; her boy was gone.

In the mission, word had come through that the *Enid*,

and all hands, was missing. Martha, Lillian and Willy's daughter, started waiting on the same day every week for the provision truck. She would leave her school duties early on that day and sit under the big tree in the centre of the mission, where all the visitors stopped. She spread a blanket and sat in the shade hours before the truck was due. The younger children, who weren't at the school yet, thought this was comical at first, and a good excuse for teasing. But Martha gave one of them a good thrashing for pestering her too much. Too thorough, his mother thought grimly. In other circumstances she would have fronted up to the girl, or the girl's mother, to seek justice — to see that the girl also got a belting from her mother, or to belt the mother herself. But the girl's family was having a bad time and had enough grief before them.

After the bashing incident, the little children left Martha alone. But later, some of them forgave her her temper, and quietly started to keep her company. They would sneak onto her blanket and sidle up to her, leaning gently against her silent form. Knowing she was sad, they imitated the comfort that adults gave them when they were sad. They sat with her only for short times and then they would get bored and take off to play, screaming and running, full of life.

Each week, on the same afternoon, the nuns would see Martha sitting under the same tree. The nuns discussed the situation and decided it was best that Martha continue her hopeless vigil. She was advanced in class, and the missed school afternoons could be afforded. Better this wait than that uncomfortable wild grief and anger that would certainly come. The nuns were fearful to mention Willy's name, not only out of respect, for cultural reasons, but also because they might provoke the madness they saw in the girl. In the first week after hearing the *Enid* might be missing, Martha had gone mad, rushing around screaming and shouting, blaming the missionaries and the mission people for his disappearance. To her mind, they made him dead by believing it and saying it out loud. There was no point trying to talk sense to the girl, or taking a firm hand with her, she just became more agitated and aggressive. Once it had taken two of her uncles to hold her down during a fit of rage, and they had dragged her off to old Jurud's place. It was not right. She had confronted Father Max in the meat cool room, threatening to assault him because it was he who had brought the news back from Broome! Lillian, Martha's mother, was paralysed with shock and grief, but even without this tragedy, she would not have been any help. Lillian had always been soft; they had all protected her from the day she arrived at the mission. Martha was always a strong personality, but this behaviour was not right. The other women were looking after Lillian's young children and house. Young Mary, the eldest girl, seemed to be the only capable one in the family. Everything had changed in the instant it was known Willy was not coming home.

It was a bad year. Everyone had loved Willy so much, and there was shock and grief enough at this loss. Now they had to cope with his daughter's apparent madness.

Jurud let Martha beat the ground, all the while sitting calmly, chewing her tobacco. She had important work to do: she was getting ready for the ceremony to send William's spirit away in the old way, and Martha needed to take part in this, never mind all that Jesus talk. Martha was craving for the mourning ceremonies, because to her, they didn't mean her father was really dead, or that she had made him finished because she believed he was gone. She would wail with the others, and strike her head with the special stones, and make blood come. The pain of the striking might reflect and ease the unbearable anguish of her heart, to take away some of the grief that was drowning her. If she really thought he was gone, she, too, would be in an underwater world of despair, like Lillian; she would be lost there. Acts of denial can save your sanity sometimes.

I thought about my grandmother, Martha, and how she had never spoken about her father's death, and how desperately she must have missed him. In writing this story, I discussed what had happened with my mother, Willy's grand-daughter, Christine, and we talked about the kind of man her *ynummi* (grandfather) would have been. We were certain he would have been handsome, dark, tall, and hardworking, with a caring heart and generosity of spirit. My mother's *ynummi* had disappeared long before she was born; her mother, Martha, had been only thirteen years old when that tragedy took place. It was a tragedy, not only because he died but also because it left the family vulnerable. A couple of years after that, Lillian, his widow and his daughters, including Martha, started being named in the Native Welfare records. But that is another story, one about Aboriginal women trying to live a free life under state surveillance and control ...

We decided Willy Munget must have been handsome because he had married Lillian. She had been taken into the mission from Gija country in 1911. Apparently, a priest and some helpers had undertaken a journey around the Kimberley rounding up any part-Aboriginal children so they could be bought up as civilised people. Lillian was nine years old when she arrived at the mission. My mother's

Pat's mother, Christine Grimm,
Darwin, 1975
Courtesy Pat Dudgeon

memory of her *mimmi* (grandmother) is of an old, small, pale-skinned, grey-eyed woman. Her pale skin and light eyes would have been valued back then because they made her look more like a white girl. In their minds, this would have made her more 'civilisable' and, therefore, more human. She would have been a favoured child and eagerly sought as a marriage partner. She would have chosen only the very best man, or more likely the missionaries would have chosen him for her. Willy Munget would have been the best man, despite his dark skin. Their children were dark, and so he had to have been very dark. Despite the racist myths, Aboriginal people do not 'throw back'. So I asked Mum what type of man would have been a good catch for Lillian. He would have been someone the missionaries held in high regard: hardworking, easygoing in character, kind — especially kind, because Lillian was small and soft natured. My grandmother, Martha, was a tall, straight-backed, handsome woman with skin the colour of rich dark chocolate. So we surmised that Willy would have been tall and also handsome, because we think men from the Kimberley are mostly good looking.

Willy must have been responsible and trustworthy as well. Why else would he have been on the *Enid* going to Fremantle, with a family back in Broome? Being an Aboriginal man as well? White crew members would have appreciated the paid or even unpaid trip down south, back to the populated civilised centre that they missed so badly living out in the frontier. We don't know if this was Willy's very first trip or one of

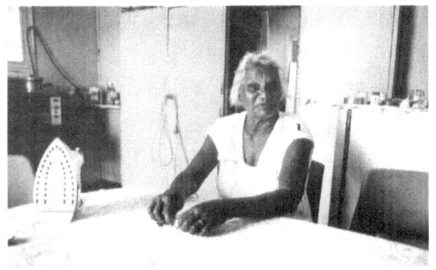

Martha Hughes
Courtesy Roger Garwood

several, but the skipper trusted him and chose him and one other to go on the trip. The crew must have been paid because Willy had a family back in Broome to support. I thought at first that the family might have been living in Beagle Bay Mission at the time, but Mum felt they lived in Broome so the family would have got Willy's salary. Indigenous people did not get equal pay then, and whatever they did earn usually went straight to the government. So, if they were living at Beagle Bay, perhaps Willy's wages would have gone straight to the mission without his ever seeing a cent, or a penny, as it would have been then. But if they lived in Broome, the situation might have been different, and he might have kept his wages. So we decided that they probably lived in Broome for a couple of years around that time. Willy may have wanted independence and success for his family, and moved away from the mission into town in hope they would have better resources and life chances. Perhaps they lived in a shack on the fringes of town, in the coloured camp called Indian Territory, where no white people went. My grandmother was there years later, when my mother left the mission and lived with her. From my conversations with my mother, about the implications of Willy's place on the ill-fated *Enid* and the reasons behind his marriage to Lillian, Willy soon emerged as a full person in my mind's eye; the ghost of an unknown skeleton became clad in the flesh of an intelligent, hardworking, responsible, kind, loving father.

William was a happy man. He seemed to be everywhere at once. He would work for the community, fixing up houses and any machinery when it broke down. He knew all the cattle and livestock on the mission, helped with the sick animals and even the slaughter when it was time. He was the one person Father took to Broome when they sold the vegetables and other produce from the mission, returning with provisions for everyone. In pearling season he would go out with the pearling boats. They would not see him for weeks on end, though sometimes he would talk the skipper into docking at Beagle Bay for fresh water and wood. Then there would be precious hours, with him swooping into the school to carry off the children, Lillian tucked under his arm, peering out, like a bright-eyed possum as he strode about, laughingly greeting everyone, missionaries and community people alike. Then, like magic, he would be gone. Lillian would cry and go to bed. Martha would wonder about these magical appearances: one moment, seemingly out of thin air, the boat and her father were there, and then, just as quickly, the boat and he were gone. Was he ever there at all? Sometimes, when she was sad or lonely, she would go to where the boat would dock and sit there conjuring him to appear. But he never came.

The best was when he was back for a long time. In the afternoon, after school and chores, the children would run home and cluster on the benches around the cooking fire, telling their mother and father all the things that had happened during the day. Other children and adults went to the dinner hall for supper, but Willy and Lillian usually liked to have supper with all of them together. Lillian would dish out stew and rice, and hand around cups of tea to the children and the uncles, aunties and other cousins who drifted in. After supper, before the light faded, the children would beg Willy to play monsters.

'Go on then, take off!' He would wave them off to find hiding spots.

They ran screaming and all would be quiet as they muffled their excitement. The smaller ones obviously couldn't stop giggling while they were hiding, but Willy would magnanimously ignore them as he growled and noisily searched for his victims. One by one he would capture them, roaring and throwing them over his shoulders while they shrieked and kicked, until inevitably one of them would start crying and run for Lillian. She would shout at Willy not to upset them or be so rough, taking up a stick or shaking a wooden spoon at him. He would roll onto his back, legs and arms in the air, pretending fear and contrition, and all the children would rush to jump on him and batter the monster until he begged for mercy. Then the little ones would cry for Willy. Lillian would shout at them some more and they would promise not to play the game again. As the evening came on, they would sit and lie on blankets around the fire, talking and calling to others walking by. Sometimes someone might strum a guitar and start a song. Later, Martha and the bigger sisters would walk back to the dormitories, tired, and happily go to sleep.

The week before the news of Willy's disappearance, Jurud, Lillian and Martha went out for ashes for the last time together. The trips were special outings that involved just the three of them. Jurud liked to take Martha out because it was her way of telling Martha about the country she was born into, and to make Lillian feel a part of the different country she had been taken into. The trips had important objectives, but the most important was to gather bark to make ashes for tobacco.

The Europeans had introduced tobacco to Aboriginal people. Prior to that, some tobacco-like substances, such as *piturari*, had been used, but not to the extent that tobacco was consumed. It probably was not available in large quantities. Aboriginal people loved tobacco and it was part of the rations they were given. My mother's generation smoked tobacco but earlier generations had chewed it. There was a complex protocol about chewing tobacco, which was used with the ashes of certain tree barks. I heard that scientists thought these ashes had medicinal benefits. That might be a myth, but gathering and making the ashes were important. They took people back to country. That Aboriginal people had adapted an introduced product and enhanced it by using the local native flora was impressive. My mother and I discussed this and wondered how the old ones would have known to mix ashes with tobacco, how they would have known which trees were safe and best. I only know of my grandmother and her generation chewing tobacco. Further up north, the old ladies smoked theirs in crab claws that they modified for the purpose. Ashes were called *gudgewt*.

Jurud would take Lillian, Martha and the girls out to find *gudgewt*. She'd order them to tell the missionaries they had to stop work and help her get ashes for her tobacco. They didn't really mind, because they all chewed tobacco too, and would share the catch. Sometimes the tobacco came in hard twists, but stick or plug tobacco came in small blocks, wrapped in waxed paper. The blocks were in layers, maybe a dozen blocks per layer. Martha loved the smell and sight of the hard, nuggetty, variegated dark brown tobacco, tucked neatly into the waxed paper with hard golden logo pins nailed into each block. One block could last at least a week. The women would bite off pieces starting from one corner, crushing and chewing it, rubbing it in the palm of their hands until it was soft and pliable. The chew was called *ngumeree*, but was in a raw state and needed to be 'baked' in ashes. They kneaded the *ngumeree* into the ashes, *gudgewt*, made from the bark and sometimes the leaves of special trees. Jurud's favourites were the white gum and the *jiggil* tree, another gum. The bark had to be right; it had to be old bark peeling away from the tree to make room for new bark to come out. This peeling also signified other events, such as the seasons when certain sea animals, like sharks and stingrays, would come in. Bark was good: it could be used to make cradles and carriers. Martha would strip the bark from the white *goonerral* tree to make small diamond-shaped boomerangs that she would spin through the air among the trees.

The chores were finished quickly, little children left with aunties and Martha slung over her shoulder an old sugar bag of provisions and a tomahawk. They would walk along the tracks and into the bush, Jurud singing up the country as they went.

One day Martha asked, 'Mimmi, why are you singing that old blackfella stuff?'

Jurud looked at her hard, and replied, 'Eh, when you go into your church; you knee down, you talk 'im up, you don't barge in any kind, frightening those spirits. Here too, don't be scaring things, they might get angry!'

It did not seem quite the same to Martha, but she stayed silent. It frankly scared Lillian, all that blackfella magic. She would murmur Hail Marys under her breath to keep the devil at bay.

Martha never told Lillian about the night she had camped out in the bush with Jurud and her sister Jundo. They had set out too late and Jurud decided they had to set up camp rather then rush to get to the mission before nightfall. Jurud was pleased to camp out and was glad to instruct Martha about how to gather dead wood, chop branches for a lean-to and pull soft grasses and leaves for a bed, while Jundo wandered around the creek, gathering cockles and small fish. By nightfall, they were snug under their branches with the coals of a small fire cooking their food. Jurud and Jundo told Martha stories in the flickering flames of the fire. Jurud's eyes twinkled and glared as she played out the roles of people and spirits. Her hands wove the stories: fingers walking for the long walks, fanned out to make the swooping wings of graceful birds, and darting for sharks. They gradually dozed off huddled together warm and tight. Sometime in the night, Martha woke with a start. Jurud, her thin body tense beside her, hissed quietly at Martha, signalling for silence. Martha followed the outline of her grandmother's stare, her face profiled against the starred sky.

'What, *Mimmi*?' she whispered cautiously.

Jurud drew in a breath and replied, 'Look there, a little devil-devil is here … over there across from the fire.'

Martha moved her head slowly and turned her eyes to where Jurud was looking. 'Where?'

'Look out, he is over there', old Jurud whispered, staring

at the darkness. 'When he opens his eyes and turns this way you can see him.'

Martha looked and looked, her eyes aching from the strain and trying not to blink, and all she could see was the black of the bushes and the dull red glow of the spent fire. And then, suddenly two shining little points of green light appeared:; eyes, looking straight at her.

'What do we do, Mimmi?'

'Nothing; he won't hurt us, he just checking up on us,' replied Jurud, and she relaxed back down into the bed of leaves. 'But you better watch out, in case.'

Soon her gentle snores joined in harmony with Jundo's. Martha lay stiff and transfixed by that patch of darkness until dawn finally washed away the shadows. Only the red sand, grey ashes of the fire and scraggly bushes were revealed in the first weak light.

They would go to all the trees they knew, and sometimes, if the bark was not ready, they would go out farther to find other trees. Finally, when they found the right tree with the right bark, they cleared a space to make a fire and boil the billy for strong, sweet black tea. Cooking the bark came later, back at Jurud's place where there were sheets of iron.

Back at home, Jurud stoked up her fire and placed the sheet iron on it while Martha chopped the bark, cleaning and tidying it ready to be laid out on the hot sheet. Lillian and Martha left to do chores and Martha returned later in the afternoon, inspecting the soft powdery ashes, white and smooth like talcum powder with veins of grey tinges. She stirred it with a stick under Jurud's watchful eye. 'All cooked, *Mimmi*, finished now.'

As Jurud went to get her old Sunshine Powdered Milk tin, Martha carefully removed the sheet from the banked fire and sifted through the ashes with a stick, flicking any lumps away. Jurud returned with her old battered container and a big spoon and carefully scooped the fine powder first into her tin and then into Martha's, one for her and one for Martha. Finally, when there were no ashes left on the sheet, she whacked down the lid on her tin with satisfaction. 'Big mob now, last for long, long time. Eh, you gottem fluff?' she asked Martha.

Martha shook her head, but said she would find some for her *mimmi*. Later, Martha went to the mission store and cadged the worker there to let her pull the loose fluff from the hessian bags of flour. Jurud liked to use the fluff to make a little nest for her *mooligin*, which was the end product of raw chewed tobacco kneaded with ashes. *Mimmi* said that storing it in fluff kept that *mooligin* fresh for days. Martha thought Jurud never had her tobacco out of her mouth long enough to let it go stale, but a nest of fluff was better than tucking the ball of tobacco behind her ear, like the other *mimmis* did, ending up with yellow-stained hair on one side of their heads.

Jurud took the raw chewed tobacco from her mouth and kneaded it in the fresh *gudgewt*, and rolled it around in her mouth with satisfaction. Good *gudgewt* could be stored for years —not that anyone had tested this belief, too many others were always asking for it. Top-quality *gudgewt* was very important to *mooligin*; if the bark was too old or wrong, the *mooligin* had to be baked everyday. This was a top-quality batch. *Mooligins* varied from the size of marble size to that of a small plum. Martha started small but progressed to huge *mooligins* late in her life. She would keep her *mooligin* in her Log Cabin Tobacco tin. Sometimes it would be eaten by unsuspecting grandchildren or family pets. Unlike Martha, Jurud shared her *mooligin* with other people; she would just take it right out of her mouth, break it in half, and give it to the other person, who would put it in their mouth straight away. Martha shuddered with disgust at the thought. Jurud and the other women — and later, even Martha — always had *mooligins* in their mouths. Some kept them tucked under the tongue or behind the bottom lip if it was small, but most had big wads bulging in their cheeks. They only took them out when they were sleeping or showering. Tobacco chewers were always spitting. My mother said that in the old days, there were spittoons everywhere, even in the hospital, for tobacco chewers. When we were discussing how the later generations smoked tobacco, my Aunty Dotty told me that Martha and her generation of women were not messy in their habits, and spat out their tobacco juice in a very ladylike manner. Like many of the changes that had come to Jurud's country, tobacco was now part of the old people's lives.

Things were not the same for the family after Willy Munget disappeared. The magnetic force that had bound them together, and to others, had suddenly vanished. While some found themselves out on their own, others, however, seemed thrown together even more tightly and closely than before. The measured, certain journey of their lives, the roles they had taken for granted, the contented future they had unconsciously anticipated was gone. Lillian lost her husband and the rock that had anchored her; she had lost her breadwinner and independence in a matter of weeks.

A few months later, still angry and full of grief, Martha went on her own on the long walk to the creek where the family had last fished with Willy. She walked for half a day in the hot sun. When she arrived, what she was looking for was there, still there, not washed away by rain or king tides yet. In the black mud, high on the creek bed were the ashes of the fire they had made many months ago, littered around with old bleached fish bones and cockleshells, remnants of their great feast. She wished they could have that feast again; she wished she had known it was going to be the last fishing trip with her family intact, not fragmented and despairing like it had become. She would have been nicer to everyone; she would have carried the water and made the tea with joy, not with complaints. The dry summer was at its end and the muddy banks of the creek were dry and flaky. Some way down from the old fireplace, she found the churned mud, hard and dried. This was where Willy had played, pretending to be caught in quicksand, shrieking and calling to the children for help, much to their shouting excitement and horror, with the dogs yelping and jumping, until Lillian had growled at and threatened them all — man, children and dogs — with her stick and made Willy go down to the creek to wash the black mud off.

Martha remembered how his footprints had been perfect on the walk back from the water. His feet were wet and the mud was just the right consistency to make perfect impressions of his footsteps. They were still there now, even though he was gone; his footprints were there, moulded perfectly in the hard, marbled mud. Martha's tears turned the grey mud to black, as she looked over each precious footprint, touching it and placing her hand in the hollows all the way to the waterline. Standing there alone, she looked out over the sea that had claimed her father's life. Then she turned and carefully placed her foot in a footprint of her father's. One step followed another until she had walked in his footprints all the way up the rise.

BILL JONAS

is a Worrimia man from the Karuah River area of New South Wales. He was the Aboriginal and Torres Strait Islander Social Justice Commissioner until 2004 and was also the Acting Race Discrimination Commissioner.

Places of Wonder and Fear

I was raised in the beautiful Karuah River valley, in New South Wales. My story of country is based on two places, Hells Gates, which is part of that river, and a large unnamed lagoon nearby. When I was a child, these were places to wonder about and to fear. As I grew up and learned more about them, they became places of imagination and awe, but my childhood feelings about them remained the same. Now that I am far away in time from my childhood and have learned about tragedies in adjoining country, I find myself thinking about these places with great sadness. Now, my thoughts about country are layered and complex, but my youthful feelings for these places have not changed and, despite what I've learned, my love for my part of the river and the valley remains as strong as ever.

The Karuah River begins in high country north of Newcastle and it flows mostly eastwards to the Pacific coast. Unlike the rivers to the south, such as the Hunter, or to the north, such as the Manning, the Karuah is relatively small and has carved no grand valley, nor has it deposited deep layers of rich soil on extensive flood plains. However, it does have a fairly impressive estuary that extends from its mouth, at Port Stephens, to about twenty kilometres inland. I grew up near the head of the estuary, close to where the tidal salt water is met by the fresh water flowing downstream from the hills. I lived in a tiny village called Allworth. This village was too small to support a school, so each school day we travelled by bus for about an hour each way to and from a larger town in the Hunter Valley.

Our family was very poor and our little house, with its walls made from hessian sugar bags and its dirt floors, did not provide much room for playing indoors. This, too, was the time long before television and computer games. Indeed, it was not until I was about ten years old that electricity reached Allworth. Consequently, we spent most of our non-school time out of doors. I have to say that this was just wonderful for us young people, both boys and girls. We played seemingly endless bouts of sports like rounders and cricket on any piece of flat land that we could find. There were wooded and cleared hills to be explored, creeks and the river to be swum in and fished, the narrow river flats to be searched for mushrooms and blackberries, and any number of bush hideouts and trails where we could play whatever games our imaginations allowed. We used to get very excited when the river was in flood, not only because of the spectacle of the water racing through this narrow valley, but also because the late summer floods would often bring down melons and pumpkins from upstream farms and this produce would be left in trees and on banks when the floodwaters subsided. We knew our country very well.

In the estuary opposite Allworth, there is a very large, long island. We often rowed across to the island where there was a dairy farm, and we would share our time between helping the farmer milk his cows and fishing from the island banks or from our boat. One of the places in my story was connected with this island.

Being an estuary, the river here is tidal and the tide flows in and out around the island. When the tide is going out and the water level is dropping, one section of the river, on the upstream side of the island, becomes like a boiling cauldron of torrent and foam. The water swirls around large rocks and through narrow channels and it is very difficult to steer a rowboat through it without hitting the boulders or the equally rocky shore. This section of the river is called, perhaps poetically, Hells Gates. If we were fishing from a boat and found that we had to navigate this section, we always felt a mixture of apprehension, even fear, and certainly excitement. If we concentrated on steering and were quick to make adjustments, we were probably never in any real danger, but certainly all of our attention and strength were needed at that point.

My Uncle Dick used to take me fishing and sometimes he would tell me stories about the places we were going to. I remember one of the earliest stories I heard was about Hells Gates. It seems that one of the first white people in that area was navigating his craft through those wild waters and his hands were fully occupied in this task when he saw an Aboriginal man with a spear on the shore. The boatman had a gun, and for whatever reason, reached for it to shoot the Aborigine. He lost control of his boat, his aim was very much off course, and he was in turn speared by the Aboriginal man. Every time I went through Hells Gates, no matter how wild the water and how daunting the task, I always had an image of the missed shot being fired and the spear being accurately thrown.

On the western banks of the river, across from Hells Gates, there is a strip of flat land that becomes inundated in times of flood. This narrow flood plain contains a lagoon, which is permanently filled with water. It is clearly a former channel of the river and the river reverts to it when it overflows. At most other times it is covered with water-loving plants like reeds and rushes; there are lots of water-dwelling birds; and though they are too muddy for pleasant eating, there are plenty of fish as well. On the inland side of the lagoon, the land rises steeply for about fifty metres and then it levels out again. This flat land is far, far too high above the river ever to flood, but it contains several lagoons like the one down on the flood plain. One of these is a small but deep waterhole that, many years ago, my grandmother used for washing clothes. A narrow strip of swamp joins this waterhole to another large curved body of water that looks just like a bend in the river but certainly not at the level of the river as we know it today. This lagoon is the second place of my story.

The big lagoon seems to hang suspended in the air. Water plants do not grow on it like they do closer to the river, and I cannot recall ever having seen birds swimming on it or swirls or ripples on it that were evidence of fish. On the few occasions I dared to get close to it, I remember its water being reasonably clear near the surface but a brooding dark brown in colour which became almost black in the very deep parts. I say 'on the few occasions' and 'dared' because we were warned specifically not to go near it. No reasons were ever given for this, but the message that it was completely out of bounds was continuing and strong. We certainly would have lived in fear of a great thrashing if we had ever gone swimming there. This in itself was strange, because we were good swimmers and any other body of water was fair game: the river, even though sharks were sometimes sighted and the depths in part were great; the creeks with their stretches of muddy mangroves, their stingrays and their crabs; and the freshwater farm dams with their murky, opaque water and often bone-chilling temperatures. But never the big lagoon. That lagoon and Hells Gates were childhood places of wonderment and fear.

At high school, one of my favourite subjects was geography. This was not surprising, perhaps, because my Uncle Dick knew our country very well and on fishing and walking trips he taught me to read it. Understanding and being able to describe our own landscapes came easily to me and I was able to extend this to describing the lands in other parts of the world. Then, in my two final years of school, when I was actually studying with the old Correspondence School at Blackfriars in Sydney, I had a wonderful teacher, Miss Robertson, who taught me to add another dimension to my geographical studies.

Miss Robertson had been one of the first women to graduate in philosophy from Sydney University and she brought an intellectual rigour to bear on the subject of geography that I had not previously experienced and which I immediately warmed to. I did not meet her until my school years were over, but in those two final years of teaching me by mail, often in her own distinctive handwriting (no email back in those days), she instilled in me the need to be constantly asking questions about my environment, what was written and what was said. She taught me to seek answers to those questions and somehow the theoretical side of the subject began to make as much sense as the practical side of Uncle Dick's teaching.

Looking around at the world I grew up in and loved and knew well, I began asking myself questions about how things might have come into being. How, I wondered, did those swirling rapids at Hells Gates come about and why were they located precisely at that part of the river? Why was the seemingly flat stretch of the river turned almost into a mini-waterfall? How did that big lagoon get formed so high above the present river? Surely the river couldn't have flowed

Looking upstream towards Hells Gates
Courtesy R and S Filson

up there in the past. Or could it have done just that? But how, then, did it get to carve its present channels so much lower down? And if the flat land containing the lagoon was formed as a flood plain of a river, how big must the flood have been to have formed a plain so high? These questions, I thought, were reasonable for someone who loved his country and was also learning more about how it had been formed. These were the questions of a schoolboy geographer who was incredibly happy in his country but who still had so, so much more to learn.

Some of this learning took place when I left Allworth and my schooldays behind me and went off to study at university. My studies there enabled me to gain more understanding about some of the things I had been told and the places I had come to know as a child. Both Hells Gates and the big lagoon took on some new meanings for me as I began to learn how they might have been formed. I continued to study geography at university, and though the approach to it was far different from that of school, the subject was to provide new perspectives on my early experiences.

One strand of university geography was about the shape of the land and rivers and the conditions and processes that result in the forms or shapes that these can take. My lecturer for that subject, a great man who had come from Holland, was a world authority on past sea level changes and the ways in which these changes in the past affect the land and its rivers today. He taught us how, over millions of years, the oceans had risen and fallen relative to the land: sometimes the seas had fallen, sometimes the land had risen, sometimes both had occurred together. This meant that, in the past, the sea level had sometimes been higher and sometimes lower than it is today. When the sea level rose, some of the land became submerged. When the sea level fell, some previously submerged land was now visible above the sea and some previously formed features became located high above where the sea was now. These changes rarely happened suddenly (like with a tsunami). It could take hundreds of thousands, even millions, of years for it to occur and for the various processes to be completed.

When the sea level falls, a river may begin to erode headwards from the river mouth. Depending on where this upward moving erosion has reached, there will be what is called a 'nickpoint'. Some of the features of nickpoints can be waterfalls, rapids and swirling waters and quick changes in the river depth, in fact, all of the things that were to be experienced at Hells Gates. This stretch of the river then seemed to me to be a classic example of a nickpoint. As I then saw it, this was where the river was making a big adjustment as a result of a past change in sea level. This was where the erosion, which was moving headwards, had so far reached.

Interestingly, the same process of a falling sea level also can result in the existence of those high or 'perched' lagoons.

I now saw those lagoons as having once been part of a river that had formerly flowed much higher up, at a height that was related to the old, higher sea level. This former river had its own flood plain, which was the flat land that now contained the lagoons, and it too was formed before the sea level fell. When the sea level fell, and the river had to carve a new and much lower course, the old flood plain got left behind, as did the old meander. This, at least to me, explained why both the big lagoon and its surrounding flat land formed by a river, were now much higher than the course of the Karuah River today.

When I was at university, and for some years afterwards, I used to return to Allworth and, just as I had when I was a child, I used to go fishing. But with my new knowledge about rising and falling sea levels, I now had a different perspective on Hells Gates and the lagoons. It took little imagination on my part to picture the river flowing along its old course, much higher than the present one. I could then envisage the sea falling and, like in slow motion scenes from a film, imagine the river eroding its way headwards. I could also envisage the lagoons being left behind, perched above the new and lower course that the river was carving. But this new and different perspective did not alter how I felt about things. I had new and more information. And I had worked out in my head a 'scientific' explanation for the way in which these features had been formed. Though the word 'awesome' has been overused and devalued in recent years, I did think of these past processes with a great deal of awe. But in my mind I also still saw the shooting and the spearing at Hells Gates and I still feared that powerfully brooding lagoon.

They have the same effect on me today. I haven't been fishing from a boat in the river there for years. I have no relatives living at Allworth anymore, and I certainly would not feel confident of having the strength or skills to manage the rapids on my own. However, I can picture Hells Gates as clearly as if I were there and, yes, I understand the geographical processes but I can also see the results of that early colonial encounter. As I did when I was younger, I can still imagine that the Aboriginal man had such an intimate knowledge and understanding of his environment that he knew exactly where to stand and just how and when to launch his spear.

I also recently telephoned the owner of the property where the lagoons are located to see if my memories of them are correct. She assured me that they were as I remembered them and the large one certainly seems to be a meander of the former river which now flows much lower down. Again in my mind I can see the sea falling and the river making the necessary adjustments, which include leaving the old course abandoned and high. But, again, the childhood fear comes back and though the owner kindly offered to arrange an inspection of the property and a ride around the lagoon in a four-wheel-drive vehicle, I declined her offer.

Now, though I left university with some understanding of how parts of the present-day valley might have been formed, I must say that I knew very little about its more recent human history. I did study some history, but in those days the courses were about the European Renaissance and constitutional conflicts in seventeenth-century England. I did not have the opportunity to learn about Australian history in general, or anything specifically about my part of the world. And even when we were growing up, we were told very little of the history of the valley in which we lived. This may explain, in part, why I was never a very good history student (though I must confess it would not account for my appalling inability to remember dates). Whatever the reason, some years went by before I began focusing on the human past of the valley.

One of the very few stories from my childhood which could be called 'black history' and which indicated that this was Aboriginal country was an incident related to the spearing at Hells Gates. This was despite the fact that this part of the valley must have been an excellent place for people to live in pre-colonial times. There was access to fish in both the fresh waters and the salty estuary. The fish varied in abundance throughout the year, but there were always some available. Perch and bream were most plentiful in spring and summer, the mullet arrived in big schools in early autumn followed by blackfish off the rocky banks as the weather got cooler, and the big jewfish swam to the head of the estuary in winter. Even by the time of my childhood, when commercial net fishing began to deplete stocks, we could always catch plenty of fish to eat. If Uncle Dick or my grandmother said we were to have fish to eat one night, then that is exactly as it would be. We would simply gather our rods and lines and go and catch the fish and the idea that we would not catch any was unthinkable.

There were also crayfish in the fresh waters; we often ate wallaby, and my grandmother used to talk of catching and cooking the smaller pademelons. Wild ducks might be on the menu, there were fruits and yams that were easily collected, and the estuary abounded with oysters. These grew on the mangroves and on the rocky outcrops, and in one part of the river they even attached themselves to water-worn pebbles so that dislodging them required just a simple tap with another stone. Indeed, the presence of large shell middens was and remains evidence of people eating these shellfish over many, possibly many thousands, of years. But we were not told about these people.

Similarly, we were told little of 'white history'. The last of the big logging ships used to come to Allworth to collect timber when I was a small boy, and I remember being told that the village, near the head of navigation, was once an important river port for people and produce coming and going along the river. At Booral, and especially Stroud, upstream from Allworth, there were very 'historic' houses and grain silos which were visibly from another era, but no information was ever forthcoming to us about their origins. Perhaps in the middle of the last century people were not interested in local history. Perhaps if we had gone to school in the valley our teachers might have told us something of its background. Perhaps people had forgotten the past. And, perhaps there were some aspects of that past which people had decided should be left untold.

From research which I have done in more recent years, I now know that the little Karuah River valley played a very important role in early Australian colonial history and had the climate there proved more favourable it would have been very significant indeed. It was near the mouth of the Karuah River, at Port Stephens, that the famous Australian Agricultural Company began its farming operations. The AA Company, as it has long been known, was formed in 1824 with a capital base of one million pounds, an enormous amount of money in those days. Its aim was to produce fine wool from sheep and to grow the crops of the Mediterranean, such as wheat and grapes. No doubt the landscape might have seemed like that surrounding the Mediterranean to the early Europeans, and the mild winters and hot summers reinforced the comparison. But the rainfall pattern is very different. Instead of being concentrated in winter, leaving the summer months hot and dry, the timing of rainfall at Port Stephens is unpredictable. Rain can arrive at any time of the year, especially in summer when crops need dry weather for ripening and sheep need dry conditions to avoid parasitic, fungal and other diseases which thrive in heat and high humidity. Farming here proved to be a complete failure.

The AA Company moved quickly and fairly soon after its establishment to country further north and inland. Other settlers soon followed them and there were the perhaps inevitable clashes between the company and settlers on the one hand and Aboriginal people on the other. While some of the colonial conflicts have been written about for some time, it is only in very recent years that a more complete and accurate picture has been emerging. And even today there is a silence about movement through this part of the Karuah River valley.

This silence has become of increasing concern for me. Now, when I think about the valley that nurtured me, I see this lovely part of the world in yet another light. In some ways it is a gloomy, even sad and tragic imagination that now takes hold of my thoughts. I find myself constantly wondering about what happened to the people who once lived here. Did the original inhabitants suffer the same fate as Aboriginal people in the surrounding valleys? Was that spearing at Hells Gates an isolated incident or, as now seems likely, was it part of a broader pattern of Aboriginal people being forced to defend their country and their lives? What awful secrets may lie hidden in that large lagoon?

We now know that atrocities took place not far inland from the Karuah, near Gloucester, and in the adjoining

Manning River valley. That these terrible things happened is being revealed as academic historians search for truths about the past, and also as descendants of early white settlers reveal their family histories. In those valleys adjoining the Karuah, there are also oral histories which have kept previously unwritten stories alive.

One now well-documented atrocity was at a place called Baal Belbora, on the Upper Gangat River, not far from Gloucester. It was here that the AA Company had established a cattle station and, in retaliation for the theft of some young cattle by some Aboriginal people, dampers were made of poisoned flour and left for Aboriginal people to eat. The result was that many Aborigines died. This was not an isolated incident. There was in fact a practice called 'the harmony', which came from a belief that poisoning Aborigines was a way to achieve peace between the invading white people and the resisting Aboriginal people. So widespread was the practice in the Manning Valley that there are contemporary reports of Aboriginal corpses being found in every creek near where the present town of Wingham is located.

In the other direction, but again not far from Gloucester, near the area known as Rawdon Vale, there was a horrific massacre of an entire tribe of Aborigines in 1835. It was known as the Mount McKenzie massacre. Men, women and children were rounded up and, so the story goes, forced to leap to their deaths from a cliff top in this very rugged terrain. Some modern historians now think the people, especially the Aboriginal men, were most likely shot and then thrown over the cliff. Whatever the truth, the remains of these poor people were never buried and their bones lay bleaching on the surface of the ground and in the bush for many decades. I have been told by a friend, who had these bones pointed out to her from a distance when she was a child, that they looked like white handkerchiefs tied to the limbs of the trees.

Other historians now talk of hints and rumours of killings at most places surrounding the Karuah River, at specific locations in the Manning River valley and around the Soldiers Point area of Port Stephens. Settlers are reported to have formed hunting parties and, on horseback, shot Aborigines or drove them into swamps and rivers where they drowned. Arsenic was mixed with flour or treacle or put into tea and given to Aborigines to kill them. Poisoning waterholes had the same tragic results.

Even where the killings were not deliberate, Aboriginal people suffered catastrophic consequences from the effects of introduced diseases. Smallpox resulted in many deaths in the nearby tributaries of the Hunter River, and again there are reports of corpses stretching across the countryside. Even diseases that we would consider less serious today were the cause of tragedy for people with no immunity to them. Measles and influenza proved to be lethal. There are, in fact, reports of people experiencing the fever of measles leaping into the waters of Port Stephens to reduce the heat they felt. Their actions only made their conditions worse and they died. Around Port Stephens itself, where at least some counting of people was carried out, the Aboriginal population declined in only a few years to about a quarter of what it had been when the white people first arrived. I've also read reports in the State Archives of cases of emaciated women and their ill children being found in remote bush areas around Gloucester. The whereabouts of their men appeared not to be known.

We also know that a large mission was established in the early 1900s at Karuah itself, the town at the mouth of the river that began its existence largely as a sawmilling enterprise. Many of the surviving Aboriginal people from around nearby Port Stephens were taken to live on this mission. They were joined by people who had survived the killings further inland, around and beyond Gloucester. We used to visit the mission when I was at school; my aunts used to tell me that they had many visits there as children, and mission people visited and often stayed with us. My grandmother and my father had very close friends there. But as far as I can determine, none of the mission dwellers came from our immediate part of the world, the bountiful and generous part of the valley where I was raised.

The nagging question for me now is 'where did the original inhabitants from around here go?' or, perhaps more appropriately, it is 'what happened to the people from around here when white people arrived?'. My ancestors moved away for a while, but they had come back by the 1920s. I have located my great-grandfather's death certificate (he died in 1908) and it lists both his parents' names as 'unknown', and in the space for 'father's occupation' it simply says 'Aboriginal'. Given that he died at a recorded age of about sixty-five, these unnamed people, my great-great-grandparents, must have given birth to him in the early 1840s. This would have been the time of increasing movement and activity throughout this valley.

I don't know why my people left here. But sometimes when my imagination really flies free I think back to the spearing story my Uncle Dick told me. He knew the story (and he was never one to make up tales), but I never heard others tell it. Is it just possible that the man who threw the spear at Hells Gates was his grandfather, my great-great-grandfather? Could this have been one of the reasons that those unnamed people fled this area?

When I am being less fanciful, I nevertheless cannot escape the conclusion that Aboriginal people around here must have suffered the same fate as in nearby country. I see that spearing as the act of an Aboriginal man fighting for his country, his people and, indeed, his own life. I see it as an act by a man who clearly knew his country very well. And I imagine that it was one of the few successful acts of retaliation by a man whose people were under threat of losing all that they had known and loved. Certainly, that accords with what we now know happened in the nearby valleys and in many other parts of Australia.

Obviously, when I am thinking these sad thoughts, my mind also wanders to the big lagoon. Again questions come flooding in — and persisting. Why was this stretch of water forbidden to us? What secrets are hidden in its brown depths? Why do birds and fish avoid it? Was it, too, a place where 'harmony' was practised and, by whatever means, Aboriginal people suffered greatly? Was it a poisoned place that contributed to the demise of people who went there simply to drink as they and their ancestors had done for untold centuries? Is it just the fact that it was forbidden to us when we were young which makes me fear it, or did I as a child catch hints or parts of adults' conversations which have led me to fear it still?

I probably will never know the answers to these questions. But the fact that they enter my mind and stay there adds another layer of complexity — indeed character — to country that I have known for all of my life. And it seems that as I get older, I can recall things I was taught, explanations that I learned or made up, and the way I have felt about places in that country with increasing clarity.

The river, island and hills where we played as children

Courtesy R and S Filson

Hells Gates and the spearing, along with the lagoon as a place to avoid, are as clear to me as they always were. But I now know and appreciate the fact that we were taught things about country for good reasons, and it is those reasons I try to understand. I know, too, that there are scientific or academic explanations for the world that I see around me and I am able apply those reasonings to places that I know. This is exciting too. But in no way does this dull the images of the rapids or the lagoon. If anything, it just makes them clearer in my mind.

And in a strange way so does not knowing some of the events that happened. Perhaps the stories about tragedies were deliberately kept from children. Perhaps we were meant to learn these truths when we had grown up, but sadly all of the old people who could tell us are now gone. Perhaps it was meant to be that we reason things out for ourselves, aided by gradually emerging knowledge and our own imaginations.

What I can say, however, is that country, like people, is a complex and many-layered part of our lives. It has those simple aspects which we learn about when we are young and for which we will always have strong feelings; there are the parts and patterns that we learn more about as we get older and hopefully wiser; and there are those places and events which remain partially hidden or secret to us forever. The Karuah River valley and my relationship to it fit exactly into this description. And I would not want it to be any other way.

TJALAMINU MIA

is a Nyungar woman with bloodline links to the Minang and Goreng peoples of the South-West. She works as a research fellow in oral history and the arts in the School of Indigenous Studies at the University of Western Australia.

Kepwaamwinberkup *(Nightwell)*

In 2000, an opportunity of cultural rejuvenation was presented to me: to step out of a fast-paced city life and to return to country. Just on forty years had lapsed since I'd last walked as a child in country, in the footprints of my grandfather, Lennard George Keen, so I was really looking forward to it. When you live in your own country, there is a quiet serenity and connectedness, a feeling that is sometimes hard to express because it's so deep. I was eager to experience that again, because, through circumstances beyond my control, I'd been robbed of it. I am a survivor of the Stolen Generations. When I was younger, I was incarcerated in Sister Kate's Children's Home in Perth, along with my six brothers and sisters. After that, I wondered if I would ever go back to my people's land again. Being put in the Home was very traumatising, and it left me feeling displaced in the scheme of things, torn away from the spiritual and cultural connections I had known when I had walked in country with my grandfather as a child. But now I was going back once again, and I felt really excited about it.

In my early years I had lived a rich life. We camped out in the bush and listened to stories told by our old people — about the animals, trees, birds, the waterways, the stars, the moon and the sun and how we are all connected to them. We had journeys out bush to be shown the different types of foods we could eat, like *cumuuck*, a bush berry, as well as the wild bush potato and carrot. We were shown how to track *yonga*, kangaroo, in the saltpans, where the *gnamma* (fresh water) holes were and how they played a major role in connecting the different groups for community Law business. Life in my younger years was culturally and spiritually grounded. I remember the sense of freedom and connectedness to the natural world, the different sounds, smells and the landscape. There is nothing better than smelling the earth after a rain, or listening to the wind in the trees, and seeing the first lot of wildflowers bloom. I longed to return to the days of my early childhood and experience all that again. That is what I had lost when I was institutionalised in a place determined to break my cultural bonds, connections and understanding. And I needed to reclaim it, because it is a part of who I am.

My people are the Minang and Goreng, whose bloodline links to country encompass a large area in the lower part of the Great Southern region of Western Australia. My father was a white man, so my Aboriginality comes from my mother: both her parents were Nyungar, which makes me a Nyungar person. My great-great-grandmother was a traditional Nyungar woman, her name was Tuglaranu. From her, my links to country take in the area where now there are the towns of Katanning, Tambellup, Gnowangerup, Borden, and Albany, as well as the Stirling Ranges. My mother's father's mother's mother — my great-great-grandmother — was also a traditional woman. My links to country through them is land that also borders the same areas of my mother's people, but extends from Broomehill down through the

Stirling Ranges, out to Esperance and Ravensthorpe and over to Thomas River near Eucla.

Nyungar peoples were the first people in Western Australia to be invaded, massacred and oppressed when Captain James Stirling established the Swan River Colony in 1829. We were disenfranchised from our land and our hunting and food gathering rights were denied us. We were forbidden to use language, or undertake men and women's business, which included ways of looking after the environment, like seasonal burn-offs of particular tracts of land, maintaining *gnamma* holes, ochre deposits, and food resources, such as the fish traps along the Kalgan river near Albany. This dramatic change in our circumstances meant that our people, our countries and all the living things within our countries were decimated. Yet despite this trauma, we Nyungar peoples have survived. As a Nyungar woman, I can honestly say we continue to celebrate our identity as a distinctive people in Western Australia. Collectively, we stand strong in our Nyungar identity and heritage, our cultural and spiritual knowledge, and our connection to country, and all this reinforces our sense of place and self. Nyungar peoples and Nyungar country are one, because since time immemorial we have belonged together. This has been explained to me through my old people, who have told me about *koondarm*, or Nyungar Dreaming. There is no English word that truly captures this concept: *koondarm* reflects a Nyungar understanding of creation, time, land and all human and animal existence — we see it as a continuum of Then, Now and Tomorrow. Like all Aboriginal people in Australia, who have their own words for it, Nyungars understand that *koondarm* is never-ending; it is eternal.

In Aboriginal culture there are 'differences and sameness'.

Aboriginal people are the first people of country in the many lands that make up Australia, but we have distinct cultural and spiritual autonomy over particular areas of country. Regional diversity between Aboriginal groups is clear to us, though many of our groups share *koondarm* — Dreaming storylines. These places were and are still linked by the travels of some of the Ancestral beings, like the *Waagul*, who is the creator rainbow serpent, and the Seven Sisters, to mention a couple; so it was possible for groups along a track of an important Ancestor to share the same spirit story. Spirit journeys embraced large areas of country, and so bought people together in an enduring way. When Nyungar people made their journeys, they maintained their knowledge about water sources and bush foods while at the same time teaching the younger members of family groups about the geography of the land. This is what my grandfather did with me until I went to live in children's homes in the 1960s. In doing this, he carried on a Nyungar tradition and his teachings have held me in good stead because they had a deep impact on me, and that eventually played a role in bringing me back to country.

This brings me to a story that spans a decade and a half. It is about returning to a particular area of land in country in the South-West with some of my older family members, who are Elders. To put this story in context, I need first to tell the story of an earlier trip I had made with a close Nyungar sister, Alta Winmar, in October of 1992. My aunty, Joan Winch, who founded the Marr Mooditj Aboriginal Health Foundation, sent the two of us on a trip down south to collect bush foods and medicines for the foundation's display at the Kyana Festival, which was to be staged early the next year. My Elders took us to

Kepwaamwinberkup (Nightwell), which is a part of Beedalup Creek. These two sites are associated with a waterway that is part of a river system that runs between Borden, a small country town, and *Bula Meela* — Bluff Knoll, in the Stirling Ranges. Both are significant to Nyungar people in that region. Beedalup Creek is a freshwater source traditionally used as a camping ground; it was close to a waterway that supplied fresh drinking water for Nyungar people travelling around country. *Kepwaamwinberkup* derives its name from a particular part in the creek where the water runs over granite rock. There is a hole in that rock that was either dug out by the water which has flowed over it for eons, or it was chiselled out by Nyungar people long ago. At night, the water rises up in the hole, but it disappears during the day. There are various *gnamma* holes throughout Nyungar country and knowledge of them was imperative to the survival of Nyungar people, so they were respected and maintained over millennia. *Kepwaamwinberkup* was no different.

When Alta and I were travelling with the Elders, who were several aunties and uncles related to me through my mother and grandfather, there was one day when we visited quite a few sites and the last one was *Kepwaamwinberkup* (Nightwell). By then it was mid-afternoon and the Elders told us we had to get in and out quickly because it was a long drive back to Albany, and the light was fading fast. Also, there seemed to be some anxiety about going through *Bula Meela*. *Bula Meela* is a place of many faces and eyes: it sees everything and is important because it is where Nyungar people's spirits from the Great Southern go after they depart their physical lives. Though it is significant, and held in great respect, it is not a place to be near come nightfall. We had about three hours of daylight left and the Elders wanted to get us home without any mishaps, so we had to make our visit to *Kepwaamwinberkup* a quick one.

Kepwaamwinberkep *(Nightwell), near Borden, Western Australia, 1999*

Courtesy School of Indigenous Studies, University of Western Australia

Piled in the four-wheel drive heading towards Beedalup Creek, the Elders yarned about the traditional history of the land; the many waterways and the animals, birds and plant life that Nyungar people used to hunt and gather in that area. As we drove along, I noticed the bush was getting thicker and it was an isolated place. Finally, we came upon a river, though the Elders saw it as a creek. At its lowest point there was a small bridge so you could drive over to the left bank. We drove over and parked the cars, then walked back across the bridge into the bush, so we were then on the right side of the creek. We walked until we came to a rocky outcrop that the creek ran across, and that is where *Kepwaamwinberkup* is. It saddened me that though Beedalup Creek is traditionally seen as a fresh waterway, it was a bit murky from the fertilisers farmers use around that area, year in and year out. When it rains, the water drains off from the paddocks into the creek, polluting it. But *Kepwaamwinberkup gnamma* hole was remembered as fresh and clean.

In this part of Beedalup Creek, water flowed over the rocks and cascaded down into a deeper pool. Uncle turned to us all and said, 'Right, we've got to wade across now. I know we've all got boots on, but they might'n grip on the rocks and you'll slip and fall into the creek, so shoes off, it's bare feet for us all. None of us younger ones wanted to test out the depth or discover what could be lurking in the creek, so off came our shoes. Everybody waded across in bare feet, all meandering one behind the other, making sure none of us slipped. The men walked in front and the women came up the back. One of my aunts and I took it a bit slower, but we finally reached the other side. By the time we did, no-one was there; they'd already moved off into the dense bush and we could not see them. Aunty went ahead to find the rest of our mob, but I was a bit slower in following. I was slipping on my shoes and about to head off after her when I was suddenly stopped in my tracks. My senses became magnified to the point that I could hear every sound in the bush as well as the running water in the creek — loudly; then, strangely enough, there was nothing, complete silence. I just stood still, listening and looking around because I instinctively knew I wasn't alone at that moment. I waited, not really knowing what was in store for me, but knowing well enough that if spirit was around, then anything could be on the cards. Then it unfolded — a little bird flew down to sit on a branch of a jam tree near where I was standing. It looked at me, stayed for a few moments then flew off. I really didn't know it then, but that was my sign. I mentally prepared myself for whatever was about to play out, because things didn't seem right

Though I had my eyes open and saw only bush, in my mind I could see a faint image of a Nyungar man standing in front of me holding a big stick, which he suddenly swung — and I felt it hit my left arm between my shoulder and my elbow. I winced, as the pain was quite intense, but it only lasted for a few moments and then was gone. Then my aunty came back, looking for me. I didn't tell her what had happened because I thought it might be better to keep it to myself for a while. Eventually, we emerged into a clearing where everyone was waiting for us. It felt strange, because while the rest of the bush was thick and dense, this area was flat and didn't have much flora at all, apart from a couple of trees and some grass. As I was looking around, taking this in, someone mentioned that Uncle had had an experience with spirit and was still recovering from it. He had been hit in the stomach and it had doubled him up with pain. I decided then to tell everyone what had happened to me. All of the Elders, including Uncle, said, 'Don't worry, everything is fine. This place is very significant. This is where Nyungar people used to camp and the old ones are most probably making their presence felt.' Then the oldest uncle said, 'It might seem like it's a bad way to let us know they are here, but it's not really, considering what happened to them. We will talk more about this tomorrow, but we have to go along now and make our way home. But before we go, I want to show you girls where Nyungars got their flint stone to make fire.'

This site was not far away, on the bank of the big pool near where we had parked the vehicles. As we were going to the site, we all stopped and stood still because something had caught our eye. None of us spoke, we just looked at each other and looked back at the water. What we saw was a big, single bubble that rose out of the water and into the air. It was beautiful, glistening with the colours of the rainbow. It hovered in front of us for a while then floated off into the bush. There were no rocks or cascading water in the pool to make any bubbles, and this is why we all thought that what we were seeing was made from something else. Because of our experiences at the campsite, we felt this was special. On the surface of the water we saw ripples slowly dispersing out to the water's edge, and though this was a strange occurrence, it had a calming effect on us and made us feel that everything was going to be okay.

We reached Albany mid-evening and felt quite relieved to be home as a lot had happened that day and we were tired and just wanted to jump into bed and go to sleep. We were staying with my aunty, the one who had been left behind with me when we crossed the creek. She is a revered Elder and the sister of the uncle who had been hit by the Old People, like me. Her house was not a bad house, it was a good one; but still, it had a strange energy about it. It was said that *woodachis* or little fellas, congregated there, and though we were aware of this and were slightly apprehensive, that is where we were to spend the night. After a barbecue, Alta, her young daughter, Deda, and I settled down on a mattress on the floor. We noticed that a couple of the aunties were putting blankets up at the windows, and when we asked them why they said, 'Never mind, it's okay, we'll talk in the morning. Now go to bed and have a good sleep, and if you hear any noises in the night, don't worry, it's nothing.'

We settled down on the mattress in an alcove in the middle of the house, with rooms running off it. One room belonged to my young cousin who was known to be visited by little people, and being so close to it worried us a bit. As it turned out, we had a very restless night. We could hear funny noises in various parts of the house. We heard someone or something in the kitchen and it sounded like they were pulling the knife-and-fork drawer out every so often, rattling the contents, then putting them back again and scampering off. As well, we heard them opening and closing the cupboard doors in the kitchenette, which made a real racket. But it was the scampering sound on the lino that really put the wind up us. Because whatever was running around in the kitchen frightened us, and we were glad they were on the other side of the closed door.

Alta Winmar and her oldest daughter Deda, c. 1995
Courtesy Tjalaminu Mia

But then the door handle started rattling, and we knew our feeling of security wouldn't last long. The energy suddenly changed in our room. The end of the mattress was in an open doorway, and in the darkness I could feel something touching my feet. Well! I pulled my legs up quick smart and then lit myself a smoke to calm my nerves. Then I heard Alta's girl, Deda, whisper to her mother, 'Mum, tell Aunty to stop pinching the skin on my back.' This is when Alta turned around and saw me sitting up with my back against the wall, away from them both. I said, 'It's bloody not me. Quick, get up and turn the light on.' But Alta was apprehensive, because Deda and I were the only ones being tormented and whatever it was would be starting on her next. She said, 'No, what if they grab my hand when I turn it on? I don't want their little hairy hands on me.' This turned into a bit of a stalemate, but Alta did eventually get up and turn the light on because Deda became really scared. And that light ended up staying on all night.

Everyone else must have been so used to the little people being mischievous that they were snoring their heads off. It seemed that whatever was in the house wanted to let us know they were there. Either that or they just wanted to have some fun. Nyungars often say that the little fellas can be real cheeky when they put their mind to it, especially if you are new on the scene. Sometimes they just want to warn you, or tell you something. They are a part of Nyungar culture and live in the bush around the hills and caves.

When I finally dropped off, I fell into a very deep sleep and just before I awoke, I had a vivid dream — so vivid that I can recall the smells, colours, sounds, and emotions even now. I dreamt I was back at that camping ground, not far from *Kepwaamwinberkup* (Nightwell). I was standing in the bush camp area, it was light and I was alone. I was looking towards the creek when I felt a strong sadness. Then I heard rustling in the thick bush to the left of me and I don't know why, but I closed my eyes. I heard more movement, louder, with a heavier sound to it. When I opened my eyes and looked down towards the creek, I saw this huge *Waagul* slipping into it; and it was the most vivid emerald green I have ever seen. The colour was brilliant, wet, shiny and mesmerising. I felt both shock and excitement because I could not believe what I was seeing. I did not know much about the *Waagul* then, only that there were males and females, and they lived in and looked after the waterways.

I instinctively felt that this *Waagul* was female, and knew this waterway very well. As it was sliding down into Beedalup Creek, it turned its head and looked directly into my eyes. I don't know whether *Waaguls* can smile, but it had a friendly face and it gave off a feeling that it cared. It also radiated an energy of security; that I would be all right and everything else would be too. It was like receiving a message saying something like, 'We are still here. Everything will be better soon, don't worry, just remember, we are still here.' The tone of those few words was assertive, caring and knowing, with an emphasis on 'we are still here'. Then, as suddenly as it had appeared, it was gone. It just slipped into the dark pool, leaving virtually no trace of having ever been there. The ripples it made were few and vanished quite quickly, and the deep pool was restored again to a deathly stillness. Then I woke up.

When I opened my eyes I felt at peace, but within a short time I felt depressed, like I wanted to cry out in pain. It was as though I was experiencing pain that did not belong to me, but to someone else. It consumed me for only a short time then faded, but I still felt very sad. I mentioned this to Alta and she said, 'Though it was a wonderful dream, there is something that is not quite right. Why would you want to see this beautiful female *Waagul* and yet feel pain and want to cry?' It baffled us both. The next day, one of our group's senior Elders was told about the dream and how I was feeling. He put his hands on me in a healing way and said, 'You'll be fine. The Old People came to you in your dream to let you know what had happened to them out there. We'll talk about it when we get out to Redmond. Things will make sense soon. Don't worry'.

At Redmond, we made a fire and cooked some mallee hen eggs that we had gathered the day before from one of the sites with some other bush tucker. We were all sitting around the fire and were about to have a bit of a yarn, but more excitement was in store for us: a couple of tiger snakes slithered out from where we were sitting. Out came the .22 rifle and they were shot, because there were kids running around and we were a long way from medical aid if someone had been bitten. Once this was sorted out, the Elders went back to their yarning and that's when we were told the story of *Kepwaamwinberkup* and what had happened out there. They said I had had the dream, and felt pain, hurt and sadness, because that was exactly how the Old People were still feeling, and the *Waagul* wanted it to be known that she was there to help heal them and country.

The story went like this. Nyungar people from that part of country had been pushed off their land and incarcerated in the camp area where we visited, because that is where the fresh water was. At that time, as with now, *wadjela* (white man) had taken ownership of the land, so those Nyungars used that site as their main base because they were not allowed to move around country anymore. But because of spasmodic resistance by those Nyungars, either those *wadjela* farmers, or people associated with them, took things into their own hands and poisoned the *gnamma* hole. When the Nyungars went down at night to drink and collect water to take back up to the camp, they started dropping like flies. There were Elders, men and women, young people, youth and babies. It might not have been a massacre with guns and bullets, like that at Pinjarra, in the south, or at Forrest River in the Kimberleys, but it was a massacre nonetheless. A lot of Nyungars from that region were killed — but a lot more could have also lost their lives if they hadn't been warned by other Nyungars, who knew about this event and passed the word on. This is why it is now such a sad place, though it is a place of healing, too, because the *Waugul* showed itself in spirit there, through my dream.

After I got home, these feelings of sadness over what had happened lingered for a while, and I also felt something with me: spiritual presences — three men and one woman, it felt like, who were not at peace. I couldn't see them, but I felt they were a little hostile and sad. They started causing me problems because I'd wake up at least three or four times a night, restless and agitated. In the end, I had to smoke myself, my house and also my car, the places where I felt them the strongest. Elders in my family, who live in Perth now but are versed in the old ways, told me what was needed and how I had to do the smoking ceremony. I followed their instructions to the letter. As I was doing the smoking, I spoke to these spirits in a manner that was quite assertive, explaining to them that I did feel their pain, I did acknowledge that they had been wrongly treated and that I appreciated them letting me know that they were there, but they couldn't stay with me; they had to go back to country, to *Bula Meela*, where all Nyungar people from the Great Southern go after they depart this world. They needed to go back to the Stirling Ranges. A day or so after I'd done this, I felt free, clear-minded and focused. I knew then they had gone.

This leads me to the next part of my story, and once again it is associated with this area of country. This time, I was travelling with a good friend and cultural brother Ronnie Gidgup, a Nyungar artist, who was working with me on a project called *Ngaluk Ngarnk Nidja Boodja* (Our mother: This land). We were working with the same Elders and visiting Nyungar sites in the Great Southern for an oral history publication. Since we were going to *Kepwaamwinberkup* (Nightwell), I thought I should share with Ronnie what had happened to me the last time I was there, so he would be prepared if something unexpected happened again.

This time, we drove over the same little bridge and parked the car in exactly the same spot. It was later in the afternoon, and it was a bit darker, so again we worried about the light fading fast. Ronnie and I were following the Elders into the bush. But there came a moment when I stopped, feeling I didn't want to go back to that place because of what had happened before. The Elders were forging ahead and Ronnie wasn't far behind them, but when he looked back he realised I wasn't close, and said 'Hey, what's going on, Sis? Come on, we've got to go along or we're going to get left behind and lost.'

'Sorry Ron,' I replied, 'I just can't go in there.'

So we both headed back to the four-wheel drive to wait for the rest of the group. The Elders must have realised something was up because they came back not long after. The senior Elder, the uncle who had been hit in the guts by the waddie stick on that first trip, came towards us with a sparkle in his eyes. He understood I was feeling apprehensive. He stood with Ronnie and me for a moment, and it seemed time was suspended. It was getting dark by then, and you could hear noises coming from the bush animals starting their night hunting. The frogs were also serenading to each other, and the water in the pool was turning a dark colour. This is the same pool near which Alta, Uncle and I had had our spiritual experience on the last trip. I looked towards the pool, recalling that moment from eight years ago, when suddenly I was jolted back to the present: something similar was happening.

'What the hell is that?' I quietly asked Ronnie, pointing to the water.

And he replied, 'Buggered if I know, but it's big, whatever it is.'

There were air bubbles and ripples in the water; it looked like something was swimming or gliding underwater. We watched this thing circling, then it would stop and be still for a moment, before taking off again with the same thing happening. The water was dark and the light was fading, so there was no chance of seeing anything clearer. By this time it was in the middle of the pool. It let out some more air bubbles then disappeared, leaving the pool as dark, still and picture-perfect as it had been earlier. Uncle just smiled at Ronnie and me in a very knowing way; no words needed to be spoken. I understood then that the emerald-green female *Waagul* I had seen eight years earlier in my dream, and who had given us that rainbow-coloured bubble as a gift, was in the water now. She'd come to show us she was still there, and always would be.

In 2006, when I approached several Elders to contribute to *Heartsick for Country*, I told one of them what I was planning to write about. He was quiet for a while and then said, 'Tjalaminu, are you aware of what you have just shared with me?' I said yes, and then no, because I wasn't really sure if I had spoken out of turn, or where he was going with his comment. I needn't have worried, though, because what he then told me was that the experience and dream I had had were good things, not bad. They were to reinforce my connection to my country, my people and my Nyungar culture.

Then he shared with me a story that had been passed down to him from his Elders. I didn't know it then, but it would bring me full circle and help me appreciate what I had experienced over the past fourteen years. This is what he told me.

At the time of Creation — in the *koondarm*, the Nyungar Dreaming — many things happened, but one major story was about the female *Waagul* and her travels across all parts of country in Australia. Her journey started out from the waters of the *Derbarl Yerrigan*, or the Swan River as it is known today, which is sacred to Nyungar people. This took millennia, but nearing her end, she came up around the southern part of our land near Adelaide, went down again, and came up to scope the landscape at Beedalup Creek — *Kepwaamwinberkup* (Nightwell).

I was lost for words when he told me this. I hadn't known the full story of the female *Waagul*, I'd just heard bits and pieces over the years. What this Elder relayed to me did, however, affect me in a positive way, because it reinforced my understanding of what my Elders had continually explained to me: that Nyungar culture is one of the oldest living cultures in the world. It is ancient, and we have to acknowledge every part of it and respect it.

I would like to end by saying that, on reflection, the years I spent in children's homes didn't break my spirit or my connections to country. They are still strong. These years may have numbed me for a while, but I think now nothing can rob me again of my cultural heritage. The spirit of my country and the strength of Nyungar people are in knowing who we are and where our place is in the world. And we are proud of that. Even though I see myself as a young student in the cultural and spiritual scheme of things, I appreciate the knowledge that is now being passed down to me from my direct and other Nyungar Elders, and I embrace it. We all need to recognise the spiritual nature of country and care for it and the environment in an appropriate manner. This is respect that we all need to take on board in our lives, because if country dies, then all of us will meet the same fate. And I really do think that this is what the *Waagul* was telling to me when I went back to country on those two trips.

BOB MORGAN

is a Gumilaroi man from the western plains of New South Wales. He is an educator and has an indivisible commitment to Indigenous social and restorative justice. He believes that, above all else, Indigenous people must never surrender the right to be Indigenous, or their connectedness to land.

Country — A Journey to Cultural and Spiritual Healing

The Indigenous concept of country is difficult for many people to grasp. Some people see it as involving considerations of land and territory, while others see it as something to do with geography and the notion of a nation state. When country is viewed through such a lens, people and other living creatures are often absent and therefore the interconnectedness of all living things is lost and never truly appreciated.

For me, country is fundamentally about community, culture and identity. Country serves to link us to our past and provides a space within which family and community can be acknowledged and celebrated. Country is more than issues of land and geography; it is about spirituality and identity, knowing who we are and who we are connected to; and it helps us understand how all living things are connected. The symbiotic relationship Indigenous people have with country and how it defines our identity are as old and profound as the land itself.

When Indigenous people become disconnected from country, their teachings, steeped as they are in generations of traditions and wisdom, are open to abuse and indeed systematic erosion. Disconnection from country is pivotal to the dysfunction that sadly can be found in the lives of far too many Indigenous people across the nation. Government policies and programs that fail to incorporate country and the relationship Aboriginal people have with it are fundamentally flawed. Real and sustainable changes to that dysfunction will only be witnessed when country and culture return to the centre of our existence as a people.

This is not to suggest that simply restoring and reconnecting people to country will necessarily be the answer to Aboriginal dysfunction. Rather it is an argument that the issues of identity and culture, both of which are intrinsically bound to country, will better position Aboriginal people to reject the destructive elements of non-Aboriginal teachings and values. Government policy, not to mention Aboriginal governance, that is culturally grounded will allow us to move beyond the illusion of self-determination that has impeded meaningful growth and development in our communities.

The journey

This is a personal perspective of one man's continuing struggle for spiritual health, cultural reconnection and wellbeing. Both the narrative and the journey are connected to and an extension of those of the countless generations who have gone before, involving thousands of years. The story is not a simple historical picture, but more a mega pixel in the bigger image of Indigenous spirituality, cultures and philosophies. Though it is a personal account, it is reflected in the experiences of other Indigenous peoples around the globe.

My journey commenced in Walgett, a small largely Aboriginal community in the land of the Gumilaroi nation, in the plains of western New South Wales. This is the centre of my universe. My culture and worldview are centred in Gumilaroi land and its people. This is who I am and will always be. *I am my country.*

Growing up in Walgett was wonderful, an experience filled with so many of the joys and heartaches that helped shape my identity and kept me grounded. I am passionate about striving to assert the wisdom and philosophies of my ancestors. For me, wisdom and philosophy are not simply about how we think about the world and our place in it, they are about how we live our lives. Put another way, wisdom is not simply what we think; it is also about what we do with what we know or believe.

My journey has not always been pure and I have strayed from the teachings of my Mother and our extended family. But this says more about me than about my teachers. I have felt the impact and contamination of experiences and the teachings of the majority culture. I have taken tools from it and I use these to supplement the Gumilaroi skills and knowledge as I navigate both the perils of life and celebrate its special gift.

For me life is like a river that starts from the collective life pools and wisdom of past generations. There are many currents, some more powerful than others; the most powerful are at the centre of the river and the more one strays or is enticed from the nurturing strength of the currents at the centre, the more chance there is of being stalled or diverted. Diversions can take many forms, such as the seductive lure of the teachings and cultures of other rivers. And in the path that the river etches, and at its periphery, there are also barriers that will impede a safe and meaningful journey.

I see four distinct, yet connected, stages to life's river. Each has its own individual strength and current, but all inevitably head in the same direction. The *first* stage is birth and renewal, a time of new beginnings and hope, conception and childhood, a time of nurturing and growth. The *second* stage involves adolescence and youth, when meaning and purpose are constant companions to discovery and growing independence. The *third* is adulthood, when a mate is chosen and hopes and aspiration are shared, informed by the experiences and wisdom of others we share this stage with. The *fourth* and final stage is a period of reflection, of rediscovery and of reconnection. It is also a period of heightened awareness and compassion, a time to counsel and protect those in the earlier stages of growth and development.

In this narrative I will seek to define and offer a glimpse of my journey on life's river, and how I have contended with its currents, diversions and barriers. I will conclude with a snapshot of a journey of reconnection, an attempt to return to the teachings and wisdom of country, the river and its people, to the current at the centre.

My personal experience of disconnection began when I was seventeen and travelled to Sydney, the 'big smoke', to pursue my dreams. One of the motivating forces behind my decision to travel to Sydney was the Freedom Rides, in 1965. A group of university students, led by Charlie Perkins, an activist who was one of the first two Aboriginal students enrolled at Sydney University, decided to drive a bus through rural New South Wales to expose the Third World living conditions of Aboriginal communities. His aim was to combat the racism and discrimination that had given rise to and allowed such conditions to exist.

I remember standing in the crowd on the steps of the Walgett Returned Services League (RSL) listening to the words of Charlie and the students. Aboriginal people, including those who had fought in wars defending Crown and country, were not allowed to enter the RSL. I can't recall Charlie's exact words, but I will never forget how his words made me feel. They were my inspiration to go to Sydney in search of a new world, where racism and prejudice were not always constantly biting at your heels. Of course, while I was growing up in Walgett in the 1950s and '60s, I never really knew the extent of the racism and prejudice that permeated our community. As a kid, all you want to do is enjoy life with your mates; the fact that you couldn't go inside the homes of your white mates didn't seem to matter, because we didn't know any different, we just thought that this was the way the world was for everyone.

Sydney was a revelation. It provided a totally different perspective on life from the one I had been accustomed to in the small community of Walgett. I enjoyed the pace of the city and the fact that white people appeared to be more accepting. It seemed that employment and training opportunities were there to be taken. It was the time leading up to the 1967 referendum, and the Foundation for Aboriginal Affairs, at 810 George Street, was the mecca for Aboriginal people who had found their way to the city.

But even with the appeal of the bright lights, sport and music and girls, I longed for my country and the people back home. I returned to Walgett every chance I could to catch up with my mates and to spend time with family. During my visits back home, I used to tell my mates about

Sydney and all it had to offer and soon a number of them took the plunge and moved there with me.

The decision to leave my community and country was a form of disconnection and, at the same time, an awakening to the possibilities that existed beyond the world that I had been born into. I have never regretted the decision to leave all those years ago, but with each passing year and with an ever-increasing desire to know more about why I see the world differently from non-Aboriginal people — and, indeed, even some Aboriginal people — I continue to strive for more cultural understanding and spiritual growth.

For all its attractions, Sydney never held the special appeal of Walgett and its people. Nor did it have the bush and the river to sustain me, and though I no longer live there, Walgett and all it represents will always be home and country.

Pathways to spiritual and cultural disconnection

For most Aboriginal people, the first Australians, the path to disconnection commenced with the arrival of a profoundly new and different cultural order: the Newcomers and colonialism. These were people whose worldview and life journey revolved around the notion of domination and cultural imperialism. This new order was, and in many respects remains, bewildering to most Aboriginal people.

Historically, Aboriginal societies were just and egalitarian, with structure provided for a clearly defined, strict and uncompromising social and cultural order. This provided the values and lessons important to living a good life. Life's journey was about honouring the past and celebrating the present and, it served as a roadmap to the future.

After contaminating and destroying most of the Aboriginal nations that had first tasted the toxins of colonialism, and driven by their rapacious greed and sense of superiority, the Newcomers soon arrived in the lands of the Gumilaroi. They used massacres and other forms of genocide to usurp the land and destroy its people. They saw land as a commodity, a possession, to be exploited and, when its usefulness was exhausted, to be disposed of. For the Gumilaroi, like other Indigenous people, land, more precisely country, is the source of life and identity, not to be traded or, for that matter, surrendered, for with it would go the soul and spirit of its people.

As a nation, Australia continues to struggle to come to terms with its colonial past. Its history of denial and oppression of the First Australians frames much of what masquerades today as public policy. This struggle revolves around the method of dispossession and the continuing failure of the nation to accept and acknowledge its legal and moral obligations.

'Civilising' Aboriginal people through Christianity was the Newcomers' primary objective, and one of the preferred methods was to separate children from the nurturing influences of parents and extended family by schooling them. Aboriginal people first experienced this with the establishment of the Native Institution at Parramatta in 1814.

Country has always been core to Aboriginal knowledge, and it is the absence of this core that contributes to the continuing failure of non-Aboriginal knowledge and education systems to provide adequately for the intellectual and cultural development of Aboriginal students. Another contributing factor is that ever since the arrival of the

Newcomers, Aboriginal students have been treated as guests in education systems, particularly at school level.

There were other experiments with Aboriginal schooling in the colony and the primary objective of each was the separation of Aboriginal children from their families. Early attempts at Aboriginal schooling provided little or no access to parents and family for students, a point graphically illustrated in the following observation in 1848 by Mr E Merewether, the Crown Lands Commissioner:

> *The ill success which has attended the efforts to reclaim the children has been in my opinion caused by their being allowed to remain within the influence of their parents and tribe, and however arbitrary and unnatural it may sound, I am convinced that no real advance towards the end desired, their civilization, will be obtained until they are taken from the locality in which they were born and thus removed from all chance of being tempted or forced to return to the savage mode of life of their race.*[93]

Of course, the trauma stemming from the removal and separation of Aboriginal children has continued in a variety of forms for generations, and resulted in a royal commission whose report was tabled in 1997. Ten years later, the Aboriginal people who were traumatised and brutalised by this system still await an apology and their families continue to seek justice, even if it is a simple sorry.

Communities in crisis

In many Aboriginal communities, people exhibit character-istics similar to those of people who have been traumatised by war. There is evidence of an alarming escalation in incidences indicative of communities in crisis: child abuse; family and domestic violence, including attacks on the elderly; drug, alcohol and other substance abuse; and a rate of youth suicide that is one of the highest in the world. Clearly, something is terribly wrong.

There is also ample evidence that since the 1967 referendum, which gave Aboriginal people citizenship status and rights, millions of dollars have been spent trying to discover the cause of Aboriginal misery and pain. Governments have devised what they consider possible interventions and remedies, but forty years later, effective and sustainable solutions remain as elusive as they've ever been.

Australian governments began to adopt a more progressive social justice agenda following the election of the Whitlam Labor government in 1972, but generations later Aboriginal communities are still struggling to survive. Aboriginal-controlled health services, in partnership with State and Federal health authorities, try valiantly to ameliorate the general state of ill health and disease that continue to cripple most Aboriginal communities. Aboriginal legal services struggle to achieve justice for their clients amid an ever increasing rate of Aboriginal incarceration. Aboriginal Land Councils and Native Title claimants strive to promote, gain and protect land rights and other freedoms, but are forced to spend most of their time, energy and resources defending rather than celebrating their hard-won gains. Aboriginal employment opportunities, especially those outside Aboriginal affairs, are almost non-existent, while education, particularly schools, continues to fail most Aboriginal students.

Government policies of protection and integration, welfare and assimilation and, in more recent times, shared responsibility and partnership have all been adopted in efforts to address Aboriginal social and political injustice. All policy approaches have failed or at best have achieved questionable and debatable outcomes.

Addressing what he called the 'welfare-based' model of social justice policy, Mick Dodson, the Aboriginal and Torres Strait Islander Social Justice Commissioner with the Human Rights and Equal Opportunity Commission from 1993–1998, argued:

The welfare-based model relies largely on government initiatives and government discretion to identify priorities, formulate policy and deliver programs. It is essentially a model based on a benignly intentioned but destructive paternalism, which underpinned past assimilation policies. It is fundamentally antagonistic to the exercise of self-determination by Aboriginal and Torres Strait Islander peoples.

Dodson added:

'The recognition that social justice is about the enjoyment and exercise of human rights establishes a framework in which indigenous peoples cannot be regarded as the passive recipients of government largess but must be seen as active participants in the formulation of policies and the delivery of programs. The rights of Aboriginal and Torres Strait peoples are at issue. We have a right to determine the manner in which they will be enjoyed.' [94]

The spiritually debilitating impact of the individual-focused 'welfare model' of social policy is a sad and tragic feature of contemporary Aboriginal affairs, evidenced by the fact that many Aboriginal communities have ceased to be communities in the broader sense but have instead become 'families' associated with organisations. Put another way, in many Aboriginal settings the sense of community has been superseded by an affiliation to a particular organisation often run by a single or extended family. Parochial and often self-centred interests often occupy the activities of these so-called community-based Aboriginal organisations, usually at the expense of broader community interests and need. This is one of the consequences of the teachings of the majority culture and the erosion of Aboriginal cultural values and traditions.

This is not to suggest that Aboriginal community organisations do not need to be accountable and responsible. They do and, indeed, most are. In fact, Aboriginal community organisations are required to comply with public accountability measures that for the most part are not found in the non-Aboriginal community.

Disconnected voices and visions

Today, modern labour market forces, poor education and training opportunities, not to mention racism and prejudice, have seen a significant drift of Aboriginal people away from their traditional country into larger rural and urban communities.

One of the interesting, and at times disturbing, features of contemporary Aboriginal affairs is the emerging presence and growing influence of Aboriginal people whose vision and voices are informed more by heritage than any notion of cultural or community affiliation or involvement. These people can point to Aboriginal ancestors or family, but they have had little if any real contact with them. Some claims to Aboriginal ancestry are vague and tortuous, a fact which naturally engenders serious doubt and suspicion among longstanding members of the Aboriginal community. For such people, connections to country are almost always non-existent. There are exceptions, of course, but they are few and far between.

It is argued that reconnecting through heritage or ancestry is one thing, but to understand the culture and traditions that are woven into country is something entirely different. But it isn't just the emergence of 'heritage-driven' policy that should concern us because there appears to be an increasing lack of awareness of the history and the struggle for Aboriginal justice as well.

During a recent camp for Aboriginal high school boys in western Sydney, I was concerned to discover that when I showed a video and images of some of the key Aboriginal activists (Charlie Perkins, Sir Doug Nicholls, Lowitja O'Donohue, Faith Bandler, Chicka Dixon, Pat Dodson, Aiden Ridgeway, and others), none of the boys had any idea who these people were and what they were fighting for. The boys all had sporting heroes, and this is understandable given the curriculum of the schooling system and the sport-mad society we've become. In years gone by these boys would have sat at the feet of their Elders and learnt about the world and the important people who were struggling to make it less racist and more just for them and those who come after them.

As with so many other Aboriginal students, these boys are

both victims and products of Eurocentric schooling, which plays a pivotal role in disconnecting Indigenous people from country. Though many Aboriginal people excel academically in the non-Aboriginal intellectual domain, more and more people are returning to their cultural roots in search of meaning and purpose.

Voices from the past — visions of the future

Outside, the old people had gathered under the old gum trees, sitting around the circle sharing life stories as was the custom on hot summer's nights in Walgett. The exact nature of the conversation was lost in the laughter and muffled voices that came flooding into the room. I loved these occasions, because this was when the old ones would share their stories and adventures, igniting visions of wonder and amazement that filled my youthful imagination. Many nights were spent in this fashion and, looking back, I now realise this was an important method of connecting and sustaining the small group who had gathered together because of our common heritage and ancestry. The stories from the circle were often about a place and time long ago. But there were also other stories, which connected people, animals, and all things that shared the country. These stories had their origins and were grounded in the journey of the storyteller, a ritual passed down from one generation to the next. This is how it had been for our people, for untold generations before the *Wundas* [95] came with their technology and teachings that changed our world forever.

Home was a shanty built on the banks of the Namoi River that meanders through the township of Walgett on its way to join the waters of the Barwon River, just a few short kilometres downstream. This was home, the centre of my universe, the place where I felt safe, comfortable and connected, the place that defined my past and was to shape my future. This was and remains country, where I had been raised in poverty but never in the absence of love.

My uncles and some other kin had built our shanty on the banks of the Namoi to house our family after my father and a sister had lost their lives in a boating accident some months earlier. The shanties of other members of our extended family and clan formed a small community that was filled with laughter and happiness.

But safe and comfortable were the last things I felt this night, because in the darkness that filled the room, I sensed the presence of something gently tugging at the bedcovers. My brother Ken, who slept at my feet in my bed, stirred and told me there was something in the room.

The tugging of the covers became more intense, but I couldn't move.

I was frozen stiff with fear and the covers were now up over my head. After what seemed a lifetime, someone was screaming and people rushed into the room carrying fire sticks and the old lamps that we used at the time.

Men and women were running all over the place, yelling and trying to understand who had screamed and why. Only after the commotion had settled down did I realise that it was in fact I who had screamed, having somehow broken the grip of fear that had paralysed me. My mother and aunties, who came into the room carrying kerosene lamps, were most upset because they couldn't work out what was going on and I was too terrified to make them understand. Ken tried his best to tell people what had happened, but there was too much commotion.

Monty, my elder brother, who was about nineteen at the time, had been one of the first people in the room, and I recall that he chased something or someone out the back and down the path to the river's edge. In the lamplight, someone noticed a small puddle of water at the foot of the bed and the words 'water dog' were soon bandied around. As a young boy I'd heard the old ones tell stories of the water dog and other mystical beings that filled the circle with both fear and wonder. According to the story, the water dog was a creature that lived in the river and occasionally climbed its banks to seek out prey. Stories like this are bountiful in Aboriginal knowledge and learning circles.

One of the most important teachers as I approached manhood was my maternal grandfather, Tom Hickey Snr. He was a mountain of a man and the leader of our extended family and clan. Amid the many special loving memories I have of him, one has remained vividly etched into my mind through the years. One of my earliest images of Grandfather was of him sitting on his favourite seat, a four-gallon drum that he had fashioned into a chair. He would sit for hours, strumming his fingers on the sides of the drum while he sang his songs. On such occasions I would sit somewhere close, silently watching him as he sang his songs, the words of which I never understood. A distant view would creep into his eyes and he would seemingly be transported to another time and place. Knowing what I know now, I realise he was connecting with his spirit world and telling those who had gone before him that he would soon join them.

Growing up surrounded by family and country, I was able to learn some of the important values that had sustained the Gumilaroi for thousands of years, but I am sad that I never had the opportunity to learn more from the teachings of my grandfather and the other old people. To be denied the fullness of their knowledge and wisdom is tantamount to cultural genocide. Government policies of protection, welfare, and, perhaps more insidiously, assimilation, prevented the teachings of the old people and so critical cultural knowledge and skills have been lost.

With grandfather, Tom Hickey, Snr

Courtesy Bob Morgan

Schooling and other assimilation practices of the Aboriginal Protection and Welfare Boards under which Grandfather had survived meant successive generations of his extended family were denied the teachings of their past. In many Aboriginal communities, stories exist about the brutal methods government authorities would use to prevent the spread of traditional culture knowledge and values. People who spoke in language were often punished, perhaps more than most. There are reports of government officials torturing such language speakers by burning their tongues with lit cigarettes or hot coals.

Growing up in Walgett under the oppressive policies and practices of the NSW Aborigines Welfare Board meant that life for Aboriginal people was what the AWB determined it should be. But amid this oppression and racism, the people of the Gumilaroi learnt to survive and adapt, though the teachings of our distinct culture, our worldview and the pivotal role of country were slowly eroding.

Sites of cultural and spiritual affirmation

Just as there are many sites and episodes of struggle for Indigenous people across the world, there are also an ever-increasing number of incidences of cultural affirmation and spiritual reconnection. From the mid to late 1960s, and motivated by and linked to the Civil Rights Movement in the United States, Indigenous people across the world started to organise themselves to consider ways to combat the legacies of colonisation. Of course, people had been mobilising in the 1920s and 1930s, but in the 1960s there seemed to be new hope, a sense of grand expectations that captured the hearts and minds of a younger generation. I was swept up in this vision and hope for a new deal for Aboriginal people.

Two events of cultural and spiritual affirmation were the World Indigenous People Conferences on Education (WIPCE) and the Healing Our Spirits Worldwide conference, gatherings that offered a time and place for Indigenous people to get together and celebrate what it meant to be Indigenous. A Canadian friend of mine said she looked forward to our education conferences (WIPCE) because it meant she could spend at least a week of her life mixing with and being inspired by people with a common history and experience, a sort of primacy of place and of purpose. There is increasing evidence that Indigenous people globally are beginning to seek answers to our continuing social and spiritual needs and aspirations in the teaching of our traditional knowledge.

These conferences are held every three years and provide an opportunity for sharing and celebrating Indigenous pathways to spiritual healing and wellness. Such initiatives suggest Indigenous people everywhere are tired of being defined and marginalised by members of the majority culture.

At local community levels, Indigenous peoples are rejecting the assimilation objectives of the majority culture, instead asserting their cultural and political rights and freedom. They are developing and embracing land rights, language revitalisation and other forms of traditional affirmation. And other Indigenous peoples, particularly in Canada and New Zealand, have more successfully developed education systems that reflect and celebrate their knowledge and wisdom.

My work with Aboriginal men and boys is also a feature of my personal journey of reconnecting and rediscovery. The 2006 Aboriginal men's learning circle, which was held in country, was a success largely because it gave men and boys the opportunity to consider important issues in a setting appropriate to our ways of knowing and doing. Had it not been held in country, the outcomes would not have been achievable.

Conclusion

This short essay provides only limited opportunity to identify and consider some of the experiences, challenges and insights that have shaped and influenced my journey as a Gumilaroi man.

Of course, all cultures are dynamic, changing and ever

adapting to the forces of social, political and cross-cultural interaction. But the tools we take from other cultures can never totally replace those that are at the centre of our personal and cultural stream; unless we allow it to happen. As Aboriginal people, we must be prepared to draw upon the traditions and values inherent in our past and allow them to inform and shape the future.

Reconnecting with old values and traditions is critical to the future of all Aboriginal peoples.

We must act as the nations we once were and indeed still are. Our existence as self-determining nations and the veracity of our claim to social and restorative justice are not dependent on the sanction or approval of non-Aboriginal society. Coexistence and reconciliation are possible only when there are equality and honourable reciprocity between Aboriginal and non-Aboriginal people. The concepts of minority and majority are loaded with negative and burdensome values and judgements that only further marginalise us. But whatever the future holds for us, country, with all its special meaning, must once again become central to our lives.

This is what I strive to achieve as I reach the fourth stage of the river's journey. As I indicated earlier, this is a period of reflection, of rediscovery and of reconnection. It is also a period of heightened awareness and compassion, a time to counsel and protect those who are in the earlier stages of growth and development. Country and all it represents are pivotal to this journey.

JOAN WINCH

*was born in 1935 and belongs to the Nyungar and
Martujarra peoples of Western Australia. She is a
well-known fighter for Aboriginal rights and was
awarded the World Health Organisation's Sasakawa
Award in 1987 for creating the best Indigenous
primary health care system in the world. She is
writing a history of the Marr Mooditj Foundation,
which she established in 1983.*

A Feeling of Belonging

The feeling of belonging that you, as an Aboriginal person, have to country is very strong spiritually. I have this in two ways, because my mother was a Martu woman who was born in a place called Lake Way, near the town of Wiluna, in Western Desert country in Western Australia. Her family name was Wongawol, but Mum was given the name Lily Booket by the Native Welfare Department when she was very young, because she had been taken away from her people. Wongawol though, is the true family name, and because of that it is very important to me. The Wongawol family are a very strong traditional family who belong to the Dingo Dreaming, which links them and me to many different places. My father came from a different place in country. He was Phillip Heath, a Nyungar man born in Katanning, in the south-west of the State. His own connections to country are through the Menang and Goreng peoples. Though my parents were from different areas of country, they were both strong spiritually in their own ways, and I learnt a lot from them when I was growing up. I am a strong person too. The spirits have always guided me throughout my life, so I am following in their footsteps. My mum and dad told me that even when I was a little baby the spirits worked through me.

They used me to warn them of impending danger. When I was about a year old, we were living in Collie, because Dad had a job on the railways. They were the only adults in the camp and then there was my elder brother, Brian. We had only a makeshift toilet, like a lot of Nyungar people who lived in the bush in those days. It was wedged in between the truck of a large tree near our camp. One day, suddenly, a willy-willy sprang up and circled the toilet.

'That's strange,' Dad said to Mum, 'I think the spirits are trying to tell us something. I think something is going to happen, Lil. We'll have to be watchful.'

At the end of the day, Dad doused the fire and he and Mum and us kids settled down to sleep. In the middle of the night, though, a bad storm blew up and it raged with such a mighty force that I woke up and began to cry my head off. Mum got up to tend to me and in that instant all hell broke loose. There was a mighty crack, then a crash and the roof fell in followed by a large tree branch. There was mayhem for a while because it was dark, we couldn't see Dad, and Brian and I were both screaming our heads off in fear. As it turned out, Dad was okay. Though the branch had pinned him to the bed, there was a curve in the branch that protected him. Mum though, wouldn't have been that lucky. If I hadn't cried and she hadn't got up to tend to me, she would have either received some very bad injuries or been killed. For many years to come they told that story because they reckoned it was me who saved Mum's life.

It is because of my parents that I can put my feet in two camps because through them I have my feet in two lands. Knowing what my connections are to my mother's and father's peoples gives me a strong sense of place and a feeling of deep belonging. Connections like these are very important to Aboriginal people because they tell us who we are and influence the way we see the world.

My father's country

It was through my father that I learnt about the Nyungar side of my culture, the old ways to do with the land and Nyungar spirituality and all the spirit creatures that lived in Nyungar country. When I was a kid, we would always be sitting with Dad and other people in our family group around the fire, or out on the lawn in the summer when it was warm; listening to the old stories being told about what had happened, and who was who. The old people loved telling stories and they were about all sorts of things. It was a wonderful way of teaching, and through listening to them you soon learnt who you were related to, and came to understand the huge amount of relatives you had. That was how knowledge was passed on in those days, because there were no radios or televisions or public libraries you could visit to find things out. It was all word of mouth, so it was that oral history tradition that I got off my father from when I was very young. I understood early on that I had been born with a passion and feeling for country. It's a feeling that sits in the pit of my stomach, it's been with me all my life, and it will never go away.

When I was little, everything in the natural world was a wonder to me because it was so beautiful. We were in the bush all the time on weekends and on school holidays, because the suburbs of Willagee and Melville were mostly bush in those days. We'd take the dogs and go exploring and smelling all the different bush smells. We felt a part of the place, of the country that we were in, and it was a part of us too. I remember there were these beautiful berries we used to eat that were a limey green colour, we used to call them swanberries. They were sweet and delicious and we loved finding them. My brother Brian and I often went down the hill to explore, because up the other side from our place was a piece of bushland loaded with thick carpets of catpaws, which are beautiful little orange flowering plants that grow about fifteen to twenty centimetres high, and lots of other native plants and wildflowers. We loved it when the wildflowers were blooming and we could have a good look around and see what was new in the bush. I used to marvel at everything and our dogs would sniff out the blue-tongue lizards from underneath the balga bushes. There were all kinds of wildlife in that area then. The trees were huge and friendly and you could stand underneath them when it rained and never get wet. Sometimes we followed the track that wound through there. Nowadays that track is called Stock Road, and it is quite a busy road with a lot of traffic, but then it was just a rough track that they drove the stock along; mostly cattle and sheep headed for the abattoirs down at Robbs Jetty near Fremantle.

Sometimes we would sit outside with Mum and look up at the sky and watch all the little woolly clouds coming in. Some of them looked like baby sheep. You would always get a cloud play there, at the edge of the Continental Shelf, because that's where the clouds would rise. If it was nearing sunset, Mum would say it was the little lambs going home to rest. That was also her way of telling us that because the sun was going down, we had to come inside as well. She never liked me and my brother wandering around at that time of day, and that was partly to do with the way the Welfare took Aboriginal kids away. Mum had been taken away from her own people when she was only two years old. There was a story that went around in her day that if you didn't stick together then the lady with the elastic arms would get you. She was always telling that story to Brian and me to warn us.

'What if I hid around a corner?' I asked her once. 'Would she get me then?'

'She will still get you,' she replied. 'Her elastic arms will come right around that corner and pick you up and take you away.'

The lady with the elastic arms, I will never forget her. I realised later, of course, that that was Mum's way of describing the Welfare and the power it had to take Aboriginal children to a place they didn't know that would be strange to them. It makes me feel very sad to remember it. In the past, many things have happened in Australia to force people away from the countries of their ancestors. I'm proud to say, though, that even when that happens, we still have the feeling inside us for where we come from, and we find different ways to go back so we keep that connection to our Ancestors.

It is strange driving through the areas of Melville, Willagee and Fremantle now and seeing all the houses, where once there was mainly bush filled with native plants and animals. When I grew up, I left Western Australia for a while and went to live on the east coast, but when I returned in 1953, I went to visit the bush I had loved so much as a child. I was shocked by what I found. Everything had been bulldozed, and I felt so sad that I just found myself standing there in a hollow between two hills, surrounded by a vast sea of sand, crying while the wind whipped the sand into my face. I have got a big feeling for my father's country, and I hate to see any of the natural world destroyed.

Right across Nyungar country now there is a lot of change going on in the environment. There are many problems. Too many trees have been chopped down, there is a huge issue with salinity and there are many threatened and endangered species of plants, animals and birdlife. Government and industry haven't been accountable enough in what has happened. At Dwellingup, there was a secret site where chemicals were dumped. I was walking along there one day with a friend when we came across some huge mature trees that were dying. I was very surprised, because I had never seen big trees like that dying before and I wondered what on earth was going on. It turned out that drums filled with toxic chemicals had been illegally buried there and harmed the trees and other plant life. That kind of thing has to stop.

My mother's country

I have said that I have a big feeling for my father's country. Well, I have a big feeling for my mother's country, too. Unfortunately, I never had the opportunity to return to my mother's country until I was a young married woman, so I missed out on knowing her place when I was a child. As I have already said, my mother had been taken away from her people when she was only two years old, and then, when I was just thirteen, Mum died. This meant she never had a chance to reunite with her people and her land, but I went back and so did my daughter, Lillian. My daughter's ashes are buried in that country now, so she is at peace where she belongs. My journey to my mother's land began with three dreams.

In my first dream I saw the big dingo painted on the flour

mills at North Fremantle. I felt scared about what this might mean. Why had it appeared in my dream? I often drove past those mills and I wondered if it meant I was going to have an accident there. From then on, I was always very careful to watch out for the other traffic, because I knew there was something very significant about that place.

In my second dream, I went over the hill from that dingo place at the mills. I walked past the low bushes and the limestone and some older Aboriginal people took me to where there was a limestone cave on the north bank of the Swan River close to the ocean. Who knows, it could even have been under the ocean at one time. I know there is another trail that goes right down to the big rocks at Albany, where they have Dog Rock. I think all these places link up together through songlines. It is a huge area and what I didn't know at the time was that it was a very significant place for me, because that site at North Fremantle is the beginning of the Dingo Dreaming trail that runs right through to my mother's country.

In my third dream, I was hiding on the riverbank behind some trees watching these little boats going up the river. A huge V-formation of black swans was flying in front of them. As I watched, a terrible feeling of doom came into my heart and I said to myself, 'This is the beginning of the end.' When I looked down, I saw that my feet were not mine; they were big chunky ones. I think I was in someone else's body and I was seeing what they saw and feeling that same feeling of doom in my heart, because of what the coming of the first white people would mean to my people. So these three dreams came to me to link me back up to the country I belonged to and to help me understand my cultural inheritance better. So then the dingo on the flour mills took on a different, more positive meaning. Many years later, I found out that my mother belonged to the Dingo people. You see, whenever I get anything from the spirit world it is usually pictures and I have to work out from the pictures what it means. I felt really good about it once I understood what it really meant, because then I could put all the pictures together like parts of a jigsaw and understand the great importance of it.

I remember when I first went back to my mother's country, I was twenty one and newly married and my husband had a job on a station in the area. I really didn't know anything about traditional people at that time, but the old people would be sitting there every night in front of the fire and singing their songs in language. I couldn't understand the words, because I'd been brought up in the city and didn't speak their language. It was really very awe-inspiring for me to be a part of that. They were a wonderful group of people and I was very impressed with the way they conducted their lives, how gracious they were, and all the lovely little fat babies running around enjoying themselves. It is wonderful to feel one with people and country. Your heart just expands in that situation, and when you are walking around the land, you can feel it deep inside you.

Due to our history, our people have been forced to deal with a lot of things that are foreign to our culture. And because of my interest in spirituality and healing, and also my training as a nurse, I have always considered all the different ways in which we can be healthy, and especially how this might have worked in our communities before the British came to colonise this land in 1788. There are many small things which, when you put them together, add up to health and wholeness. For example, I know that vitamin A is essential for healthy skin and things like that. But the day we stopped giving our babies the tail end of the goanna, which is jam packed with vitamin A, and bought them a teething ring to chew instead, was a backward step for us. Our ways were different, but they worked. Our people had tested them for thousands of years. We knew how to be healthy. We were active and vigorous in our own countries. We never had processed foods with no goodness left in them, instead we had what the land provided: low-fat meat, vegetables, fruits and fresh water. It was all very balanced. Governor Arthur Phillip even noted in 1788 that Aboriginal people looked much healthier than many Englishmen. Now, over two hundred years later, our whole health status has been reversed and we are struggling to survive. The introduction of tea, sugar, flour, sheep and cattle was devastating. Sometimes we were herded together by the authorities and forced to live in one place; our bush medicines couldn't cope with this kind of static environment and neither could our people. It caused us a lot of harm and the introduction of other animals, like foxes and rabbits, harmed all the natural resources of the land so it made it impossible for us to live the way our ancestors had. Our people lost heart because of all the changes that affected every aspect of their lives and their countries. It was like being caught up in a big willy-willy of change and not knowing what the new rules and regulations were or why they had suddenly come.

The problem with uranium

My mother's family, the Wongawol family, have a culture deep in spirituality and healing and are tied closely to the land and environment and ecosystems. They feel very concerned with the damage done to the land. In our way of thinking, if the land is in bad repair, then so are the people. If the rivers dry up and become polluted, then this

Joan's mother's country — Lake Way, Wiluna, c. 1986
Courtesy Joan Winch

can be equated with the body's lifeblood, and it means that life can't be sustained. In my mother's country, the government has allowed large drums of nuclear waste to be buried, and this has caused a lot of destruction to the underwater system and consequently to the land and the people. We are spiritually tied to the land, so whatever happens to the land has long lasting effects on us as human beings.

My mother's birthplace, Lake Way, is seventeen kilometres south-east of the town of Wiluna, and six hundred kilometres north of Kalgoorlie. Uranium was discovered there in 1972, with the ore deposit sited on a channel on the northern end of the Lake Way salt lake. In 1978, bulk ore samples were taken and used for a wide variety of purposes, including a pilot plant project for uranium extraction. In the early 1980s, the government gave permission for mining the ore, but this project never came to fruition. However, the radioactive ore that had been irresponsibly left lying around the old mine sites has caused a lot of problems. In June 2000, scientists determined that there were areas of extreme radiation scattered around the

Joan, with her daughter Lillian and her cousin Nellie Farmer (Wongawol) at the orange orchid outside of Wiluna, c. 1986.

Courtesy Joan Winch

former site and these areas were unmarked and unfenced, so Aboriginal people living there had never known of the danger. Corroded forty-four-gallon drums and piles of uranium ore exposed to the wind were found on the shoreline; and on the lakebed itself, where the ore samples had been kept, ground radiation levels were found to be seventy times higher than the background radiation level. This area has always been an important and popular hunting ground for Aboriginal communities, so what on earth did the mine workers think they were doing leaving radioactive ore lying around like that? I just can't believe the mentality of it all.

Lake Way is called Lake Way for a reason. The water goes underground and all the rivers run into that area, so of course the waterways, which are so important to life in that desert area, will be affected. This was a great meeting place for peoples from throughout the desert country and extending right into Central Australia. Large groups always met where there was fresh water and good game, but the mining industry in general has given very little consideration to factors such as this. If you know anything about mining, any kind of mining, then you will know that by the time the miners have finished with the land, it's absolutely ruined. They rip the guts out of the country, leave big slag heaps behind them, and spend as little as they can on rehabilitation. There is very little accountability in terms of looking after the place for future generations.

What kind of world?

There is a battle looming over uranium and the government will want to win because of the amount of money involved. Our old people have always told us that there are some things you leave in the ground, and uranium is one of them. Huge mistakes have been made in the past, but the lessons still haven't been learnt. The increased use of nuclear energy that is being proposed now in Australia could end up destroying the cradle of civilisation in the oldest land in the world. Look at the Rum Jungle uranium mine, south of Darwin, in the Northern Territory. It was Australia's first large-scale uranium mine and while it was closed in 1971, it is known all over the world as one of the worst cases of pollution. The radioactive tailings and other poisons got into the waterways, especially the Finniss River, and when the wet season came and the rivers and dams flooded, it helped to spread the poison. The traditional owners of the place warned everyone about what would happen, but no-one listened. 'Don't dig those holes in there because it is really very bad, it is big trouble,' they said. 'A big monster is going to be released out of the ground. Just leave the monster in the ground. Don't disturb him. He is asleep.' They knew the uranium shouldn't be disturbed, but their warnings were ignored. The fish and the shrimp all died, the trees, palms, grass, plants and other vegetation all died, and you couldn't drink the water. Even today, the sources of contamination still haven't been contained and heavy metals, including uranium, continue to leach into the waterways. How long will it take people to learn that what happens to the land also happens to us?

I feel very concerned about the whole uranium issue because Western Australia's largest uranium deposit is at Yeelirrie, which is right smack in the middle of my mother's country. For many years, thousands of tons of powdery radioactive rock was left lying around there, exposed to the elements and causing harm to the land, water and air. No warning signs were posted, there were no fences to keep people and animals away either. When ore is exposed like that there is a danger of radioactivity entering the food chain, if that happens then you can't clean it up; and it can lead to all sorts of cancer and other genetic diseases, especially if the poisons have built up in bush foods that people are eating, like the wallabies and kangaroos. The people who created the mess didn't want to clean it up. It took a twenty-year campaign before the ore was finally reburied, but who knows what damage it did in the meantime. It's really quite horrific if you think about it. Scientists tell us that it takes hundreds of thousands of years for plastic to break down in the environment, but when it comes to radioactive waste, it is with us virtually forever. So why do governments and multi-national companies want to fill the earth with nuclear waste? If it becomes too dangerous to breathe the air, then money won't help you. I have seen first hand the effects of nuclear weapons. As a nurse I went to Japan, where the first nuclear bomb was dropped. It was very distressing to see babies in the hospital in the 1980s who had been born with cancer. Their families were still suffering from the effects of what had been passed on with the dropping of that first bomb. Is that what we want? It is just too terrible to think about.

The way forward

I am hoping I won't be alive to see what governments and multi-national companies will do to the world. If they have their way, they will destroy all the beautiful natural things and it will all be in the name of the dollar. So how are we going to protect Australia? How are we going to protect the people and the country? What will happen to the babies and children when the world is turned into a giant nuclear dump? Will it be the beginning of the end? Is there nothing we can do about it? All over the world there are already unsolvable problems with nuclear waste, and now governments are talking about creating even more. Let the people who advocate this live next door to the reactors and the waste dumps with their own families. What will they think about it then? Will they feel safe? Or will they be terrified about the effect it is having on their children and grandchildren? Children are the heritage of Australia, and they are the ones who will be dying of cancer and other diseases if all this rubbish isn't stopped.

I look back on my own experiences and there are two things that give me hope. The first is that our people have always had their own protocols when it came to caring for country. I can explain this best by sharing a story. There was an old lady I knew who went through the Law when she was young. In those days, you were given a role to play and you were also given a tract of land to look after. Her tract was hard to look after because it was at Meekatharra and there was a lot of mining in the area. Though the miners were there, she still thought of it as her tract of land and she felt responsible for looking after it. When I went walking with her, it was like walking through her own garden. She would show me this

A visit to the Emu Farm when it was operating outside of Wiluna, c. 1986

Courtesy Joan Winch

tree and that plant and tell me where the water comes in the winter and it was just magic to listen to all the things she knew about that land. She had the ownership, she felt the responsibility, she did her job caring for it as best she could. It hit me, then, that if you multiplied that many thousands of times over across Australia, then that was how this continent and all its flora and fauna got looked after in a very particular way. Everybody had a job, everybody had a role to play. It's the same to day. We all have to be responsible for what happens.

The other thing I think about is a woman's Dreaming site in the Perth area, which is called the Butterfly Dreaming, and it is tied to the beautiful blue and black butterfly. The butterfly lays its eggs in ants' nests near a small shrub we call a bacon-and-egg plant. The ants carry the larvae up to get the nectar from the shrub. Then they carry the larvae back down again at night and the larvae exude this nectar, which the ants collect for food. This is a symbiotic relationship, where what is good for one is good for the other. That's how we have to think about the natural world, because in the long run, when everything is in balance, what is good for the earth will be good for us as human beings too. Life is dynamic, we need to harness it positively, not negatively. If we don't all work together to find a way to do that, then at some time in the future there will be no safe place left for anyone's children.

JOE BOOLGAR COLLARD

is a Nyungar from the South-West region of Western Australia. He is an associate lecturer in the Indigenous Community Management and Development Program at Curtin University.

A Strength that Can't be Broken

Ngany Deman Gaa Maanga Moort Baalup Ngany Ang Ngientj Collard — a Koonyart, Bennell — a Koonyart, Thorne — a Koonyart, Garlett — a Konnyart, Winmar — a Koonyart, Bilya, Derbarl, Moorda, Ngany Boodjar Gaa Ngany Djurit. Ngany Koort Djerb Kartinjin Nidja. In my Nyungar language, this means my grandmother and grandfather's family, they are with me. I am a descendant of the Collard, Bennell, Garlett and Winmar families. The rivers, the estuaries, the hills and valleys — are all my land, my tracks. My heart is happy knowing this. My name is Joe Boolgar Collard and I was born on Moroo Boodjar country, which is the Perth area; they are the kangaroo totem people. I am a freshwater Nyungar and a Bibbelman man on my mother's side from the Nyungar nation. If I was to explain to someone who my people were, then I would say 'I am from the land of the grey kangaroo, *yonga*; land of the grasstree *balga*; land of the long trees. We are a proud and fierce people. My skin name is Nagarnook and my moiety is the *wardong* or black crow.'

I have always had a special affiliation with the black crow and right from an early age my Pop, Rod Collard, called me 'Joe the black crow from Popo'. Popo was short for the town of Popanyinning. I spent a lot of time with my Pop when I was young, we were very close to each other and he taught me many things, so it was deeply hurtful for me when he passed away. When it comes to crows, though, right to this very day they are still with me. Red-eye crows are from here and blue-eye crows are from Wongi country, in the Goldfields area. They will talk to me two or three times a day and sometimes it is a sign or message for me. I just can't get away from them. I can just be standing on my front porch and a couple of them will even land next to me and start talking. I don't even need an alarm clock to get up in the morning, because the crows will turn up early and say 'It's time for you to wake up!' They have been coming to me for a long time now, and there is something very special about them.

I have a lot of respect for the older people who have shared cultural knowledge with me right from when I was a young fella, especially my family Elders. I have learnt a great deal by listening to them talk at home and around the camp fire. I am still fairly young and I have many years ahead of me before I become an Elder myself, but in the meantime I make it my business to learn as much as I can. I want to be knowledgeable enough to be able to teach others and pass my culture on to my children, my grandchildren and other

Joe with his uncle Venis Collard, who is a respected Nyungar Elder and a role model for him, 1995

Courtesy Joe Collard

Nyungar people. When kids are grounded in culture and country, then they have a positive way forward because they have something special to offer the world. This gives them the confidence to make good choices for themselves, and hopefully it will generate in them a strength that can't be broken. I take this seriously and I work hard to achieve it.

Creating positive change

I have always had a desire to make things better for my people and because of this I have deliberately developed a mentality of being part of the solution, rather than being part of the problem. I am all for creating positive change and this is what I try to do in my work with the environment and also culturally, so I am always learning. There is a lot that can be learnt from my Nyungar culture, especially when it comes to looking after the land. I believe that if we all work together, then it is possible to create a better place for future generations. As Nyungar people, we know from our ancestors that a detailed knowledge of our land has always sustained us. We actually excel at having an intimate relation with the land, including its spirit and the songs, dances and rituals. In the past, every landmark had a name and there were stories and meanings connected to those landmarks. Many of them still survive today. Special places often required a ritual that had to occur in order for people to be able pass through that particular spot safely and in the right way. In the old days, our people often travelled vast distances. Walking the songlines was an important part of our life, because it continually connected us to our beliefs and to the land through story and art, song and dance. These travels also helped us to understand the creation in our country and why we should protect it.

Nyungar country

The South-West region of Western Australia is home to over 30,000 Nyungar people and it is considered by many to be the most fertile land in Western Australia. This land, which our people occupied for thousands of years, was where the British came in 1829 in order to establish the Swan River Colony. They settled on the banks of the Swan River, or the *Derbal Yerrigan* as we call it, and over the years this settlement has grown into the city of Perth that we know today. There was plenty of food and fresh water and other natural resources, so it was a good place for family groups to live. For thousands and thousands of years, Nyungar people had lived, hunted, traded and travelled all through the Perth area, so you can appreciate that it would have been a very puzzling event when the new arrivals first came to our country. There is a story that has been passed down from our Bennell relations about those early days, when the *wadjelas* (white people) first sailed along the river towards our people who were living in the Kings Park area. Nyungars thought their big rafts had clouds on the top and when the newcomers, dressed in their red coats, climbed onto horses, they thought they were riding on large dogs. This was because our people were seeing things they weren't used to seeing and they were trying to make sense of them. Our old people would have talked about this event for many years to come, and that is how this story would have been handed down through our family over the generations.

It is true to say that the invasion of Nyungar country

deeply affected our people, and its ripple effects are still being felt to this day. Following that first contact, the relationships between Nyungar and *wadjellas* quickly deteriorated into violence and mistrust. While a lot of the killing is unrecorded, reports of much of it have been passed down orally through families like mine. For example, there are many stories about how our people had to hide in the rushes and among the paperbark trees around Lake Monger in order to protect themselves from attack. In Karragullen, up in the Hills, there were massacres that our family have talked about, and in York, the fighting was horrendous and went on for many years. Members of my own family were among the victims of the Pinjarra Massacre of 1834, when Governor Stirling led a dawn raid against a group of Nyungar people who were objecting to the invasion of their lands and to the destruction of the bush, which had sustained our families over the generations.

The Kings Park area is a very special place to Nyungar people for many reasons. In my own family, we have always been told that our relations are from this area; and I know personally that every time I go there and sit down I get a spiritual high. You can only feel it strongly like that when you know you are from that area. That knowledge makes it very strong, because you know your old people are there. This is why, when I sit up at Kings Park, I don't see the skyscrapers and all the cars going back and forth across the Narrows Bridge to the city. Instead I see the old people. I see the campfires, I see the smoke from a long way away that belongs to another family group, and I see the other large extended family groups who would have travelled throughout the whole of the Swan coastal plan before the white people came. This makes it an important place for me. It's good that the Kings Park area has the protection of being a park, because it is rich in plants and wildlife, but it is also an important *Waugal* site.

The *Waugul* is the greatest of all the creator rainbow spirit serpents; he is the main spirit being for Nyungar people. He played a major role in the creation stories for Nyungar people and while there are many Dreaming creation stories of epic battles between different spirit animals, the *Waugal* is always revered and honoured. He formed many of the landmarks that we still see today and traditionally he controlled every aspect of Nyungar life. My old people have taught me that we shouldn't talk about the *Waugal* too much, not unless we really need to, because he is very special and dear to us. In order to show respect, we talk softly and humbly about the *Waugal*. He created the valleys and the hills and the rivers that flowed through him. Even today, we can still see his tracks along the rivers because when he went through the country he shed his skin and in so doing he left marks and other things behind. Sometimes today, people are confused thinking that they are just shells on the sides of the riverbank, when really they are actually the scales of the *Waugal* that came off as he travelled along on his journey. Also, as Nyungar people, when we look at the different colours in the landscape, we see the *Waugal*'s colours, because when he went through country, he left his colours in the environment.

There are many stories about the *Waugal*. Different people from different parts of the country tell different stories and they are all important. For example, if there was a dry season in the old days then sometimes our people used to sing and cry out to the *Waugal* that they needed rain to replenish the land so they didn't die out. They would even do a certain ceremony and sing and do the right ritual to bring the water. This was a very significant thing. All the stories about the *Waugal* are significant, because he is the chief of all the totems. He is the punisher. If anyone disobeyed, he would punish people to keep things in balance. This made him the judge, jury and executioner. Because the *Waugal* is so important, we get very sad when things are destroyed or damaged. I am thinking now of some of the special landmarks that used to be here, such as the *Waugal*'s eggs and holes and the many freshwater springs that have been destroyed through either ignorance or re-development. Even today, the *Waugal* has a role to play, because we are now learning different ways. Also, things are going to happen in the world. In fifty to one hundred years' time we may actually have to go back to the old ways, because the oils and the different resources that we have come to depend on for modern living are going to dry up. When that happens, then we will need the old wisdom and knowledge to help us survive.

Legacy of the past

The damage to the environment has made it hard for everyone and now we are in a situation where there needs to be some healing. Some of the destruction has occurred because the land was seen as a means of gaining wealth, so people didn't think too much about the long-term consequences of what they were doing. But there has also been a lot of damage done through ignorance, too. For example, traditional fire burning techniques have always been important in the maintenance, use and care of our country. Burning-off was carried out as a necessary part of the cycle of life. It had a number of purposes, some of which included helping with regeneration and regrowth, attracting game and encouraging the development of desirable food plants. The fires were skilfully managed, they were fairly low in strength and did not needlessly damage or destroy large areas of country. However, in 1840, traditional burning techniques were banned. Any Nyungar people who were caught were publicly flogged. This happened because the burning was seen as an act of hostility against the new arrivals. They didn't understand that it was a land management practice that we had been carrying out for thousands of years, or that our own laws protected the plants and animals so that our way of life was sustainable for future generations. Every family group had its own special totem that protected their people, and there was a very strict law that determined if and when a family could hunt or gather their special totem. Nothing was ever hunted to extinction or needlessly destroyed, so the way our families lived supported the cycle of life.

Sometimes, things were destroyed simply because it made things more convenient for the oppressors. For example, in the 1860s the mouth of the Swan River was blown up by the invaders who had come to Nyungar country. My old people have told me that this was a very upsetting thing to have happened, because the area had a lot of cultural significance. The ocean and the mouth of the river and the spiritual stories to do with the *Waugal* and our ancestral spirits that were associated with it, were very important. Then later, another law was passed which caused further devastation because it allowed for the destruction of all the fish traps on the river simply because they interfered with boating traffic. These kinds of things greatly affected Nyungar people at the time, because they had an impact on our spiritual beliefs and interfered with our way of life.

We followed the cycle of the six seasons. This meant our families went to specific places in the right season and at the right time. The seasons put things in perspective for us and dictated what our focus was. For example, in *Maggoro*, which is June/July the cobbler fish were plentiful. In *Dilbar*, which is August/September, the potatoes along the river were plentiful. Then there is the *moonja* tree, or the Christmas tree as many people call it today, which was very special to us as well. It blossomed in the season of *gambarang*, which was October/November, and it signified a new season coming into being. The *moodja* tree, though, is also special to us spiritually, because when someone dies our people say their spirit goes to the *moodja* tree. After that it goes on its journey to *Karranup*, which is over the sea. In traditional times, when they buried someone, they buried them in a certain way so that their spirit would travel through the country following the *moodja* trees.

The seasons determined how our families interacted, and they were part of our social and cultural calendar, which also included our own festivals and ceremonies. In Kings Park, we had the kangaroo festival, because that area was a good hunting ground for kangaroos. Then at South Perth, near where the Narrows Bridge is now, we had the honey festival. The honey came from the flower of the banksia tree and they used to put it in the water where it would ferment. In the old days there was a big lake there, but it has been filled in now. The fish traps were important too, for high tides and low tides we had certain techniques for catching cobblers and all the other types of fish that venture through these waters.

The changes that were made to the land, like the infilling of many freshwater springs and lakes, the way our land was given away in land grants, and the ways that water was wastefully used, made it impossible for our people to continue to live in the way they once had. And of course, this caused a lot of distress.

Our spiritual connections to country

Nyungar people have always been, and continue to be, closely connected to country in both physical and spiritual ways. We have spiritual experiences with country that we respect at a very deep level. I would like to share something that happened to me when I was younger, as an example. I was at Walyunga National Park, which is about thirty-seven kilometres north-east of Perth, doing a cross-cultural awareness session for the Department of Conservation and Land Management. Older Nyungar people were there, too, and it was my role to learn more and to keep on learning. That was my job. Over the years I have learnt from many experienced people and I am very grateful for it. On this occasion, I was very happy to be at Walyunga. I felt strong walking through there because my old people are there and they protect me and look after me when I am in my country. Anyway, we were looking at the traditional potato grounds that are there. The bush potatoes were a food source for our people in the old days, and even today there are some old people who can tell you where to get the potatoes and how to identify them. This is because there is a certain feature in the ground that shows you that there is a potato underneath. The same people can also tell you how to get wild onion and wild carrots. Anyway, while we were on this trip sharing this kind of special information with the participants, there was one man from the Kimberleys who unfortunately wasn't that respectful to our knowledge or our generosity in sharing it. You have to be respectful when you are in someone else's country, so he wasn't really doing the right thing.

But then something happened. When it came time to leave, I suddenly saw three old people with red bands on their heads appear. They were sitting down with their legs folded they and gave me a nod of approval for being respectful in the country. Shortly after that, that man from the Kimberleys who hadn't had the right attitude was hit on the head by a branch. No-one said anything, but we all knew why it had happened to him and he knew as well. The action of the tree showed that he had been disrespectful, so he was reprimanded for it.

You see, we live a spiritual life and we are spiritual people, and without spirit we are nothing. From a young age I was taught about spiritual things and some of that was to teach me respect and also to keep me safe. For example, as children we weren't allowed to kick the dirt or whistle at night because the *mamurries*, the little spirit people who live in the bush, might come and get us. I remember the old people used to break certain leaves off certain trees and put them where we were camping to keep the bad spirits away. Sometimes they'd keep the fire going most of the night to keep the bad spirits away, too. The spirits are very strong at night, so we always made sure that we had a little bit of light: if not a fire, then an old lamp. Fire was very important because it kept us warm and a lot of the old stories were passed down around the camp fire. Fire also kept predators at a distance — both physical and spiritual predators. Also, smoke was used to cleanse people and to get rid of bad spirits. We liked our families to be strong, because families came first with us. In traditional times, when a baby was born it would get smoked and possum skin would be put over it to make the baby grow strong. They would also tie possum skin on the baby's ankles and arms for about a year to help it grow big and healthy. These were the kinds of things that were handed down, so we knew what and what not to do. The spirit is important and we are sad people if we lose our spirit because then we don't know what we are doing. That can cause us to get caught up in things like drug and alcohol dependency. That's why you see some of our people walking around with those kinds of problems, because their spirits have grown weaker.

Being responsible in country

Everyone has to learn to be responsible for our families, our community and our country. There is a lot that our Nyungar values can teach us. Water is a problem now, but it is going to be an even bigger problem in the future. One of the major issues we have now is protecting our wetlands, waterways and significant sites on the Swan Coastal Plain from further development. The wetlands, which are a series of lakes and swamps, have always been important to Nyungar people. They are rich in wildlife, especially birdlife, and many birds, animals and plants depend on them. Unfortunately, since Europeans came, eighty-five per cent of the wetlands have been destroyed; they have been drained, filled in, or made into artificial lakes for new housing estates and other kinds of development. Perth itself is sited on reclaimed wetland. For example, where the Perth railway station and the Perth Entertainment Centre are located, as well as large areas of Northbridge, there were once lakes. Everyone knows that groundwater levels are affected when natural vegetation is cleared, but the clearing still continues and so do the problems with salinity and very high levels of sulphur in some of the remaining lakes and the soil. Over-demand by the general population and by industry for groundwater has created a major imbalance in the environment.

The difficulty with many land developers and some local governments is that they don't understand why wetlands are important or how they work. Councils are up to their necks in paperwork approvals for new developments and developers like to get in and get out quickly in order to make as much money as possible. No-one is taking enough time to seriously think about the long-term effects of what is happening. Some wetlands are seasonal and all wetlands support each other, but the continued development is affecting the whole system in a very negative way. Instead of detouring around wetland areas, the newer suburbs are encroaching on them. There are some homes in Perth that are actually about a metre below sea level, and if the prediction about a hundred-year flood comes true, then perhaps at some point in the future they may even become submerged.

Over the years, Nyungar Elders have often told developers not to build in certain places because of the damage that it will cause, but most people don't want to listen. Proper consultation with Aboriginal people is seen as a burden. It is time consuming and they think we are anti-development. In most instances, government agencies, developers and industry don't know how to put proper processes in place. We need knowledgeable Aboriginal people in identified key positions who have a voice that will be valued and acted upon. They could also work on developing sustainable strategic practices. If non-Aboriginal people could learn to appreciate our relationship to country in a deeper way though,

Joe as the Wetlands Indigenous Project Officer, when he was working at the Swan Catchment Council, Herdsman Lake, 2006

Courtesy Swan Catchment Council

then it might be possible to make more positive progress. People seem to find it easy to forget that Australia is the driest continent in the world. Protecting our wetlands, our waterways and our underground water reservoirs is critical. Take the Gnangara Mound for example, which is a big underwater source. It is sensitive to climate change and to changes in rainfall, but what have you got sitting on the top of the mound? A large pine plantation! That plantation is sucking out far too much water from the aquifer below and it is one of the reasons the water table in the aquifer has been lowered. Even our winter rainfall is a concern, because over the past few decades it has fallen, so there is less water being caught in our above-ground reservoirs. This has led to the use of water from under the ground for public drinking water. Around forty per cent of our water is now drawn from underground sources. However, with the population growing rapidly and more and more housing estates being developed, how and when groundwater continues to be used needs to be very carefully looked at.

The environmental damage that we are seeing now is growing, and unfortunately there are also many areas where the disposal of poisonous waste is not being properly policed, so this is adding to our pollution problems. Pollution affects the fish and the mussels and everything that lives in the water, so you have to be very careful what you catch and eat now. Our rainfall is also decreasing, so in the future the groundwater levels in some aquifers will get lower than they are now, and it is only commonsense that this will lead to further water restrictions. We need to take a really good look at ourselves, because our lifestyles need to change. We need to plant bush gardens, use less water and protect and manage the water we have left so everything becomes sustainable. In the early days, our old people taught the white settlers many things, such as how to read the landscape, how to read the signs through nature, how to find the *gnamma* waterholes and the bush foods and how to walk the tracks across Nyungar *boodjar*. The Nyungar wisdom and knowledge from the likes of Kaiber, Miago, Dylan, Windich and Kikit also helped the white explorers to reach other lands throughout Western Australia where they wished to live. This exchange should have been a two-way process, but it wasn't. While it is our responsibility as Aboriginal people to maintain and protect our natural and cultural heritage, there is also a collective responsibility to take care of this country and to be strongly involved in environmental sustainability. This hasn't happened in the past, but it must happen in the future if we are to survive and look after this country.

SALLY MORGAN

belongs to the Palyku from the Pilbara in the north-west of Western Australia. She is a writer and artist and is employed in the School of Indigenous Studies, at the University of Western Australia.

The Balance for the World

They set sail with noble endeavour
to possess with the owner's consent
mystical lands beyond Never Never:
terra nullius awaits those who dissent.

Graeme Dixon, Nyungar poet, 2003[96]

The world is an old, old place and this island continent is the oldest of all. For thousands of years it lay hidden between Antarctica and Asia, pounded by the great swell of the Indian Ocean on one side and the reef-studded Pacific on the other. Here our many peoples lived from generation to generation in a vast dry land, one-third desert, with the world's smallest rivers and mountains and with plants and animals found nowhere else on Earth. Down in the valleys and along the blue and purple gorges, in the rippling red desert, and on the plains and sandy ridges, along the winding, weaving gum-lined rivers and around the inland lakes, among the glistening forests and shady woodlands and throughout the meandering coastal plains. Each nation made its own way, living life by following the laws laid down for their country by their spirit ancestors in the first creation. Through songs, stories, dances, art and ceremonies, the keys to life and wisdom were passed down, ensuring the survival of our world, including all the plants, animals and life-giving water sources. We knew everything there was to know about our countries; the strong and special places, the flash of silver lightning signalling a summer storm, the feel of the air before the heavy rains, the churning of the cyclone clouds, the roaring of a river running a banker, the whirling willy-willy, the whispering wind, the smell of the earth wet and dry, dust storms and a starry sky. This was how it had always been. This was how it would always be. And so it was for thousands of years, until the day when the oceans became a pathway to any land with a coast, and men of fear and men of faith took to the sea in ships to conquer the globe.

The lost garden

One of these hardy seagoing adventurers was a working-class man from Yorkshire named James Cook, England's hero and the nemesis of my people. On the eve of the America's giving birth to the idea that all men were created equal, with the right to life, liberty and the pursuit of happiness, and of the French taking up the cry, '*Liberté, égalité, fraternité, ou la mort!*'[97] — freedom, equality, brotherhood, or death! — Cook brought the winds of change to our shores, only he blew in on a mighty gust of Empire, not revolution.

He was born in the Age of Reason, when the prophets of his time boldly declared there was nothing in the universe that couldn't be known, ordered and understood. Even problems of human nature could be unravelled by using reason, and in the future reason alone would provide the happy-ever-after ending that troubled humankind had always longed for. Though nominally a Protestant, he prided himself on being a hard-headed man of science, not a superstitious observer of religion. So unlike other explorers who launched into the deep, he did not pray before weighing anchor, read the story of Jesus calming the storm to his crew in turbulent seas, or think the Southern Cross was God's wonky thumbs-up sign in an unsaved southern sky. In James Cook's eyes, the world existed to be explored, analysed and investigated, not saved; and if he was lucky and worked very, very hard, he might gain for himself a great deal of status and wealth in the process.

Although the voyage of discovery he was secretly ordered to undertake by his no-nonsense superiors in the British Royal Navy was cloaked in science, it was based less on reason and more on imagination. For centuries men of learning had argued it was likely that a large rich continent lay hidden somewhere in the southern hemisphere. This was only logical. The landmasses of the northern hemisphere needed a counterweight, otherwise the globe would wobble and wobble like a giant bowl of Aeroplane Jelly until it destroyed itself. Cook's mission then, was to find this magnificent missing country which, since time immemorial, had been the balance for the world; a silent, secluded land that for a thousand years the intelligentsia of Europe had imagined but not known, drawn on maps but not found, yearned for but not understood.

Strangely enough, the continent which sheltered the country of my own ancestors lay in the south too, but it wasn't our land they were searching for. Cook's people dreamed of a fabulous lost paradise, a promised land where the streets were paved with gold and the inhabitants lived idle lives in polished marble palaces. There was none of that fatty, roasting woodsmoke smell you get from the campfire at dinnertime. And no sharp smell of eucalyptus, either. No plump death adders were lying in wait in the long damp grass and hungry crocodiles weren't floating like bumpy logs beneath the salt water. There were no buzzing blowflies, stinging mozzies, croaking crows, swooping magpies or kookaburras laughing their heads off high up in gum trees. Nor were there any muddy rivers, beaches littered with seaweed, crazy cyclones, wicked willy-willies or droughts and flooding rains. The pitiless blue sky of a sunburnt country, the beauty and terror of a wide brown land, were not for these dreamers. They were haunted by a place of perfect happiness which they called *Terra Australis Incognita*, Latin for 'the unknown south land'. And because of where their dreams would one day lead them, peoples like mine would become haunted by a Latin name too: Aborigines, Latin for 'from the beginning'. One dead Latin word to describe hundreds of living nations. Like the mystical, magical land of *Terra Australis*, we would bear the burden of the dreamer's inability to see clearly and intuitively.

By the time James Cook set sail, Europeans were well aware of the existence of the west coast of our continent, which they frequently referred to in disgust as that 'infernal southland'. When the winds and currents were too strong, their ships ran aground on our rocky shore and sank below the heavy, pounding, grinding swell of the Indian Ocean. On the seabed they rotted and fell apart, sending up bits of broken mirror, china, beads and gold and silver coins to litter our reefs, islands and long sandy beaches. Hard-nosed merchants and shrewd investors were convinced our treacherous and barren coast had nothing to offer. It was simply the barrier to the promised land they were all searching for. The real *Terra Australis Incognita* lay deeper in the South Pacific. Perhaps it might even encompass our enigmatic eastern shore in some way, if only it could be found.

This wasn't the first time an Englishman had been sent forth like a dove in search of a land where the rivers flooded with rubies and diamonds and the beaches glittered with gold. Finding it was a dream that had preoccupied the minds of kings and queens, priests and prophets, soldiers and sailors, and wheelers and dealers for as long as anyone could remember. On ancient maps, the lost country of *Terra Australis Incognita* was drawn as a mighty southern continent stretching north from Antarctica into every ocean. On some early, yellowing charts, the fearful warning, *Here be dragons,* was hastily scrawled across the land in thick black ink. Monsters might be found in the topsy-turvy land down under, or miracles. As for its location, all anyone could ever say was that it lay somewhere at the ends of the earth, down near the bottom of the world, below the equator, past the sunset and over the rainbow.

For the English, this was the third time they had gone a-hunting; but this time they thought they had an ace up their sleeves. Captain Wallis, of His Majesty's ship, the *Dolphin,* had just hit port with exciting news of the beautiful island of Tahiti. Better still, he'd glimpsed what he thought were distant mountains to the south, which might well belong to the fabled missing southland. Wallis' crew were ordered to zip their lips, but sailors on shore leave aren't known for their discretion and they were soon singing hearty songs about a tropical Garden of Eden in the local alehouses. 'The beautiful Queen of Tahiti,' they bragged drunkenly, 'thought the English were Gods and felt very proud to embrace King George!' There was no Queen of Tahiti. The *Dolphin* was a thirty-two-gun frigate and Wallis had bombarded the island to a bloody truce, then taken possession for Britain. Now it was to be Cook's port of call on the way to *Terra Australis.* From Tahiti, he would disappear into the world's largest ocean with the intention of scouring it for a land which, if found, would offer King George III more plunder than a pirate could poke a stick at; and guarantee global dominance for the wet and windy British Isles.

Brave and stalwart men had tried before and failed at the goal Cook hoped to achieve. In earlier times, some had even set sail with visions of this mystical land being a lost Garden of Eden. There were some very old tales, passed down from one crafty grandmother to another, which said the Garden lay in the south. But when the Garden eluded their beseeching prayers, they decided that God must have hidden it from the greedy eyes of humankind until the coming of a Chosen One. In the history of humankind saviours have always been few and far between, and while ale was plentiful in dockside inns and taverns, sober seafarers with a sense of their own spiritual destiny were not. Even if one were found, some captains considered such a man would be a dubious asset. A tirade about the Fires of Hell would spook any crew in a lightning storm. In the seventeenth century though, over one hundred and sixty years before Cook set sail, a Portuguese sailor announced that he had been anointed to find the missing Southland. Fernandez Quiros was passionately religious, wearing rough goat's-hair shirts to ward off the temptations of the flesh and keep his thoughts holy. He impressed the King of Spain and Pope Clement VIII with his colourful tales of endless riches and his heart-rending warnings about the fate of millions of lost souls in the South Seas if the Protestants reached them first. In 1605, with the mutual support and blessing of these men of power, he set sail. Along with him went a small gift from the Pope, a woodchip from Christ's cross to ensure the success of his journey. There was an ancient story which claimed Christ's cross had been carved from a tree which had once had its roots deep in the soil of the Garden of Eden, so perhaps the woodchip was meant to be a talisman of some kind, or even a homing beacon.

Quiros searched in vain, but when he finally landed on a large lush island in a group of islands later named by James Cook as the New Hebrides, he convinced himself he had found God's own country and named it the *Southland of the Holy Spirit*, claiming it for Spain and the Church. Here he meant to build a new Jerusalem and use it as a base to convert the whole southern hemisphere to Catholicism. The owners of the island where he built his small wooden church were suspicious of the bearded strangers who sang religious songs while pointing muskets and cannons at them from the beach. Open warfare soon broke out and Quiros's crew, whom he had dubbed the 'Knights of the Holy Ghost', turned out to be a bloodthirsty lot. In the end Quiros decided to leave. Three young boys were kidnapped with the intention of whisking them away to Spain, where they would learn the Spanish language and be trained in Spanish ways; then they would be returned and used to infiltrate their own people in order to spy out the coveted location of any secret treasure. Sadly, the boys died en route to Europe and when Quiros arrived home empty handed, he plunged from the dizzying heights of spiritual tall poppy to religious nutter. Within ten years of setting out to find *Terra Australis* he was dead, but not before he managed to utter a final deathbed prophecy. The Southland, he warned the true believers gathered around his bedside as his life was going out on the tide, would one day fall into great evil.

Perhaps in a strangely ironic and perverse way, it did — at least in Quiros's eyes. When Britain eventually committed to a colony on the east coast of *this* Southland, King George III banned Catholic priests from sailing with the First Fleet to Botany Bay, so Protestants could get a head start in the land down under. But if the passionate Quiros ever looked down from heaven he would have drawn consolation from the fact that the first Protestant preacher to alight on our shores was more adept at growing pumpkins and cabbages than harvesting the souls of humankind; and for many years the Catholic Church in Australia faithfully taught that the *Southland of the Holy Spirit* was actually located in Queensland, and therefore a devout Catholic and not a heretic Protestant deserved the glory of 'discovery'.

First contact

When James Cook at last brought the turbulent winds of change to our shores, they beat down upon us with bewildering speed. Cook never walked in the west, it was only in the east that he cast his shadow; but even here he remains a poignant symbol of a conflicted past steeped in layered denial. My people were lucky in the sense that we were able to hold onto our country longer than many others. The north-west of Western Australia remained free of the intrusion of pastoral stations until the 1860s, and it wasn't until the 1890s, when gold was discovered, that the population of men seeking their fortunes swelled dramatically. For many of our old people, the distant past is not so distant, and over the decades I have been honoured to spend time with some who marvelled at all the changes, both small and large, their families had seen. These conversations were always both funny and sad. Humour has made us great survivors.

'Straight lines, they were something new. If you see a straight line, then you know it's not our line. We follow the rivers and the hills and the curves of the land. And Western Australia, that never used to be here either.'

'Oh, there are a lot of silly things now. There's a place further inland where I can stand with my big toe in the Northern Territory and my heel here.'

'My old aunty told me when she first saw a man on a horse she thought it was a devil kicking up dust. The first horse, imagine that.'

'Oh, those early days were terrible times. I was lucky, I was born in my own country, but it was still on a sheep station.'

'Hmph, stations! They breed secrets more than they breed sheep and cattle!'

'True. My old granny told me a story once. It was just before early dawn, still cool, with the sun only just peeking over the hill, so there was a chill in the air when her boy went out with the boss. She had a funny feeling, like something real bad was going to happen, so she watched. When the boss came back she went looking. That poor boy was dead in scrub. Oh yeah, a lotta people died of lead poisoning in those days.'

This was not an unusual story. Many deaths, both of individuals and of groups, went unrecorded in regional Australia. In some places, the land still holds the memory, so the sadness and heaviness remain. If you unwittingly come upon such a place, the sense of what happened can still be felt, and conversations with the old people who know that area will soon reveal what occurred. These are not good places to stay overnight. An old uncle told me once how, when exhausted, he camped in such a place, only to be woken in the night by a terrible crying. He never went back to sleep. He kept the campfire burning.

'The birds and animals will tell you what's going on,' he advised me. 'Watch them. Your dog, is he right? What's he doing? Where's he looking? Is his tail up or down? My dog didn't like that place, but I was too tired to listen properly to what he was telling me.'

Change. Incomprehensible, often lacking in compassion and commonsense, and frequently brutal. But over two hundred years later, the hearts of our people, especially our older people, still lie within and long for country. Inside ourselves, we still feel sad for country, sorry, happy, worried, joyous, fearful and sick for country. This is because our country is alive, and no matter where we go or are forced to go, our country never leaves us. When we experience that deep longing inside ourselves, then we know our country is calling us back. It is time to go home, even if only for a short while. This is because country is far more than what can be seen with physical eyes. Our country is the home of our ancestral spirits, the place of our belonging. The core of our humanity. We recognise the connectedness of all

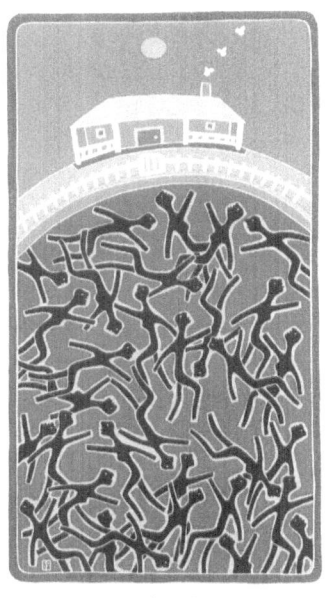

Another Story
Courtesy Sally Morgan

things in our country, both seen and unseen, breathing and not breathing. Our feelings encompass everything that country is and includes the water and stars, the plants and animals, the Creator ancestors and all the spiritual beings tied to our country; the songs, dances, pictures, stories, dreams, visions and experiences of country; and everything on every level and in every dimension that has a life in our country. And this is the great Australian conflict: conflict over country; who it belongs to, what it is, what it means, and how it should be valued.

James Cook might have set sail on his first voyage of exploration in 1768, but I never met him until the 1960s when, as an awkward and troubled teenager, I sat glued to my family's black-and-white television set watching the adventures of Captain James Kirk, of the USS Starship *Enterprise*. From then on, I was an avid fan of science fiction shows and films, but I was unaware at that time in my life that the *Star Trek* series drew inspiration from the life and adventures of the famous Lieutenant James Cook, of the HMS *Endeavour*. I remember though, that I wanted Captain Kirk to play fair when first contact with another planet was made. I wanted him to keep secret the location of any peoples who might be vulnerable because human explorers, no matter how genuine they seemed, couldn't be trusted. And I wanted him to be humane, to choose defiance of his Federation superiors over condoning harm to different races or other forms of life. But all heroes are flawed, and Kirk, like the man from whom he was cloned, often stumbled his way through the galaxy with little thought of the consequences that might follow in his wake.

Later, when I briefly read that a couple of Americans had been on board the *Endeavour* in 1768, I wondered whether it was a sign of things to come. In the future, astronauts from the United States of America would utilise space as a highway to distant places in the same way Cook had used the oceans as a freeway to distant beaches. When those first astronauts landed on the moon, they flew their nation's flag, like Cook had flown the British flag on our eastern shore. And like Cook, who left behind a carving of ownership in a giant gum tree facing out to sea, they left behind a carving on a plaque facing out to the universe. Not on behalf of a single nation, or so they said, but on behalf of an entire planet. The plaque read: *Here men from Planet Earth set foot upon the moon. We came in peace for all mankind.*[98] In 1992, they honoured James Cook by naming a space shuttle after the *Endeavour* and sending it winging its way to the stars with a woodchip from the original ship on board. Coincidentally, that same year, the High Court of Australia finally recognised the rights of Indigenous peoples, leaving the door open to a form of native title over country.

So one hot summer's night, when my grandfather and I were sitting outside looking up at the stars, I told him about Cook's spaceship and we talked about it's significance and what it might mean to anyone living happily on another planet, unaware that the spirit of James Cook and his new spaceship was about to descend on them. He laughed and said. 'Those poor buggers in the stars, do you think they'll get stuck with Native title too?' Perhaps they will. The sky is full of unclaimed real estate. And though the United Nations' Outer Space Treaty reserves space for the good of all humankind, land on the cosmic frontier is already pulling in big money here on Planet Earth. The Head of the Lunar Embassy, an American who claims to own the moon, has been selling off plots for years, and another American company wants to mine it. NASA has been sued for landing on someone else's asteroid and the Milky Way is up for grabs to pioneering space speculators, who are offering celestial bodies for sale at bargain prices. In 2007, an individual filed a claim to Venus, but indicated he was willing to share it as long as any inhabitants lived within the spirit of the planet's motto, which was 'love reigns eternally'.[99] Modern thinkers are already predicting war in what some Indigenous peoples call the sky country.

When James Cook set out to 'explore strange new worlds, to seek out new life and new civilisations, to boldly go where no man had gone before', his own view of country was simple. Land was a means to wealth, a resource that God had ordained to be tamed and utilised by 'superior' nations. Born into a blue-blooded society where your social rank and likely future were determined by your birth, Cook knew that in order to get on in the world he would have to seek wealth by any means available to him and, if at all possible, do something extraordinary. This was the only way to gain the valuable patronage he needed to rise high; the only way to guarantee greater comfort in his old age than the miserably cold stone cottage his own father had ended up with. It was ambition that drove Cook to travel farther than any man before him. Being willing to head out into a vast watery unknown and possibly never return was an amazing and exciting thing to do in eighteenth century England. And Cook did it well. In a period of less than ten years he commanded three major voyages of discovery, gaining incredible fame and winning for himself various flattering titles like 'The World's Greatest Navigator', 'Explorer Extraordinaire', and 'King of the Pacific'.

Over the centuries his character has remained almost saintlike to many writers and historians; what my mum once described as the Mills and Boon version of history, where James Cook's own story opens with 'Once upon a time in a land far away, a bold handsome man rowed into Botany Bay.' Despite his increasingly irrational and violent behaviour, especially on his third and final voyage of exploration, his reputation for being humane has followed him like a bright light into the twenty first century. In 2002, in a book titled *Cook: Obsession and Betrayal in the New World*, the author wrote:

> *But as significant as all his discoveries was his attitude towards the indigenous groups he met. Defying the colonial zeal of the day, he treated them with a decency that shattered all convention — and taught his men to do the same. This is the real legacy of James Cook, the enlightened explorer.*[100]

Yet when this 'enlightened explorer' arrived on the east coast of this continent in the wet autumn of 1770, he willingly chose to deploy a weapon which, as a science fiction fan, I think is best described as the philosophical equivalent of the Death Star in the first movie of the Star Wars trilogy, *Star Wars*. *Terra Nullius* was a legal fiction which, when activated, emptied this continent of her first peoples as quickly as God emptied the Garden of Eden in Adam and Eve's time. And like the Death Star, it was *as if millions of voices suddenly cried out in terror and were suddenly silenced.*[101] Everything that has happened to our peoples and our countries since begins and ends with *terra nullius*, the lie which said that it was fine for men like Cook to claim the lands of peoples like mine because it was like claiming empty land. Today, its seductive whisper blocks Australian courts from moving forward in any dynamic or progressive manner. The Mabo decision, in which the High Court recognised the existence of Aboriginal rights to land in the form of 'Native title', was hailed as a landmark victory for Aboriginal peoples. Unfortunately, subsequent judicial decisions and legislation have seen our peoples burdened with a legal approach focusing on an over-specific, Westernised notion of 'traditional laws and customs', which has made a mockery of the spirit of the process. Indigenous peoples are penalised for events over which they had no control. This includes no longer living in the country from which they were forcibly dispossessed; not practising 'traditional' law; not being able to speak the language they were banned from speaking; proving genealogies going back multiple generations where much of this 'proving' has to be based on records not of their own making — records whose telling silences embrace a story no court wants to hear. In other words:

Indigenous peoples are being placed in the position of having to demonstrate, not simply what Aboriginal culture is, but continuity with a Western interpretation of the minutiae of what it was at some point in the distant past. Rights to land — and future uses of land — are being constrained by a reductionist perspective that locates culture in a multitude of specific past activities, rather than looking at the holistic nature of Indigenous relationships with country.[102]

The exasperation and anger this engenders led my mother to complain to lawyers at one Native Title meeting that, 'This process is so stupid that even if it was 1770 and Captain Cook had just landed here, we still wouldn't be able to prove our connections to our own country!'

For Native Title claimants this situation is further complicated by gross under resourcing. The Native title process is so poorly funded that some of the lawyers who represent claimants have their salaries paid for from a fund contributed to by the industry groups with which they are supposed to be negotiating. Native Title meetings are often hastily called and poorly run. They begin early, finish late, force-feed participants with large amounts of information, some of it often highly technical, and frequently press for quick decisions on matters requiring thoughtful consideration or involving serious heritage issues. Then there is the silent prioritising of claims. The unspoken rule, usually denied, is this: resources are allocated to those groups whose claims are most likely to be winnable in court. This means that for many groups it's a struggle to find funding for important community meetings, and no anthropologist or historian is made available to do any sustained work on researching the claim. In the meantime, important old people slowly pass away and their wisdom and knowledge of the land remain unrecorded.

We want to protect the places where our grandmothers and grandfathers walked and talked and lived with their families. Our country is a living library, a place where the part, present and future come together in one continuing creation. There are grinding patches near the waterways — granite worn flat and smooth where the old women used to grind the spinifex seeds into flour for damper. There are standing-stone arrangements far older than anything found in Europe. And there are thousands of beautiful rock engravings; for men, for women, for families. Some of them made, according to one of our Elders who has since passed on, 'before people were walking around'. Made by our spirit ancestors who are still watching over us and helping us to be strong because we always have been and always will be their people. What a tremendous roller-coaster of emotion it is; loss, grief, anger, sadness, rage and all of it threaded with humour and the will to survive. People find the courage to keep hope alive by reconnecting with the past and with lost family members and by talking about what is happening in our country now and what we can do about it. Largely through our own efforts, our severed family trees are slowly pieced together and the group as a whole begins to understand how, when and where the lives of our people became so shattered. We have our differences, of course, but our lives are underpinned by the need to be formally and legally acknowledged as the traditional owners of our particular area of country. We carry the wounds still. When you look at us, you can see what's been done to our country.

Learning to read the signs

In a discussion with one of my grandfathers, he commented that he thought Captain Cook was a man who couldn't read the signs. He was talking about an intuitive way of knowing, a fluid and dynamic language grounded in country and linked to the wider world, that our old people are very adept at. Country is alive. The world is alive. This is the essential unchanging nature of the universe. This is the reality of life for Indigenous peoples.

'If a man can't read the signs, then he might get out of his depth and end up in dangerous waters. He might muck things up for other people too.'

It wasn't until years later, when out of curiosity I delved deeper into the life and times of James Cook, that it dawned on me just how right he was.

The *Unknown South Land* was supposed to be a place of

untold wealth and beauty — and so it was when it came to our particular southern continent, but the kind of wealth and beauty the British desired was not immediately obvious here. The Gweagal people of the Dharawal nation confronted Cook and his crew, warning them not to land, but superior weaponry won the day. When Cook and his motley crew landed in Botany Bay still searching for their own people's lost dream, God wasn't sitting under a gum tree singing 'Rule Britannia' and waiting to embrace the English with a glass of sherry and a fat cigar. No diamonds, rubies and other precious gems littered the rocks and there were no streets paved with gold or glistening marble palaces. Nor was there any smashed pottery, gold and silver coins, or beads and ribbons floating in and out on the tide. This was an ancient place, one which had never seen a group of armed European men or a ship with hundred-foot masts and great billowing white sails. Instead of vast riches, what faced Cook were giant eucalypts, clumps of grass trees, flowering banksias, brightly coloured lorikeets, noisy cockatoos, goannas, possums, bandicoots, kangaroos, and dingoes. Fat koalas were lying back in the forks of gum trees, wombats were digging and sleeping and raising their families in burrows beneath the earth, and platypuses were narrowing out tunnels in creek banks. Fresh water was streaming past the big cabbage-tree palms down in the gullies, which were alive with ferns and mosses, and the wetlands were a wonder, where all kinds of birds flew in and out to nest. The seagrass meadows, kelp forests and mudflats were home to crabs, prawns, sea dragons, molluscs and all sorts of fish. The sea mullet were plentiful, and huge stingrays hundreds of years old were sliding around in the crystal-clear water of the bay.

Unable to read the signs, all James Cook could see were too

many trees and not enough paddocks. What this land needed, in his opinion, was the plough and the touch of a 'civilising' hand. While his crew filled barrel after barrel with fresh water, Cook trotted through the bush leaving small, neat piles of beads, nails, ribbons, combs and mirrors at any dead camp fire or empty hut he came across. These were the offerings the British normally gave to peoples they considered 'uncivilised'. Meanwhile, the aristocratic and trigger-happy Joseph Banks, soon to be dubbed the Patron Saint of New South Wales for his ongoing support of a future British colony, was frantically collecting, gutting, shooting, skinning and preserving any plant or creature he came across in order to take them home to England as museum specimens. In years to come he would even send an order for skeletal remains of Indigenous people. Picture this then: strangers suddenly arrived and greedily hogging all the fresh water, a gun-toting scientist manically slicing and dicing, a tall man bearing strange gifts marching armed into people's homes without any invitation. Blind to the impact of their own behaviour, they were intruding into a country where people lived by honouring the land; taking only what was needed when it was in season in order to provide sustainability for future generations. Mystified by the lack of welcome they received, Cook even had the arrogance to complain in his journal that 'all they seem'd to want was for us to be gone.'[103]

The ever pragmatic and wickedly humorous old grannies I have known in my life would tell me plainly that Captain Cook suffered from too much pride and not enough spiritual advice, which they would be willing to provide by way of a big stick. With a wry chuckle they might advise that if I ever went back in time I should knock him on the head with one before he could name and claim anything. If there were other people present when they made this suggestion then a hearty discussion might ensue.

One old uncle, one who had been droving to Queensland in his younger days and discussed our situation with the people over there, might sing out, 'Captain Cook was as cunning as a shithouse rat, my girl! When he slipped his big ship in through that opening in the cliffs, he slipped his bag of dirty tricks in too.'

'The barrel of his gun, that was his law!' another would add. 'It wasn't long before the camp fires went out.'

Not to be outdone, one of the old grandfathers, who enjoyed a philosophical conversation or two, might remind me of the other problems James Cook had.

'The poor bugger only spoke English. And English is a terrible mean language. It doesn't have the right words or the right ideas; that's why people get mixed up when we talk about things. They can't understand what we're saying. They don't believe in spirits, so they can't see what they're destroying.'

'Haa, English wasn't all that was wrong with him,' someone else would complain, 'he was a robber after all! He'd push you away if he saw something shiny!'

Then another person might say thoughtfully, 'A long time ago now, I met this Aboriginal fella from Sydney, and he reckoned Captain Cook is just like the Phantom in the Phantom comics, he's the ghost who still walks this land.'

'Yeah,' one of the old grannies determined to have the last word would laugh, 'and he's still got that devil dog by his side! I've met him, you know. Every meeting I go to there's somebody wanting something!'

I have sometimes thought back to the time before the worlds of the first peoples of this continent and the world of people like James Cook permanently collided. Thought back to the moment when Captain Arthur Phillip, lover of law, order and agriculture, arrived in the hot sultry summer of January 1788 to establish the first British colony. By then, the children who had been playing on the beach when Cook arrived were grown with families of their own, and this time from the headlands they would have seen not one, but many ships breaching the horizon: two warships, three cargo ships and six transports. For that brief moment, as two vastly different peoples gazed at each other in curiosity across a brilliantly blue watery expanse, the future lay wide open, vulnerable to the good or evil the ships would bring. What would happen when they finally crossed that sunny, dazzling distance? How would the relationships between these strangers to our shores and peoples like mine play out? What would the Australian nation of the future one day look back on and call history?

The innocent, idealistic part of me likes to believe there is hope in every moment; that the dye is never cast until the moment has passed. Perhaps even then, despite the unlawful claiming of our land, hope lingered amongst the sharp smelling eucalyptus leaves, whose vaporised oil rises beyond the bush on warm and sunny days to cast a cleansing blue haze over the land. This was such a day. Far seeing individuals are born into every nation. This causes me to believe that the possibility of forging a just future is always present, if only we have the vision, will and courage to pursue it. Unfortunately, the first governor of the land named by James Cook as New South Wales, Captain Arthur Phillip, would choose to set a cruel precedent; one which would unfold for generations to come and decimate peoples like mine. In the years to follow a campaign to instil terror through violent action in order to quell resistance would be actively pursued. It would be initiated officially and unofficially. The little documentation that later found its way into the public record would be questioned and pedantically undermined. Brutal frontier secrets would be buried in silence and denial. There would be another precedent too, one which aimed to quell the land itself and which continues to manifest today in the wanton destruction of important heritage sites and ancient rock art.

Finding Botany Bay unsuitable, Arthur Phillip took an advance party of forty convicts and a company of marines to Sydney Cove and set about establishing an alternative site. The Judge Advocate for the new colony, David Collins later wrote:

> *The spot chosen for this purpose was at the head of the cove, near the run of fresh water which stole silently through a very thick wood, the stillness of which had then, for the first time since Creation, been interrupted by the rude sound of the labourer's axe ...*[104]

There was no distance now between those on the land and those on the water, there were just those who honoured the country and those who wished to exploit it. In the coming months the new arrivals would catch too many fish, chop down too many trees and pollute the fresh water. Soon all that would remain of the giant forests would be the blackened stumps of ancient trees hauntingly embraced by the rising salt of a weeping land.

At the end of that first long, hot day of labouring with the axe and the saw the British downed their sweaty tools and crowded beneath the flag that had sailed with them from the motherland. After a hearty round of 'God save the king' and a toast to King George III and the success of the colony, Phillip again took possession of the country. In doing so, he formally began the physical dispossession of the many nations who, for millennia, had exerted authority, custodianship and ownership over the continent as a whole. It was the twenty-sixth of January, the first Australia Day, and there were no women or children present, they were still locked away on the ships. Men, their mates and their muskets would go forth to rule this new frontier. That night, red-coated marines, their guns fixed with bayonets, patrolled the ghostly moonlit perimeter. The first fleet, the first military beachhead, the first Australia Day, the first fence, the great divide.

Of things to come

These days Sydney is the business gateway to Australia and home to the Australian Securities Exchange. It is a major international tourist destination and has a population of over four million people, of whom only around one percent are Indigenous. A few kilometres south of the Sydney central business district is Botany Bay, which historians still cite as the birthplace of modern Australia. It is vastly different now from the place where James Cook first landed in 1770. The bay has been dredged and its sand dunes mined, the groundwater flowing into the bay has been poisoned by chemicals — linked to cancer — from heavy industry, and many species of plants and animals native to this area are now extinct or endangered. In the west, the story is no different. In the Pilbara, where the land of my own people lies, we are struggling to protect the plants, animals and water sources and to save the strong and special places. One of the greatest battles we face at present is protecting our ancient rock art from an unthinking and greedy alliance of government and industry. The oldest, largest and richest rock art galleries on the planet, which archaeologists say should be World Heritage listed, are found in the Pilbara, but bit by bit they are being wiped off the face of the earth by projects which government describes as being 'in the public good'.

We all play a part in the world to come, and as the earth casts its shadow to the moon, none of us can ever truly know how far our great dreams or our crimes will take us. The era we live in now will one day be the past and the time will come when our actions will be weighed by others who will reflect on our legacy. In the tragedies and joys that unfold beyond our passing, what role will each of us have played? Is there a framework can we use then to forge meaningful and just partnerships between the new and the old, between the firstborn peoples of this land and the diversity of peoples who have been born since? What can guide and help us in protecting this most ancient and special place, this multitude of countries that together form the continent now known as Australia? If we look to all the peoples like mine, then it is clear that country has always been at the heart of every nation ever birthed here. Country makes us. This land makes us. Whether we know it or not,

We are all connected. We all exist within a nexus of relationships that link us to one another, and to all life. Everything we do affects these connections. In our different ways — we all tell the story of the world as it is, and the world as we want it to be — and in this land, stories have power. We are surrounded by the tales that shaped, and shape, this country.[105]

The possibility of good or evil, love or hate, justice or injustice, cruelty or compassion, destruction or protection, exists in every moment. But if we do not learn to read the signs wisely, then like James Cook we will find ourselves out of our depth and heading for very dangerous waters. The balance which honours and nourishes the inter-connectedness of all life and ensures its ongoing creation is missing from our world. If, 'in this land, stories have power' then we only have to choose what story we will tell, what story we will live, what story we will pass on to the children who will one day follow in our footsteps. As we make, so we are made. The unrealised possibility of the lost mystical, magical land of *Terra Australis Incognita* was not its vast material wealth, but the concept of balance that it offered humankind. The dream of a thousand years came as a counterweight to plunder and privilege, a push to pursue a path of balance in order to nourish a global future where all peoples, all life, thrived. If we, as human beings, continue to cut ourselves away from the web of life, then we embrace a story that like the bitter lie of *terra nullius* can have only one ending — death. Far better then, to embrace a story which not only honours life, but returns it a thousandfold to all those who will come after us. We are the mothers and fathers of the future, we stand at the crossroads and behind us are our children. What will we birth here, in this ancient southern land? The land which my grandmother once told me she saw in a dream as a place where everything lived and nothing died. A place far older than she or anyone knew. A place where too many people were still walking around blind. A place of much power and many secrets, if only you had the eyes to see the awe and wonder of it all.

Endnotes

1   Beryl Dixon, 'Back Home to Country'.
2   Len Collard, '*Kura, Yeye, boorda,* "from the past, today and the future"'.
3   Joan Winch, 'A Feeling of Belonging'.
4   Bob Morgan, 'Country — A Journey to Cultural and Spiritual Healing'.
5   A Kwaymullina, 'Seeing the Light: Aboriginal Law, Learning and Sustainable Living in Country', *Indigenous Law Bulletin*, vol. 6, no. 11, May–June 2005, p. 13.
6   Dawn Besserab, 'Country is Lonely'.
7   Greg Lehman, 'A Snake and a Seal'.
8   A Kwaymullina, p. 12.
9   Greg Lehman, op. cit.
10 Jill Milroy, 'Different Ways of Knowing: Trees Are Our Families Too'.
11 Tjalaminu Mia, '*Kepwaamwinberkup* (Nightwell)'.
12 Beryl Dixon, op. cit.
13 Bill Jonas, 'Places of Wonder and Fear'.
14 Bob Morgan, op. cit.
15 ibid.
16 ibid.
17 Pat Dudgeon, 'The Sinking of the *Enid* '.
18 Joan Winch, op. cit.
19 Noel Nannup, 'Caring for Everything'.
20 Joan Winch, op. cit.
21 Irene Watson, 'De-colonising the Space: Dreaming back to Country'.
22 Joe Boolgar Collard, 'A Strength that Can't be Broken'.
23 Sally Morgan, 'The Balance for the World'.
24 L Secatero, in S McFadden, *Chiron Communiqué*, April 2007, viewed 22 July 2007. http://www.chiron-communications.com/communique11-1.html
25 E Crombie, 'We are the Kupa Piti Kungka Tjuta, the Senior Aboriginal Women of Coober Pedy, South Australia', viewed 22 July 2007, http://www.iratiwanti.org/iratiwanti.php3?page=kungkas
26 B Neidjie, *Gagadju Man Bill Neidjie: The environmental and spiritual philosophy of a senior traditional owner Kakadu National Park, Northern*

Territory Australia, J B Books, 2002. p. 40.

27 The Ruddock interview was reported in *The Age* newspaper,
    3 October 2000, p. 3.

28 A Roach, *You Have the Power,* Harper Collins, Sydney 1994, p. 1.

29 Mussolini Harvey in Bradley, John (trans.) *Yanyuwa Country: The
    Yanuwa people of Borroloola tell the history of their land,* Greenhouse
    Publications, Richmond, Victoria, 1988, p. ix.

30 M Gilmore, 'Old Botany Bay', *The Penguin Book of Australian Verse,*
    Hesseltine, H (ed.), Penguin Books Australia, Ringwood Vic., 1972,
    p. 91.

31 Homestead near Hunters Creek.

32 Recently passed away.

33 L Little Bear, L 'Jagged Worldview Colliding', *Reclaiming Indigenous
    Voice and Vision,* M Battiste (ed.), *University of British Columbia Press,*
    Vancouver, Canada, 2000, p. 78.

34 ibid. note 3, p. 78.

35 R Whitehurst, *Noongar Dictionary, Noongar to English and English to
    Noongar,* Excelsior Print, Bunbury, WA, 1992, p. 6.

36 S Morgan, *My Place,* Fremantle Arts Centre Press, Fremantle, WA,
    1987, p. 356.

37 A Moreton-Robinson, *Talkin' up to the White Woman, Indigenous
    Women and Feminism,* University of Queensland Press, Queensland,
    2000, p. 19.

38 Bardi word for white person.

39 G Aklif, *Ardiyooloon Bardi Ngannka, One Arm Point Bardi Dictionary,*
    Kimberley Language Resource Centre, Halls Creek WA, 1999, p. 46.

40 Place near Skeleton Point.

41 L Marika and B Yunipungu, 'Gathering', *Elders, Wisdom from
    Australia's Indigenous Leaders,* P McConchie (ed.), The Press Syndicate
    of the University of Cambridge, Cambridge, UK, 2003, p. 41.

42 A W Nona, 'The Sea', *Elders, Wisdom from Australia's Indigenous
    Leaders,* p. 82.

43 Australian Museum Online (2004), 'Spirituality', *Indigenous Australia',*
    viewed 7 June, 2007, http://www.dreamtime.net.au/indigenous/
    spirituality.cfm

44 ibid.

45 R Whitehurst, *Noongar Dictionary, Noongar to English and English to
    Noongar,* Excelsior Print, Bunbury, WA, 1992, p 23.

46 M Hart, *A Story of Fire, Continued, Aboriginal Christianity,* New
    Creation Publications Inc., Blackwood, SA, 1997, p. 11.

47 ibid., p. xiii.

48 S Cornell and J P Kalt, *Sovereignty and Nation-Building: The
    Development Challenge in Indian Country Today,* 2006, 21/08/2006.

http://www.ksg.harvard.edu/hpaied/docs/CornellKalt%20Sov-NB.pdf

49 K Healy, *Social Work Theories in Context, Creating Frameworks for Practice*, Palgrave Macmillan, New York, USA, 2005, p. 83

50 ibid p. 83.

51 Op. cit. at Note 19, p. 85.

52 ibid.

53 V McLennan and F Khavarpour 2004, *Culturally appropriate health promotion: its meaning and application in Aboriginal communities*, Health Promotion Journal of Australia, 15(3), viewed 20 June 2007, http://www.healthpromotion.org.au/docs/mclennan_article.pdf, p. 238.

54 ibid.

55 J Walley, oral history interview with L Collard, Western Australia, 2002.

56 Welcome or hello, everyone.

57 Nyungar language group.

58 Knowledge.

59 Country, family and knowledge.

60 People from the South-West of Western Australia.

61 White people.

62 Long long ago.

63 http://wwwmcc.murdoch.edu.au/multimedia/nyungar/

64 T Bennell, oral history interview with L Collard, Western Australia, 1978.

65 A P Elkin, *The Australian Aborigines: How to Understand Them*, Angus & Robertson, Australia, p. 241, pp. 260–61.

66 G F Moore, *A Descriptive Vocabularly of the Language in Common Use Amongst the Aborigines of Western Australia; with Copious Meanings, Embodying much Interesting Information Regarding the Habits, Manners and Customs of the Natives, and the Natural History of the Country*, Wm S Orr & Co, 1842, p. 75.

67 T Bennell, *Kura*. revised edn, Glenyse Collard (ed. and compiled), Nyungar Language Centre, Bunbury, 1993. Oral history interviews with L Collard: T Bennell, 1978a; S Garlett, 2002; J Hayden, 2002; D Winmar, 2002.

68 *Ngulak Ngarnk Nidja Boodja: Our Mother This Land*, T Mia and S Morgan (eds), Centre for Indigenous History and the Arts, University of Western Australia, 2000; http://wwwmcc.murdoch.edu.au/multimedia/nyungar/.

69 Woman.

70 T Bennell, oral history Interview with L Collard, Western Australia, 1978.

71 Child/children.

72 Mother, blood/bloodline.

73 Sylvia J Hallam and Lois Tilbrook (eds), Aborigines of the Southwest region, 1829–1840. *The Bicentennial Dictionary of Western Australians*, vol 8, University of Western Australia Press, Nedlands, 1990; S Hallam, 'Aboriginal Women as Providers; the 1830's on the Swan', *Aboriginal History*, vol. 15, no. 1, pp. 38–53, 1991; R Van den Berg, *Nyoongar People of Australia; perspectives on Racism and Multiculturalism*, Royal Brill Academic Publishers, Leiden, 2002, p. xii.

74 Mother.

75 R M Lyon, 'A Glance at the Manners, and Language of the Aboriginal Inhabitants of Western Australia; With a Short Vocabularly,' *Perth Gazette*, 1833, p. 9, and *Western Australian Journal*, vol 1, no 13, p. 51–52, 30 March 1833.

76 S Garlett, oral history interview with L Collard, Western Australia, 2000; 'Goonininup; A Site Complex on the Southern Side of Mount Eliza', *An Historical Perspective of Land Use and Associations in the Old Swan Brewery area, Perth*, West Australian Museum, 1989.

77 D Bates in *Aboriginal Perth: Bibbulmun Biographies and Legends*, P J Bridge (ed.), Hesperian Press, Victoria Park, WA 1992; D Bates in *The Native Tribes of Western Australia*, I White (ed.) National Library of Australia, Canberra, 1985; T Bennell, 1993, op. cit.; E Bennell and A Thomas, *Aboriginal Legends from the Bibulmum Tribe*, Rigby, Adelaide, 1980; P Baines, 'A Litany for Land', in *'Being Black' Aboriginal Cultures in 'Settled' Australia*, I Keen (ed.), Aboriginal Studies Press, Canberra, 1988, pp 227–249; D Winmar, oral history interview with L Collard, Western Australia, 2002; E Kickett, *The Trails of the Rainbow Serpents*, Chatham Road Publications, Midland, WA, 1995.

78 T Bennell, 1993, op. cit.; E Bennell and A Thomas, 1980, op. cit.; P Baines, 1988, op. cit.; D Winmar, 2002, op. cit.; E Kickett, 1995, op. cit.

79 Means both goodbye and hello.

80 T Bennell, 1978, op. cit.

81 On 21 June 2007, the Howard government announced its intention to use Commonwealth powers to impose a number of emergency measures; this response followed the Northern Territory government's Broad Inquiry into the protection of Aboriginal Children from Sexual Abuse, Report of the Northern Territory Board of Inquiry into the Protection of Aboriginal Children from Sexual Abuse (2007), a report known as *Little Children Are Sacred* — http://www.nt.gov.au/dcm/inquirysaac/pdf/bipacsa_final_report.pdf — and an announcement by Noel Pearson, Director of the Cape York Institute for Policy and Leadership, on 19 June, about plans to impose measures in Cape York, Queensland, which would withhold welfare payments in situations

where children were not attending school and where also there were notifications of child abuse.

82 An Aboriginal word, meaning Aboriginal, the term is used extensively throughout the southern parts of South Australia.

83 Means country.

84 The Kupa Pita Kunkgas are a group of Aboriginal women Elders living in Coober Pedy. They were active during the 1990s in speaking publicly about the cultural significance of country and the destructive impact the building of a nuclear waste dump would have on their lands. Eileen Brown is a Yangkuntjara Elder and this interview was translated by Waniwa Lester.

85 The expansion of the Roxby Downs uranium mine, already the largest uranium mine in the world, was announced during 2006 by the South Australian state government, granting BHP Billiton approval for further expansion.

86 In May 2007, the Northern Land Council began negotiations with the federal government Education, Science and Training Minister Julie Bishop to allow a nuclear waste site to be situated on the traditional lands of the Muckaty community in the Northern Territory.

87 From the mid-1990s the Kungkas waged a campaign to stop a nuclear waste dump being sited in their traditional lands. The campaign was ultimately successful and the federal government now lists Aboriginal lands in the Northern Territory as one of its options for the dump.

88 *Inma* means ceremonial dance and singing; *Kungka* is women.

89 British Nuclear Weapons testing, nine were exploded in South Australia in 1956–58.

90 This conference was convened by the Cape York Institute and held in Cairns, 25–26 June 2007.

91 T Koch, 'Get Parents Who Shield Abusers: Pearson', *The Australian*, 26 June, 2007, p. 1.

92 R A Dickson, *Ships Registered in Western Australia from 1856*, vol. 3, West Australian Maritime Museum, Fremantle, 1994, p. 44.

93 E Merewether to Governor Macquarie, 11 December 1848, cited in: *Documents in the History of Aboriginal Education in New South Wales*, Fletcher, J J, p. 37, Southwood Press, 1989.

94 M Dodson, *First Report to the Aboriginal and Torres Strait Islander Social Justice Commission*, Australian Government Publishing Service, Canberra, 1993, p. 7.

95 *Wunda* was the name given to the white people when they first arrived in our country. *Wunda* is a Gumilaroi word denoting spirits, and my people believed that when they first saw white people that they were spirits returning from the other side.

96 G Dixon, *Holocaust Revisited — Killing Time*, Centre for Indigenous

History and the Arts, University of Western Australia, Perth, WA, 2003, p. 82.

97   http://en.wikipedia.org/wiki/Liberte,_egalite,_fraternite

98   http://en.wikipedia.org/lunar_plaques

99   http://en.wikipedia.org/wiki/extraterrestial_real_estate

100 V Collingridge, *Captain Cook: Obsession and Betrayal in the New World*, Ebury Press, UK, 2002, p. 5.

101 http://www.imbd.com/title/tt00765759/quotes

102 A Kwaymullina, 'Living together in country: Creation, terra nullius and the trouble with tradition', *The Trouble with Tradition: Native Title and Cultural Change,* S Young, Federation Press, Melbourne (to be published in Dec 2008).

103 J Cook, *Captain Cook's Journal 1768–1771*, Australiana Facsimile Edition no. 188, Libraries Board of South Australia, Adelaide, 1968, p. 244.

Glossary

Variations in the spelling of some Aboriginal words in this book reflect local community variations.

boodjar: land.

boodjarri: pregnant woman.

Boordier: Elders.

coolaman: wooden dish/bowl for carrying food/water/baby.

gadiya: white person/people.

gnumma
  (hole):   fresh water collected in a hole in the rock.

karrdar: goanna.

Kunanyi: Mount Wellington.

Lupaylana: Betsy Island, near where the Derwent River enters Storm Bay.

Nipaluna: the Derwent River and area around the city of Hobart.

num: the ghosts of palawa ancestors. A word used for white people who, when they first arrived, were considered to be spirits.

numlagger: 'the white man comes', from the poetry of Jim

	Everett.
Midgerigoo:	respected Nyungar Elder of the Swan River coastal plain.
rowra:	a powerful spirit, capable of great harm.
tunapri manta:	old knowledge (law).
tyerlore:	island wives, palawa women taken by European sealers and held on the islands in the Bass Strait.
Yagan:	respected Nyungar warrior from the Swan River coastal plain.
Yellagonga:	respected Elder of the Swan River coastal plain.
yorkga:	Nyungar woman.

Acknowledgements

This anthology is an initiative of the Centre for Indigenous History and the Arts, School of Indigenous Studies, University of Western Australia. Our heartfelt thanks go to all the courageous contributors who have generously shared their feelings and experiences of their own countries in this publication.

Sally Morgan, Tjalaminu Mia
and Blaze Kwaymullina

First published 2008 by
FREMANTLE PRESS

Reprinted 2010.

Fremantle Press Inc. trading as Fremantle Press
PO Box 158, North Fremantle, Western Australia, 6159
fremantlepress.com.au

Cover painting by Sally Morgan, *Wittenoom Landscape 1*, 1991
oil on canvas, 62 x 92 cm, private collection
Designed by Tracey Gibbs

A catalogue record for this
book is available from the
National Library of Australia

ISBN 9781921361111 (paperback)
ISBN 9781760991159 (ebook)

Fremantle Press is supported by the Western Australian State
Government through the Department of Cultural Industries,
Tourism and Sport.

Fremantle Press respectfully acknowledges the Whadjuk people of the
Noongar nation as the Traditional Owners and Custodians of the land
where we work in Walyalup.